Praise for
Sunrise in Florence

"Sunrise in Florence is a tonic for any reader who loves Italy, fine art and adventure. When Rose, a practical art history professor, decides to paint instead of teach, her world opens up, and with it her past, the revelation of a secret, the return of her first love and the complications that arise when a woman has the courage to change her life and choose happiness. All this and bella Firenze too! Brava Kathleen Reid!"

Adriana Trigiani
Author of *Tony's Wife*

"Kathleen Reid has the rarest of writer's touches, one that can delicately explore the thoughts, emotions and dreams of memorable characters while drawing them into situations and settings that are alternately romantic and realistic. In Sunrise in Florence, she has created a story marked by the passion of self-realization and discovery . . . In so doing, she has written a book of subtle wisdom and great beauty, something to be embraced and remembered."

Greg Fields
Author of *Arc of the Comet*, 2018 Kindle Book of the Year Nominee in Literary Fiction

"A deliciously engaging novel about adventure, art history and finding your passion under the Tuscan sun. Kathleen Reid's nimble storytelling delights as she serves up Italian romance with a Southern twist."

Heath Hardage Lee
Author of *The League of Wives*

"Escape to Italy for romance and adventure in Kathleen Reid's long-awaited new release. The city of Florence and countryside of Tuscany come alive on the pages. Rose Manning is a relatable and likable protagonist who finds herself in a love-life quandary readers won't soon forget."

Ashley Farley
Author of *Life on Loan*

"Bravo! The vivid descriptions of Renaissance art, artists, Italian culture and architectural sites are highlights of the novel. Insights that Reid provides into the artistic process and use of conservation techniques are an added bonus for fans of art historical fiction."

Lee Bagby Ceperich
Director, Library and Special Collections, Virginia Museum of Fine Arts

Sunrise in Florence

by Kathleen Reid

© Copyright 2019 Kathleen Reid

ISBN 978-1-63393-976-9

This is a work of fiction. The characters are both actual and fictitious. With the exception of verified historical events and persons, all incidents, descriptions, dialogue and opinions expressed are the products of the author's imagination and are not to be construed as real.

Published by

köehlerbooks™

210 60th Street
Virginia Beach, VA 23451
800—435—4811
www.koehlerbooks.com

Sunrise in Florence

KATHLEEN REID

VIRGINIA BEACH
CAPE CHARLES

Chapter 1

AS ROSE HEADED OUT the front door, her boss and Bellfield's headmistress, Catherine Oberlin, embraced her.

"I'm so happy for you, dear. What a beautiful adventure you have ahead."

"You have no idea how much that means to me, Catherine. This was a difficult decision and one I really struggled to make."

"Of course. I'm disappointed to lose you. Another chapter awaits, but you will always be welcome at Bellfield. You're an excellent teacher."

"Thank you, Catherine."

"Zoey has accepted our offer to become dean of the Upper School, of course. We couldn't be more pleased."

"That's great news!" said Rose, her feelings bittersweet. It was scary giving up job security and a promotion without a plan. With mixed emotions, she headed to the local coffee shop less than a block from campus to get a latte to help jump-start the day.

"Rose?" said a distinctive male voice behind her in line.

She turned and came face-to-face with Ben Pierce, who she hadn't seen in years.

"Ben," she said nervously, caught off guard by his hazel eyes. "How are you? I thought you were in New York."

"I moved back here a couple of weeks ago," he said with a wide grin as if he were the proprietor of the best-kept secret in Charlottesville.

"Uh, great," she said stupidly for lack of a better response. Her stomach twisted into knots as she recalled a fleeting image of a sandy beach at dusk when they were in high school. The intensity of that kiss and the way he made her feel was something she would never forget.

They both grew up on the same street, and he was her first love in high school. Their parents were friends, and her mother had always shared bits and pieces of his life over the years. As she recalled, Ben had successfully climbed Mount Kilimanjaro, run the New York City Marathon in under three hours and regularly spent winters skiing the powdery slopes in Jackson Hole, Wyoming. And, most importantly, he had married a model and had a daughter. Their messy divorce was all over the society pages, which Doris, her mother, had followed like a hawk in search of its prey.

The woman behind Ben cleared her throat, and Rose got hold of herself and quickly ordered a latte. As she waited patiently for her order at an adjoining counter, she studied Ben's perfect profile out of the corner of her eye, noting his cargo pants and flip-flops. When he smiled at something the cashier told him, Rose thought, *He's even better looking than I remembered.* He was now an accomplished entrepreneur at thirty.

Recalling their teenage years, she felt a slight blush stain her cheeks. *He's just being nice,* she reminded herself firmly, taking out her iPhone and checking emails to keep herself from staring at him.

"Hey, you should have let me buy that for you," he offered, coming up to stand beside her.

"Not necessary," she replied, trying to take a sip of her steaming coffee. Some foam must have rubbed off on her upper lip because he reached over and wiped it from her mouth easily, as if they were still connected. At her look of surprise, he laughed and said, "Sorry, I couldn't resist. You were always so adorable and now you're all grown up." He paused, looking at her, his gaze resting a touch too long on her collarbones. "I'm back for the summer," he announced. "I'm researching a book."

"You're a writer? Last I heard, you ran a hedge fund on Wall Street."

"I sold that business two years ago; too many greedy people in one location," he joked. "Seriously, after almost ten years, I decided I didn't enjoy working in finance, so I went a different direction. I'm researching a book on Jefferson and came home to write. My life has changed a lot. How about you?"

"You're not going to believe this, but I teach art history down the street at Bellfield."

"Ah, the Bellfield lions. I'll bet nothing's changed."

His comment touched a nerve. Of course nothing had changed in this small Southern town where predictability was the cornerstone of life.

"Hey, I've gotta go. Great to see you again."

"You too. I'm hoping you'll help me catch up on things around here," he said, walking beside her to the door, which he held open for her.

"Sure thing. Bye," said Rose as she moved into a slow jog, not sure why she felt in such a hurry to distance herself from him. After all, this was just a chance meeting. Although he was awfully easy on the eyes, Rose didn't dare spend any more time with him; he was a part of her past.

Suddenly, she recalled that she had once named her ficus tree plant in his honor. It brought back a host of other memories that made Rose laugh aloud. Ben Pierce was the ultimate success story; he was not only brilliant but a star tennis player at the University of Virginia. Rose made a mental note to tell her mother that she'd run into him. *Scratch that idea,* she thought with amusement, since Doris was more up to date on social gossip than Rose could ever hope to be.

Rose sat at her desk to enjoy her coffee and go over the lesson plan for the day. Stacy Billings walked in with her blue plaid skirt artfully covered by a long, white sleeveless sweater.

"You know, Miss Maning, it would really help my relationship with my parents if you'd give me a better grade. I'm under a lot of pressure to get into a name college."

"Well," said Rose, telling herself to give the non-anxious response. She really wanted to say "You can't be serious." Instead, she replied, "You didn't put enough effort into your term paper. My classes are about more than just getting good grades, Stacy. They're about expanding your knowledge of art history and teaching you how to research and analyze a topic."

"I think I deserve better than a B- in your class. Besides, I didn't like writing about the Renaissance."

"I understand you're under pressure," said Rose. "So, I'd suggest you rework your term paper and focus on one artist, say Michelangelo. Tell the story of how he came to win the block of marble for the David and carve one of the greatest sculptures ever made in Florence."

"How long?"

"Well, since today is the last day of classes, I want three pages of your best work by this weekend."

"Will you change my grade?"

"Maybe you should focus more on the learning part."

"My grades are the main thing that determine the college I go to, Miss Maning."

"I see," said Rose, resisting the urge for sarcasm. Students like Stacy were challenging, ultimately affirming her decision to leave Bellfield and pursue her dream of becoming an artist. *Stacy is spoiled,* thought Rose. *Maybe I shouldn't have asked her to write another paper. It's not going to change the way she views art history.*

Rose reminded herself to stay positive. She had really enjoyed being a teacher, and hopefully her love of Renaissance art rubbed off on some of her students.

Rose couldn't help but notice the gorgeous pink azalea bushes as she gazed out the window. *Spring in Charlottesville is always beautiful*, she thought, wondering what the future held for her. She was scared, but also excited.

Hurrying to her last morning assembly, Rose was stopped by one of her best students.

"Hey, Ms. Maning," called Lori, coming up to walk briskly beside her. "Say it isn't so," she exclaimed. "I can't believe you are really leaving us."

"I can't believe it either, but someday you'll understand that you have to take risks in life." She stopped to look at her. "You can always visit me." They embraced. "So, how is your term paper on Michelangelo coming along?"

"I read last night that Michelangelo used to study dead bodies in order to make his figures more lifelike. That's totally disgusting!"

Rose giggled. "It's all a matter of perspective, Lori. He was a genius."

"Come on, Ms. Maning. He had to be kind of weird. Would you really ride down to the morgue and spend your day studying a dead person's arm to understand how to draw muscles and veins? Ugh!"

A vision of Michelangelo's *David* formed in her mind. Lori was right. Michelangelo did study corpses, which was forbidden by the Church in fifteenth-century Italy. But it was only in doing so that he was able to create one of the greatest sculptures of all time. She thought Lori's paper on Michelangelo would allow her to tackle politics and art in Rome in a more engaging manner. After all, Michelangelo was caught between the powerful Medici family in Florence and the pope in Rome. His life and art were shaped by these two ruling forces.

***

Rose had made printouts of the *David* and handed them out to her students in class. In her usual manner, Rose began her discussion with a question. "What do you think? Would you go to this extreme to pursue perfection?"

"If I could create something this beautiful," said Christine, "I would definitely consider it. But it's pretty gross if you really think about it."

"Lori, you're the one that got me thinking this morning. Why are you so appalled?"

"Ms. Maning. Really? You're going to go there . . . "

Everyone laughed.

"I am," said Rose.

"I just don't get it," said Lori. "I'm not sure I have that kind of passion or intensity for anything. Michelangelo started having all of these health issues because he was hanging out with dead people."

Sherry chimed in. "Clearly, Michelangelo had a gift and he did what he had to do to create lifelike statues. But that's what made him unique and it's why we're still talking about him."

"How far would you go to pursue your passion?"

Rose smiled shyly. It occurred to her that, oftentimes, one needed to take risks in order to get what they wanted. An apartment with a balcony view in Italy flashed in her mind. She sat at her desk.

"I hope all of you are so passionate about your research paper topics that you're willing to go the extra mile to achieve perfection."

A collective groan filled the room.

"We're going to miss you, Miss Maning," said Lori sweetly. "I've loved being in your class."

"Me too," said a chorus of girls.

"I expect every one of you to keep in touch," said Rose cheerfully. "Once I buy a place, I'll give you my address so you know where to find me."

The girls cheered and Lori said, "I hope you mean it, because I'm coming to Florence!"

"Absolutely."

After the bell, Rose received lots of good wishes and hugs. After her students filed out into the hallways, she paused and glanced out the window, admiring the redbrick facade of Bellfield Academy.

Three years earlier, she garnered a coveted teaching position at her alma mater, a private high school known for academic excellence and rigorous sports programs. There was a sense of comfort wrapped in the school's 100-year-old traditions, or so she thought at first.

As Rose surveyed her classroom, she caught sight of a painting of her created by this year's graduating seniors; the picture of her with long yellow hair conjured up the moment that the girls voted her "best teacher" at the spring banquet. It was something she'd never forget.

"Hey, Ms. Maning," called Sophie. "Great dress!"

"Thanks!" replied Rose as she headed to the faculty lounge, watching the sprightly girl dash down the hall. *I'll miss them,* she thought sadly.

"There's enough there for another cup," said Zoey, an English scholar with long dark hair and tawny brown skin. "But hurry up and grab it before I get greedy."

"This is a two-cup morning," said Rose, filling up her mug. "Thanks for thinking of me. You're my favorite person."

"Flattery always works for me," said Zoey. "I'm suddenly having a vision of Forster's *A Room with a View*. Perhaps you'll fall madly in love with two men in Florence."

"Spoken like a true English teacher who looks like a model," said Rose, who admired Zoey's jewel-toned embroidered tunic. "I'm sure every girl here is going to want to know where you got that top."

"Anthropologie," she countered. "On sale."

"Okay, so, unlike the story, I'm not engaged to a handsome British aristocrat and torn between two suitors." She shifted her gaze to look out the window at the lush green courtyard. "All I know is that I'm so excited to go apartment hunting in Florence!"

"I still can't believe you're leaving!"

"You know, my dad always encouraged me to put down real roots abroad. He's the reason that I can follow my dream and afford to buy a place. I miss him every day."

"I wish I'd known him."

"I wish you'd known him, too. He had an adventurous spirit, unlike you-know-who," Rose said, referring to her mother.

"Doris only knows how to be Doris, and besides, it's not her life!"

"Yeah, I know, but it's kind of complicated. Mom has always favored Jack, who can do no wrong. My big brother married a beautiful Southern girl, bought the perfect house in North Carolina for his adorable family." She paused. "But you know I'm in love with Florence."

"What's not to love?"

"Every time I think about actually living there, I imagine waking up and looking at the Arno in the morning, drinking an espresso and soaking up all of that Italian culture. I would love to have the Duomo in my backyard. Or go visit Botticelli's Venus at the Uffizi whenever I want. We both know Doris will blow a gasket when I actually buy a place rather than rent one."

"I hope escaping your mom isn't why you are so hell-bent on owning your own place," Zoey said. "She'll always be your mother for better or worse, and no matter where you live."

"You know me better than that. I want to be in Florence because of my memories of it, because I'm still enchanted by it."

Rose recounted the times she had visited Florence with her father, and later as a student, and then while vacationing. Her most recent visit had been two years earlier. On that trip she visited the studio of Antonio Romano, who was both a sculptor and painter. His works were sought after, and he was considered one of the greatest instructors in Italy. He was also a scholar of Renaissance artists, which was how Rose learned of him. Antonio's wife, Valentina, restored the works of great Florentine masters. Rose asked a studio attendant whether Antonio held workshops.

"Occasionally, Antonio accepts a student with exceptional talent, but the waiting list is long," Rose was told. Rose was forlorn, but not surprised. As she was about to leave the studio, Valentina approached.

"American?" she asked.

"Yes, art history teacher."

"Do you draw or paint?"

"I do, but not formally. Just a dream of mine," Rose confided. "I am more of a student of art than practitioner."

"Me too," Valentina said. "But understanding art is not enough. You must find the artist in you."

Those encouraging words motivated Rose to draw and paint in her spare time in her little house across from Bellfield Academy, hoping that her dream would come true.

"The most amazing thing about Antonio and Valentina was that they were madly in love for more than forty years," Rose said. "I knew when I saw them together that was the kind of love I wanted."

Rose shared other stories about Florence, especially those involving her dad.

"Did I ever tell you about the time my dad made Jack and me climb to the top of the Duomo when we were in middle school? I got scared when I looked down at the altar and then up into that dark staircase at the top. When I refused to go any farther, he grabbed my hand and said, 'Don't ever let your fears stop you. We'll count the steps together.'"

Rose smiled at the memory.

"When we reached the top, I looked out over the city and it all seemed so magical. I'd forgotten that story until I took my students to the same spot two years ago. It was so weird. I felt this sense of calm come over me." Rose paused as tears formed.

"I just know in my heart that Dad would want me to buy a place abroad. He was upset that I gave up my semester abroad in Florence when he was diagnosed with cancer. I stayed with him instead and have never regretted that choice for a moment. During those months, he shared so many personal things about himself and my grandparents' life in Poland. My grandmother survived a concentration camp and his family came to America to have a better life."

"Your dad sounds amazing," Zoey said.

"I lost my hero, and now, for the first time ever in my people-pleasing life, I'm doing something that I want to do. Not what I think I should do." Her voice rose a notch. "I'm not going to let anyone, or anything, stop me this time. Not my mother or stepfather. And certainly not my fear."

"Well, you go, girl! Seriously, I'm so glad to support you, even though it means losing my bestie. I know you. You'll do your homework and make an informed decision."

"Thank you, dear friend," said Rose, giving her a hug; she was definitely inspired and so appreciated Zoey's efforts on her behalf. "I'm so glad you're going to help me!"

"Well, my help is completely self-serving. I'm going to make sure you have a sleep sofa because I'm booking my visits. Spring break is a given!" Zoey checked her watch. "Hey, I need to get going. The girls want me sitting at my desk so they can complain relentlessly about last night's homework."

"What did you assign?"

"I asked them to analyze how a foreign setting drove a bunch of kids crazy in *Lord of the Flies*."

"Oh, I don't like that book either," exclaimed Rose.

"You can't say that!" Zoey grinned.

"Today is my last day as a teacher, so I can tell the truth.

Oh, did I tell you that I'm having dinner with my mom and Eric tonight? I'll try to behave and keep the conversation light."

"Good luck with that."

"Thanks. I'm going to need it."

Picturing the wrath of Doris now that she had finalized her plans, Rose felt a momentary pang of remorse. But then she envisioned seeing Michelangelo's *David* at the Galleria dell'Accademia, the Basilica of Santa Croce with its frescoes by Giotto, and tasting her favorite chocolate almond gelati again. The sound of the bell prodded her back to the present as she walked out to the hallway filled with the almost deafening sound of teenage chatter. She really was going to miss her life at Bellfield.

***

That night at her mother's dinner table, Rose foolishly mentioned that she and Zoey were planning a bike trip through Tuscany.

"Why would anyone want to bike in Tuscany?" her mother said, breaking off a chunk of white roll and pushing it in her mouth. "That sounds awful."

"I think it's all part of the adventure," said Rose, who eyed her stepfather, Eric, looking for moral support. He winked at her, suppressing a grin.

"I still don't get it," said Doris. "You have a lovely life here in Charlottesville and a great job. Rumor has it that you have some news that you haven't told us."

Rose shifted uncomfortably in her seat. The fried chicken suddenly felt like a ball of grease in her stomach. The table was silent as she tactfully ignored the comment.

"There's no need to be shy, Rose. You've been on the fast track for years. You would be the youngest ever dean of the Upper School. It's crazy that you don't consider the offer."

"How did you find out? It's not public information yet."

"I'm certainly not the public," she sniffed, getting up to

lavish more butter beans on Rose's stepfather. As always, Doris garnered his support through her home-cooked meals.

"Thank you," said Eric kindly, greedily placing a heaping spoonful in his mouth. "That's wonderful news. I'm sure Rose will tell us more when she's ready."

"Well?" asked Doris. "Are we to stay in suspense all evening or can you give us a hint?" Her hot-pink manicured nails deflected the aggression in her tone.

Suddenly capitulating, Rose said, "Um, well, I was somewhat shocked that they offered me the position." She paused for another moment.

"Congratulations, Rose," said Eric, raising his glass. "It's always good to be recognized for a job well done."

"Well, I don't see any point in rushing off to Florence now. You've got a wonderful opportunity right here and you'd be a fool not to take it."

"I turned it down. Zoey is going to get the job."

"*What?*" said Doris huffed, looking like an angry Himalayan cat. "How could you be so irresponsible? You're making a huge mistake, young lady, and this whole thing is going to be a disaster."

"I'm moving to Florence whether you like it or not."

"You sound just like your father."

"I assume that's a compliment," she shot back. Her father was her hero and the one person who had always believed in her. Annoyance set in, and she wasn't in the mood to placate her mother.

Rose stood and raised her glass. "Cheers to foolish me!" she added. "I really appreciate all of your support," she said sarcastically, before excusing herself.

***

As she turned into the driveway of her tired-looking faculty house, Rose felt as if she'd been run over by a truck. Her nerves were shot, and she needed to calm down. Taking a deep breath, she decided to try out some new ideas on canvas.

Rose changed into comfy jeans and a T-shirt. The urge to paint was overwhelming, and she settled into her makeshift studio that acted as an office, guest room and storage space. Boxes lined the walls, but she didn't much care since it was a temporary rental.

Calm descended over Rose as she took out a crisp white canvas and some oil paints. With broad strokes, she began to draw the angels in a Roman floor mosaic that she had recently photographed at the Virginia Museum of Fine Arts in Richmond. Hours swept by as she fashioned an olive tree in the background. As she drew the curly locks of an angel, it occurred to her that she could copy original artwork well. While her drawing wasn't perfect, it was rather good, she concluded.

Suddenly, her mother's voice came to mind, and she remembered that day in seventh grade. Rose had come home from school and announced that her dream was to be a famous artist. Her mother had looked disdainfully at her artwork.

"Rose, you're not an artist and you never will be. Don't waste your time. Your father and I are not spending all this money on private school for you to starve. Be smart."

Rose had cried for hours and then shredded all of her pictures in a fit of anger. That moment may have, in fact, been the genesis of her desire to teach; it was extremely important to her that she use her talent to empower others, not demean them.

Rose had never talked about the roots of her career choice, and that painful night Doris shattered her dreams, until she had opened up to Zoey.

Rose was having dinner with Zoey and Stan at their apartment. Stan worked as a bartender on weekends to support his music. He played local clubs and was gaining a large following in the city with his amazing voice. His passion for music was tangible. Rose saw his eyes light up whenever he talked about writing songs. They all got to talking about finding one's bliss in life.

Maybe it was the white wine, but Rose finally shared her middle school story, trying to make light of what happened. Zoey got angry, informing Rose that she needed to reignite her passion for painting. Thanks to her encouragement, Rose slowly began drawing and working on canvas.

Fatigue won out, and she emerged from her studio feeling decidedly less stressed. Fortunately, her workload was light; she would dig in tomorrow and get going on grading those final term papers. She made herself a cup of lemon tea and opened the folder of potential apartments in Florence. The pages were filled with notes she had scratched on the sides and ideas. The colorful printouts pictured very attractive one-bedroom apartments, which to buy would cost roughly 350,000 euros, depending upon the exchange rate. "Thank you, Daddy," she said aloud, as tears misted her eyes.

The first place was located right near the Uffizi and was a clean white renovated space with a beautiful balcony, which was clearly its best feature. Rose practically gasped when she saw a picture of another Medici apartment with a fireplace, beamed ceiling and updated master bath. It was a mix of the old and the new. A third picture showed a two-floor apartment with a water view, and an old-fashioned curved staircase leading to a lower level.

Visions of the Duomo danced in her mind. Sun-dipped terra-cotta rooftops pervaded her consciousness as she envisioned herself with an easel, setting up to paint by the Ponte Vecchio. Since that school-sponsored trip to Florence, her longing to go back to the city was almost palpable. Florence always evoked memories of her father.

"My favorite city is Florence," her dad had often said. "If I could pick anywhere to live, it would be there."

Whereas her mother was controlling and pushed Rose toward what was expected, Rose's dad nurtured her intellectual spirit. He loved to hear about her passion for the Renaissance and discuss art and culture. Doris, on the other hand, was more interested in the next Junior League party.

Rose glanced at her inbox, and a red-flagged reply was there. Clicking on the icon, she saw the message was from her new realtor, Lyon Walker in Italy.

Dear Rose:

Buon giorno!
I've just learned about a price reduction on another very special apartment that you must see. I am going to set up an appointment on the third of June at 10 am. It would be very hard to change this date so please try to make it! I have selected two other options to show you as well!
Please let me know if this will work.

Sincerely,
Lyon

Rose confirmed the house appointment and forwarded the email to Zoey with a bunch of smiley-face emojis. She also congratulated Zoey on the new position and told her about the chance meeting with her old boyfriend, Ben Pierce. Was fate whispering into her ear when she ran into him after all these years? A pang of sadness swept through her, but she pushed it aside. With renewed determination, Rose planned to follow her dream and embark on the best international house hunt ever!

Chapter 2

DESPITE A LONG FLIGHT and Uber ride into downtown Florence, Rose was still full of energy, and she wanted to get outside and breathe some fresh air. She peered thoughtfully out the window of their hotel room overlooking the Arno River and observed the Ponte Vecchio bridge in the distance. Calculating the time, Rose estimated that she had nearly three hours to walk around. Suddenly hungry, she rummaged through her purse to find a granola bar tucked into a side pocket.

"You've got that David look on your face again," Zoey said.

"What's a David look?"

"All dreamy eyed. I'd say you're in love with that statue."

"And *Firenze*! I can't wait to get outside and explore."

"I'm exhausted and completely jet lagged from the trip." She punched the pillow and put her head down. "I need to take a nap for two hours. Then I should be good to go."

"I may go out and walk around a bit. I'm so excited to actually be back here!"

"Don't tell me; you're going first to Galleria dell'Accademia to see the *David*."

Rose laughed. "Boy, you know me too well." She looked at her watch. "I was thinking we'd have some dinner nearby around sevenish and keep it simple."

"Sounds like a plan. Night night," said Zoey, stretching out on the bed, and she promptly fell asleep.

Rose gingerly changed into a fresh pair of slip-on sneakers and brushed her hair. No jacket was necessary; it was a sunny, warm afternoon. As she made her way downstairs, Rose was pleased with the hotel that she had found online. It was located in the heart of Florence and in walking distance to nearly everything she wanted to explore. With its black-and-white marble tiled floors and white sofas, it boasted a frescoed ceiling adorned with angels. A white alcove to the right of the front desk contained a statue of a Roman leader with a black pot of white orchids at his feet.

Florence was draped in terra-cotta, and had the most incredibly beautiful monuments that existed, or at least Rose was convinced as much. She used her iPhone to help guide her to the Galleria dell'Accademia where there was a much shorter line than she expected. Relieved that her feet were comfortable, Rose took her place in line, keeping her travel pass handy. This would probably be her most focused sightseeing adventure before the house hunt began tomorrow morning.

The *David* towered over the crowds, and his perfectly formed body made Rose ponder how many hours per week Michelangelo worked to create this exquisite sixteenth-century masterpiece. She recalled that oftentimes he labored from dawn until late in the night with little food or water, fueled only by his creativity. David was a biblical hero and a favorite subject of many Florentine artists because he was a reminder to all about faith and the power to overcome.

While on the plane, Rose had read an abridged version of the story, which told how the Israelites and the Philistines were at war with each other during the reign of King Saul; God chose young David, a shepherd boy, to unite the two sides and become the future king of Israel. As the story unfolded, young David was chosen to beat Goliath, a nine-foot giant Philistine. Everyone thought that this boy didn't have a chance against a seasoned warrior, but young David trusted that God would lead him to victory. The boy used a slingshot with stones to hit the giant in the eye, ultimately winning the battle.

As Rose craned her neck to stare up at David's face, she was inspired by his courage and the triumph of beauty that could change the earth.

"Amazing, isn't it?" said a woman in a red scarf.

"Revolutionary," replied Rose. "You know, Michelangelo was the first artist to depict David before the battle. He looks tense, courageous and confident."

"He's larger than life in some ways, small in others."

They both laughed.

Rose walked around the seventeen-foot statue again, staring at the slingshot in David's hand and his contrapposto stance, which had him with one foot in front of the other, ready for battle. This extraordinary male nude commanded attention even without the gory head of Goliath.

Rose recalled that Michelangelo was actually the third sculptor to try his hand at this huge block of marble. The original commission came in 1463 when the members of the woolen cloth guild, the *Arte della Lana*, a very influential group, wanted to commission a series of twelve biblical figures for the buttresses of the Florence Cathedral. This project started with the great Donatello, who began the figures using terra-cotta to fashion them. The guild then asked Florentine sculptor Agostino di Duccio to create a David, likely under the direction of Donatello, and they provided him an enormous block of marble. Agostino used the marble and began the semblance of legs. Everything stopped when Donatello passed away.

Nearly ten years later, Antonio Rossellino was commissioned to finish what Agostino had started. He was soon fired from the job, and the marble lay dormant in a quarry for more than twenty-five years. Local Florentines had named the stone *The Giant*, which Rose thought was entirely appropriate. Michelangelo, at the young age of twenty-six, would ultimately earn the right to take on such a major feat. His reputation had preceded him. He began carving on the thirteenth of September and spent more than two years to complete the masterpiece.

She wasn't sure how long she stood there silently contemplating this treasure until someone stepped on her foot. Rose moved to observe the statue from the side and stood beside a group of French tourists, listening intently, pleased that she understood more than half of the tour guide's descriptions.

Hours flew by at the Galleria dell'Accademia, and Rose decided to make her way back to the hotel; she walked alone and felt deliriously happy in the evening light, eagerly peering in some brightly colored shop windows. A small leather store at the far end of the Ponte Vecchio caught her eye, and she looked at all of the meticulously crafted handbags displayed in the storefront window. Rose entered, smelling the tangy scent of new leather. She observed two young women sewing in the back area behind the counter. A young salesgirl asked if she needed help, and Rose focused in on a tan suede bag with leather trim.

"You have good taste," said the clerk.

"It's gorgeous. Are these bags made in Florence?"

"Right over there," she said, pointing to the two women who were discreetly working on new creations. One dark-haired girl looked up and smiled and then immediately returned her attention to the task at hand. "Ariana and Becky are artists who recently graduated from the leather school."

"I love that. How much is this bag?"

"One hundred and twenty euros."

"Hmmm," said Rose. "I'm a former teacher, and that bag is not in my budget!"

"I understand," said the strawberry blond–haired girl with the freckled face. "I'm Nicole and my parents own this store. They're Australian transplants here. Anyway, let me see if I can come up with a few similar options at a lower price point."

"That would be great. I'll try to come back in a few weeks

to check them out." Rose liked Nicole's friendly demeanor, and she seemed to be roughly her age. It occurred to her that she really wouldn't have any friends or family in Florence, which was intimidating.

"Sounds good."

"I'm going on a house hunt and thinking of buying a place. It's always been my dream to live here."

"That's wonderful. I've lived in Santa Croce for the last four years. I can't imagine moving back to Australia. I'd be happy to offer suggestions if you need something. Just drop in whenever."

"Thank you so much! I really appreciate it. See you soon."

"*Ciao.*"

An hour later, Zoey had showered and dressed in faded jeans and five-inch stilettos, ready for the evening. Her hair was pulled up in a sleek bun, and she wore large gold hoops.

"You look fantastic!" said Rose as she brushed her hair and threw on a pair of jean crops and a white sleeveless blouse. Her wedge espadrilles paled in comparison to Zoey's heels.

"I'm ready to start our Italian adventure!" Zoey put on a layer of black eyeliner. "I wish my man were here. What a beautiful evening! I'm so excited. Oh, and I almost forgot; Lyon called and said he would meet us in the lobby of this hotel around eight thirty sharp. The first place is a ten-minute walk from here."

"How old do you think Lyon is?" giggled Rose. "I am betting twenty-six."

"I bet you a carafe of Chianti that he's thirty-two."

"You're on," said Rose.

At the hotel concierge's recommendation, they found a traditional café three blocks north with red-and-white-check tablecloths and outdoor seating. When they had settled at their table, Rose told Zoey all about her field trip to see the *David* and, of course, the purse sighting in the small leather shop.

"Sorry to have missed the *David*," said Zoey, "but not that sorry. I feel so much better after a nap. I just can't sleep on a plane."

"Totally understand, but let me say that the statue was just fantastic."

"Alright, alright. Don't make me feel bad! I'll reactivate my brain again tomorrow and I'll pop in and see it. Maybe we should check out the Uffizi Gallery in the afternoon as well. That being said, I'd also love to go to that leather shop. So many fun things to do, so little time. This week is going to fly by."

"Well, when I live here, we can have regular adventures. So, that leather shop was so authentic; it even had that tangy smell. It's located at the far end of the Ponte Vecchio tucked in between two jewelry shops. I can't remember the name, but I'll find it for you."

"That'd be great!"

They ordered a margherita pizza with a homemade thin crust and a carafe of Chianti. Rose shared how she had spent the afternoon and wandered around the city looking at various neighborhoods. The waiter brought them some warm bread and their wine.

"I absolutely love Florence. I can't thank you enough for coming with me. It's like being a part of history all day long."

"I'm a bit jealous of your freedom to move here. This city is amazing with all of these cafés, famous works of art and museums."

"It's magical. So, I wandered about this afternoon and studied the two neighborhoods that Lyon suggested, which are Santo Spirito and Santa Croce. I particularly love Santa Croce because it's right near the Uffizi Gallery and the Palazzo Vecchio."

"You need to make a list of the most important things in your search for Lyon."

"Great idea. I am certain that I want something with modern conveniences and a view of the city."

"And the building?"

"Hmmm," said Rose, taking a sip of red wine. "I want a building with a history; maybe something built in the 13th or

14th century. I can live in a modern building in the States, but it would be fantastic to find a home owned by one of the Medici."

"Well, if that's what you really want, why not ask for something owned by Michelangelo Buonarroti's family?"

"You know me so well. I hadn't thought of that."

"I was kidding. But maybe you should text Lyon and see if there is an apartment available that was once owned by someone famous; I think the Michelangelo thing may be pushing it, but I know how important history is to you."

"Good idea. I'll confirm and make sure he has at least one historic building with some modern conveniences."

"Perfect," said Zoey. "I'll drink to that. This is going to be fun! Who knows? Maybe Stan and I can relocate too. This city is *bellissimo!*"

"A world away from Charlottesville."

"Shall I state the obvious?"

Rose eyed a statue in the courtyard and shifted her gaze to an ornate carved figure above the doorway of a church.

"I'm convinced that I'm making the right decision by buying a place. I feel like a new person here—energized and excited again. I mean, it's like living in a museum."

"Well," said Zoey, "I have a confession to make. I've been totally binge-watching HGTV and think I've seen every episode of *House Hunters International.* Just like the show, you need to make your wish list for an apartment and focus on the house hunt."

"Agreed. I want to live downtown in a 15th-century building that has some modern conveniences. I want to be able to walk to everything." She paused. "Maybe I can find something with a little extra space for a studio."

"Now you're talking," said Zoey, who added a splash of red wine to each of their glasses. "Here's to finding your dream house."

"I'll drink to that and salute my father, who made this possible."

Rose felt closer to her father now that she was in Italy. She could almost feel his approval. An image of his handsome face surfaced: dark hair, high, intelligent forehead, and gleaming blue eyes. He had this irritating habit of whistling when he saw something he liked. She recalled that she had always been able to ask him any question she wanted without judgment. It was a quality she always embraced as a teacher.

She took a sip of her wine and smiled at the memory.

Her father's older sister, Sofia, had lived in Florence for a few years, and he used to visit her there when he was a young professional. His face always lit up when he talked about her; Rose recalled her lively personality and beautiful palazzo in the center of town. A vision of Sofia's long blond hair, smooth skin, gold rings and stylish high heels came to mind. Aunt Sofia was always so sophisticated and confident, traveling from country to country. Sofia had only visited them in Charlottesville once when her father was ill, but there was no question in Rose's mind that her aunt would surely approve of her decision to move abroad.

Chapter 3

AFTER TOSSING AND TURNING all night, Rose awoke Zoey with her chatter. Her excitement was palpable as she hastily put on a simple sundress and tan suede ballet flats. A colorful scarf completed her carefree look. It was another beautiful sunny day, and she was actually living her dream.

"I'm going to head to breakfast."

"I need a triple espresso. You're way too peppy for me in the morning. I'll be there in ten."

Rose knew that meant fifteen minutes, so she made her way downstairs to the hotel breakfast area to get some coffee and refine her list for the realtor. She would tell Lyon that she had four priorities: a historic building downtown, modern conveniences, a view and maybe a bonus space for painting. Taking out her iPhone, she also made a list of her anticipated monthly costs. The good news was that she had diligently saved her own money for years, so she could go without working for a few months. Twenty minutes later, Zoey appeared in a pale-pink romper and coordinating jeweled sneakers.

"Good morning," she said, casually putting her sunglasses on top of her head. "Any sign of Lyon?"

"Not yet. I think we have ten or fifteen minutes if you want to grab some coffee. I've had my shot of espresso for the day, but I'll get a small plate of something to hold me over."

"Will do," said Zoey as she made her way to the breakfast bar.

"You know how I love options, and this spread is gorgeous. Did you try any of the cheeses or bread?"

"No, but that creamy Brie looks decadent. Doesn't cereal, fruit and yogurt taste better with a Renaissance backdrop of winged angels?" The enormous painting covered the back wall, and a small fountain gushed in front of it.

"We're definitely not in Charlottesville," joked Zoey, gingerly reaching for a few figs and some goat cheese. "And this certainly beats the teacher's lounge fare."

"Bellfield Academy feels a million miles away right now."

"Yes, but I just spied a group of teenagers over at that long table on the left. One of those boys just chucked a few ice cubes at his friends. Glad I'm not in charge!"

"Me too," said Rose as she saw a handsome man at the front desk. "Do you think that's Lyon?"

"I hope so for your sake."

"What are you talking about?"

His thick, dark hair caught her eye. Rose perused his profile and was drawn to the tall man in a navy suit. His olive skin lent him an air of mystery, and she envied his high cheekbones. He was talking to an attendant at the front desk and laughing aloud. Rose liked his easygoing manner. The man checked his watch.

"Is he really wearing a suit?"

"Very professional," said Zoey. "I like that."

Moments later, after introductions, Rose was caught off guard by Lyon's penetrating blue eyes. She swallowed hard and shifted her attention to the discussion at hand as they reviewed her wish list. Lyon said he wanted to show her a move-in ready modern apartment on the edge of the city to start the house tour.

"It's about a fifteen-minute walk from here, and I think you'll like many of the amenities. Some Americans move over here and refuse to give up things like clothes dryers in favor of a clothesline."

"I'd be okay with a clothesline on a back terrace," said Rose.

"I want an apartment that looks and feels Florentine with maybe some beams and terra-cotta floors."

"I understand." Lyon said. "House number one is a large affordable loft apartment in complete move-in ready condition. I think it will give you an excellent standard of comparison next to apartments in historic buildings. We'll look at three very different options that meet your criteria."

"Makes sense," said Zoey.

After a brisk walk, they arrived at a neat, clean stone building and began climbing three flights of a dark staircase. Zoey praised herself for her sensible shoes while Rose noted the cracked marble flooring with the freshly painted black railings. When they opened the apartment door, Rose was immediately struck by the fifteen-foot ceilings and bright open space. Light poured into the room from a large open skylight-style window. She was pleasantly surprised at how much she liked the apartment's decor even though it wasn't what she had asked for.

"This is beautiful," she blurted with excitement.

The living room was tidy and modern with a pair of beige leather sofas facing each other. A rectangular glass table with art books and a copper pot of wildflowers separated them. There was a modern cream rug and a couple of armchairs. Various-sized pictures of botanicals and vegetables adorned the walls in the salon style. Sensing her questions, Lyon offered, "Would you guess that the owner of this place is a master chef?"

"It's incredible," said Zoey. "Look at this kitchen!"

With a completely open floor plan, the living room opened to a massive kitchen with a large center island. In keeping with the modern feel, the countertops were a sleek beige granite with dark wood cabinets.

"This is so organized! I'll bet this is where the homeowner keeps his rather large collection of spices. I've never seen so many small individual spaces for kitchen items." Rose pulled open several drawers underneath the island; her curiosity was rewarded with the pungent scent of rosemary.

"This space is immaculate. Take a look at the pantry. He has jars and containers with individual labels for everything!"

"So impressive," said Rose, running her hand over the Viking industrial stovetop. "I could really entertain a lot of people in this kitchen alone."

"With all of your new friends!" Zoey chimed in. "This place is amazing!"

"Look at the built-in wine rack," said Rose, whose eyes widened as her gaze followed the unit all the way up the wall.

"Red wine is an integral part of the Italian culture," said Lyon with a wink.

"Yet another thing I love about this city!"

Lyon pointed out the long rectangular wood table adorned with silver candlesticks and steel chairs. A china cabinet was in the corner.

"Does this place come furnished?"

"Yes."

"What is it listed for?"

"This apartment is listed at 375,000 US dollars, which I know is at the top of your budget. But you wouldn't have to do a thing but unpack. Let's take a look at the master suite," said Lyon, ushering them up a small staircase to a massive top floor with skylights. A large queen bed was at the center of the room, along with an exercise bike. "You have so much room up here that you have many ways to use this space."

"I can't believe how big and open this room is. Look at the light."

"What's with the shower with no door?" asked Zoey, peering in the bathroom.

"That's an easy fix," said Lyon, ushering them over to the spacious bathroom with a modern sink and shower. "You can put a sliding door on this doorway for a few hundred dollars; I can give you the name of a contractor who could take care of it for you."

"Good to know," said Rose as she perused the space, thinking that she could put an easel by the window.

As if reading her mind, Zoey said, "The light would be great for you to paint right there."

"Not so fast," said Lyon. "I have two more important rooms to show you." He led them both out to a back terrace with a plethora of potted plants and a clothesline. "Here's your new GE clothes dryer," he said, pointing to the clothespins.

"Brave new world here," remarked Rose. "I can go and buy a clothes dryer and find a place for it, right?"

"Of course," said Lyon.

"I'm not loving this view," said Zoey, pointing to a cement courtyard that looked like it had seen better days. "What's that?"

"I think this is the neighborhood kids' spot for basketball."

"Oh no!" cried Rose. "A courtyard full of screaming kids. It'll feel just like home."

At Lyon's puzzled expression, Zoey explained, "We're both high school teachers. My friend has wisely decided to trade the world of education for that of an artist."

Rose laughed. "I would hardly call myself an artist, but at this point in my life, I want to develop my interest in painting."

"You are a wise young lady. I think finding one's passion in life is important." He took them to the other side of the loft where there was a small, brightly lit spare room with a small bathroom. "You could definitely use this room as a small studio, and have it double as a guest room when you have company."

"Now you're talking!" joked Zoey as she eyed the space. "Let's not forget about the best friend from the States who wants to come often with her husband."

"This is a gorgeous option, Lyon," said Rose as she walked through the second bedroom, noting the molding and fresh hardwood floors. "The homeowner has really taken good care of this property, and I have to admit that I do like how modern and comfortable this place is."

"Excellent," said Lyon. "This is house number one."

"We're going to call it the Master Chef Apartment like they do on HGTV."

"Master Chef Apartment. Very catchy." Lyon smiled. "I want you to keep in mind that it's in move-in ready condition when we head back to the city center to see a 15th-century building right in the middle of Santa Croce near the Uffizi."

Rose walked back into the light-filled living room of the loft and looked around again, taking in the glass chandelier in the dining room.

"The chandelier looks Venetian," she remarked as she walked around to view the ornate glass arms.

"That's right, Rose. It's absolutely original to this property— yet another old-world touch to an updated space. You can also see where the homeowner tried to maintain the integrity of the apartment if you look over at the restored corner cupboard to the right or that sconce by the front door."

"This is definitely a contender," said Rose, meeting Lyon's gaze.

"And if you tell her Michelangelo lived here, you'd have a sale," joked Zoey.

"Aha!" laughed Lyon. "So, you've got a passion for Michelangelo."

"She's obsessed."

"Good to know. I think you'll really like the next apartment, located mere minutes from where Michelangelo lived with Lorenzo Medici as he learned his craft."

Rose's eyes lit up, and she felt a blush staining her cheeks as she met Lyon's gaze. He winked at her and she smiled warmly, suddenly feeling like one of her students.

"Are you ready to see your second option?" asked Lyon.

"Absolutely," said Rose.

"This is when they go to a commercial break in the show," added Zoey on the way out the door.

"You're not going to believe this, but she's an English scholar," explained Rose with a laugh.

"All work and no play are no fun. I think being an HGTV addict is a good problem to have."

"You're making my job easy," countered Lyon. "Let's go."

***

Rose looked at *Il Duomo* and remembered that construction on the original cathedral had begun around the late thirteenth century, but its first architect couldn't figure out a way to construct a dome over its massive nave, so the building remained unfinished for nearly a century. They paused in front of the building, which took Rose's breath away.

"The second option that I found for you is a two-bedroom and two-bathroom apartment right over there," Lyon said, pointing.

"This is amazing," Zoey said, scanning the majestic cathedral.

"You know the story about how sculptor and architect Filippo Brunelleschi won the commission to construct the dome in the early 15th century?"

"Actually, I have no idea," said Rose. "Do tell."

Lyon rubbed his hands together as he looked upward at the magnificent Santa Maria del Fiore Cathedral.

"It's one of the largest domes ever created. Turns out Brunelleschi was a gifted architect who spent a great deal of time studying ancient Roman domes. No one would listen to him until the group in charge of construction held a competition for local artists on the design. Soon after, artists from all over Europe began submitting ideas."

"How did he beat out his competition?"

"On the day of the presentation, master builders arrived at the unfinished cathedral with models of their designs. Many ideas were reviewed, from the concept of using sponge-stone to keep the weight down to perhaps a giant pillar in the middle to hold it up." He looked Rose in the eye, and she practically hung on his every word.

"Well, when it was Filippo's turn to present—he went last, of course—he described his solution, which was a dome within a dome, octagonal in shape capped by a lantern, and the whole project would be completed without the use of scaffolding. The other master builders and judges demanded to see his model, which Brunelleschi refused to give them mainly because he was worried they'd steal his idea."

"Then what happened?" asked Rose.

"In a bold move, Filippo told the assembled group that the commission for the dome should be awarded to the artist who could make an egg stand on end, and it was only that man who had the necessary skill set for the job."

"Can't you just see these builders scurrying around for eggs to make their point? It must have been complete chaos!" Zoey said.

"I'm sure it was, but Filippo was ready and whacked his egg at the bottom and placed it on the table where it stood upright. Ultimately, he won the competition to construct the dome."

"How long did it take him?"

"Sixteen years, and it's the largest dome ever created with bricks and masonry." Lyon checked his watch. "Let's keep moving. We're right on time for house number two, which Zoey is going to label for us."

"I love the name game," exclaimed Zoey.

Rose looked around at the bustling activity that made up the center of town and felt as if she had one foot in the past and one foot in the present. She really couldn't remember the last time she had felt this content and excited.

The building was yellowish in color with a black door. They walked up two flights of stairs to the next showing. Lyon reached in his pocket for the keys, opening up the door to a large apartment. A faint smell of lavender filled the air as Rose took in the space. She was immediately drawn to the living room with its sloped, beamed ceiling and terra-cotta floors. The walls were a clean white and the wood was a deep rich brown. She was certain this was one of the first pictures that she had seen online a few weeks ago. The sound of keys rattling brought her attention to the task at hand.

"This apartment is 20 percent smaller than the last one but, as you can see by the terra-cotta floors and dark wood accents, very Florentine in feeling."

"Look at the ironwork on the stair railing," said Rose as she rubbed her hand over the fine metal craftsmanship.

"That railing is original to this space and hammered by hand several hundred years ago."

"I love that," said Rose, admiring the sleek, curved spinals and black finish.

Lyon guided them to the guest bathroom, which was white with bright-yellow tiles and an old shower curtain.

"This looks like an '80's throwback," said Zoey as she scanned the older-looking white subway tiles, dingy faucets and faded green paint.

"Yes, it's going to need some updating in time," said Rose.

Lyon ushered them into a spare bedroom, which he explained could be an office or the studio that she requested. Rose thought the room was small but functional with good light. A fresh coat of paint along with removing the 1980s-looking plastic venetian blind on the window would instantly brighten the space.

This kitchen was nothing like the other place; it was small and dated, but everything was white and looked clean. Zoey opened and closed several of the cabinets, studying the space for functionality.

"You could update the countertops and appliances readily and take down this wall to open up the floor plan. It wouldn't be too bad to modernize this room."

Rose pondered her suggestion. "How hard is it to knock down walls in one of these old buildings?"

"The smartest thing to do would be to go through this place with a contractor and get a bid on the job. You'll need to figure out if this is a load-bearing wall or not. Another idea would be to simply cut a large square hole in the center of the wall to open up the kitchen to this sitting room, which would also work."

"Great idea," said Rose. "The idea of taking down an entire wall seems overwhelming and expensive, so I like your solution. Is this furniture for sale?" asked Rose, eyeing the white sofa and coordinating armchairs. "This place is very nicely decorated."

"It could be, but everything has a price. We could add furnishings into an offer if you're interested. I can't wait to show you the master suite, which has been completely renovated."

They headed upstairs to a gorgeous open loft with beamed ceilings and a wall of built-in closet and storage space. Rose thought the room looked like something out of a magazine. The wrought iron carved headboard fit the space beautifully along with the white linen sheets with a gray velvet bench on the end. There were two tall wingback armchairs in front of an old fireplace.

"This is amazing!" said Rose.

"I love it!" exclaimed Zoey. "Where's my room?"

"You haven't seen anything yet," boasted Lyon. "Come this way."

He opened a door out to a beautiful balcony with a spectacular view of Florence.

"I could totally hang out here," said Zoey.

"Wow." Rose was practically speechless as she stared at the terra-cotta rooftops and national treasures; she noted the undulating rooftops and the Duomo in the distance. "Look at the Palazzo Vecchio!" she cried.

"I could see you starting your day here with a nice cup of espresso and ending it here with a glass of red wine."

"This is incredible," said Rose as she gazed all around her at the beauty of Florence. "I can see all of these little rooftops here."

"This is a special place," said Lyon, "and it's just come on the market. So, if you're seriously interested, then you'll need to proceed quickly."

Rose walked back through the bedroom, which did have an updated bathroom and more than ample closet space. There was something about this apartment that felt like home, but she just wasn't ready to decide.

"I think I need to see other options," said Rose. "I do love this place, but there are a fair number of updates that need to be done, and it's a bit smaller than the first one."

"Location, location, location," said Zoey as she looked at the living room. "And I think you could live with that extra bath for the time being. Maybe paint it and hang some nice photographs on the walls. The kitchen is all white and will work pretty well. I like the idea of cutting a hole in the wall and making it seem like an open floor plan."

"I'm glad you like this place, Rose," said Lyon. "Zoey?"

"We'll call this house number two with the Balcony View," Zoey said, rubbing her hands together. Lyon smiled, which Rose found endearing.

"I've still got one more apartment to show you that I think will be a very interesting comparison. It was once owned by Machiavelli, and it's been turned into six units. One of them has also just come available for you to see."

"Machiavelli and not Michelangelo?" joked Zoey.

"I think all of these options will put you in Michelangelo's backyard, so to speak," said Lyon. "Let's get going so you have time for sightseeing before the next one."

"I am thrilled with the first two options so far," said Rose. "But I love the idea of a 15th-century building!"

"Hmmm," said Zoey. "Let's just hope the updates are from

this century. There's no way I'd buy a place without modern conveniences."

"Wait until you see Machiavelli's palace. You may change your mind!"

Rose was thrilled with the Master Chef loft and the Balcony View apartment. She laughed. "I love the first two options. But I'm mostly worried about not seeing you every day anymore."

Zoey shrugged. "I think you're going to see more of Stan and me than you imagine. Remember, I get summers off and you may just have a spare bedroom."

"Well, we still have apartment number three to see. Let's hope it's got some extra space and doesn't need too much renovation."

"I can't wait to learn more about Niccolo Machiavelli's palace. In the meantime, let's go find that Florentine market and look around."

***

The market was bustling with activity as they wandered in and out of the aisles. Brightly colored scarves lined one stall while another contained leather wallets and purses. As they browsed through the stands, Rose paused to look at women's leather jackets. A cool black leather bomber jacket caught her eye as she reached to check out the price. The salesman spotted her and was just about to pounce when Zoey pushed her along, suggesting they eat first. They spotted an indoor market where raw slabs of meat were hanging on industrial hooks and rows of pigs' feet in jars filled the countertop.

"Don't you just love how rustic this market looks! It's like we're back in another century. Look at those cured hams over there."

"Those pigs' feet are the most unappetizing things I've seen in a long time!"

A pastry stand was located nearby, and the familiar smell of fresh baked bread wafted through the market. "How about if we get a baguette and some good cheeses to share? We can sit over there under that tree," offered Zoey.

"I'll go in search of some fruit and water as well."

"Sounds like a great plan."

There was a slight breeze as they sat under the tree to eat and discuss Rose's first two options.

Zoey took a plastic knife to cut into some fresh goat cheese and slathered it on a piece of warm bread. "Okay, the food here is absolutely decadent. I could have this for lunch every single day."

Rose savored the warm fresh bread, which practically melted in her mouth. "I'm going to have to figure out how to walk all the time so I can keep eating like this and still fit in my clothes," she joked as she unwrapped a slab of white cheese to try. "I was really surprised at how much I loved that loft. It did have most things on my wish list, but it was missing a view, which bothered me. I mean, I'd love to look out the window and see all of these glorious historical buildings. Now, that Balcony View was a little smaller but every bit as beautiful with the old beams and terra-cotta floors. It really did have a Florentine feel to it."

"I agree," Zoey said.

"I'm excited to see the third option. After all, Machiavelli's apartment has the history factor that intrigues me."

"I'm not sure he was such a great guy. Wasn't his book *The Prince* criticized for teaching power and deceit in politics?"

"Hmmm. I think that was five hundred years ago and some things may never change."

They both laughed. Rose savored her last bites of the fresh baguette. Her house hunt was both exciting and challenging as the enormity of the decision hit her.

***

Rose looked up to see Machiavelli's statue in a large alcove, and she wondered what it would be like to call this place home. Lyon was waiting for them outside a handsome building in the heart of Santa Croce. He had removed his jacket, and Rose thought he looked far more approachable and, in fact, more ruggedly handsome if that was possible. He greeted them warmly and asked about their lunch.

"This kind of history comes at a price, so I must warn you that this apartment is over your budget by 40 percent."

Zoey rolled her eyes, but Rose's curiosity was aroused, so much so that she started calculating if she would ever ask her mom for some extra money.

"This one's easy. Let's call this third option Machiavelli's Mansion," said Zoey. "Or maybe I should say Machiavelli's Over-Budget Mansion, but they certainly wouldn't say that on the show."

"Oh, and we must be true to the show," joked Lyon.

"Absolutely!" said Zoey. "I'm addicted."

Lyon opened the door to an enormous pale-yellow living room with fifteen-foot ceilings. A grand pair of immense windows looked out over a massive courtyard, letting in an abundance of light.

"The proportions of this place are great," commented Zoey as she walked around studying the living room. "But I must say that these floors don't look original to the house. Is that correct?"

Lyon agreed and said that it was possible to rip out the flooring and figure out what was underneath.

"These windows are fantastic. Look how much light they bring in, and the crest in the center looks original."

"Back when this place was built, the nobility wanted large windows to display their wealth to the community. This approach was also highly impractical as it drove up the cost of heating during the winter. Nowadays, the systems have been modernized so there is no longer an issue." He walked over to stand in front of the window. "Can't you picture what it was like to stand from this vantage point and look out over this sweeping courtyard back then?"

Rose took a closer look at the view of the immaculately planted gardens and sighed at the beauty below. She placed her fingers over the crest and felt as if she were touching history. The glass was warm on her fingertips, and she pondered what it would be like to have this view on a daily basis. It was a heady thought, and she suddenly felt an overwhelming sense of joy on this journey. Machiavelli's Mansion had such a historic feel, down to its wall tapestry and worn blue-velvet sofa.

Lyon led them to a small sitting room, which he thought could be used to expand the master bedroom. The room was too tiny to convert to anything. The master bedroom was small and more cramped than Rose had anticipated. The front formal rooms were designed for show, and the living quarters were tight and lacked good light. Lyon said that the master bath had been updated with a large shower and a jacuzzi-style bathtub.

"This is a beautiful bathroom!" Zoey exclaimed, running her hand over the gray marble tiles that made up the sink backsplash.

"This is well done," agreed Rose, who decided that she wouldn't need to do any updates in this room.

The next stop was the dining room, which featured built-in corner cabinets for entertaining. Rose marveled at the craftsmanship of the shelves designed to hold plenty of plates, glasses and red wine.

"You're ready for your next seated dinner party for twenty guests," said Lyon, who leaned on one of the wood chairs.

"Well," said Rose, "I'm going to have to import family and friends to come over from the States. I'm afraid I'm really going to start a new life from scratch."

"Don't worry," said Lyon. "There are loads of young professionals in this area. You'll meet people in no time. The Florentines are welcoming. I arrived here fifteen years ago thinking I was going to stay for a year, and here I am. It's a wonderful place to live. There's something almost sublime about experiencing history on a daily basis."

"But it comes at a price," offered Zoey.

"Yes, that's true. Rose, if you're serious about this apartment, you may want to think about taking out a mortgage."

"That's really not what I wanted to do."

"I understand, but the benefit of a place like this is the fact that it will always retain its value given the history. That's important for you to keep in mind. I'd like to show you the last room in the house, which is the kitchen."

Rose followed Lyon into a small dark space that was dated. The cabinets were old and worn, and the appliances had seen better days.

"This needs a complete renovation," Rose said.

"Yes, there is lots of work to be done here to make it meet your needs. Fortunately, the master bath has been remodeled and the formal rooms don't need much work."

Rose walked around the apartment again, taking in the size and scale of the living room and dining room areas, the kitchen and large windows with the courtyard view.

"You've really given me three great options, so I am going to have to ponder which one works best. I am hoping to make a decision in the next few days."

"I understand that this is a big decision, but don't dawdle too long. These are hot properties that will sell quickly. I'm available for questions at any time, so please don't hesitate to call or text me with what you're thinking."

"Absolutely," said Rose. "I won't drag my feet, but I want to get it right."

"Very good then," said Lyon, walking them back outside. He shook both of their hands and headed on his way. "Good luck with your decision."

Once Lyon had departed, Rose and Zoey walked side by side down the street.

"What are you thinking?" asked Zoey. "I think you should eliminate one choice and focus on the other two to make the final decision easier."

"Good idea," replied Rose.

"What did you think of Machiavelli's Mansion?"

"Well, the formal rooms are simply gorgeous with their high ceilings and grand proportions. Those huge windows are breathtaking and the family crest in the stained glass was like touching history."

"I agree, but the floors were not original."

"Yes, I didn't like that speckled faux marble or whatever that was they used in the '60s. It would be expensive to redo them."

"You could create a large master suite by using that small room, but there was no place to put a studio or have guests unless you put an inflatable mattress in the living room."

"You're right on that front. The kitchen was functional yet cramped and would all need to be updated. This place is also at the top of my budget."

"You don't want to take out a mortgage on your first apartment. I personally think that it's the wrong floor plan and way too expensive."

"But that stained-glass crest embedded in the living room window is so special!"

"If it were the 15th century, I could see why it mattered, but times have changed."

Rose laughed. "You're right. I think I can eliminate the Machiavelli Mansion from this house hunt."

"Let's clear our heads and go do some sightseeing for an hour or two while you think about the other two options. Maybe you should talk to your mom about it."

"The last thing I want to do right now is call Doris and get some lecture on how I threw away a good job to pursue a dream."

"Okay, if you don't want to consult your mom, then what

about calling your brother, Jack? He's always struck me as levelheaded and may surprise you with his insights."

"I like that idea," said Rose.

"Just don't forget to mention that your real estate agent is extremely good looking with a great sense of humor."

"*Not funny!*"

"Options are good," Zoey mused.

"What are you talking about?" demanded Rose. "Lyon is not an option."

"Hmmm," said Zoey. "I beg to differ. I saw the way he was looking at you. He's definitely interested."

Chapter 4

"ZOEY, WAKE UP!" SAID Rose excitedly.

"What time is it?" she asked sleepily with heavy-lidded eyes.

"Morning!"

"What's up?"

"I've picked an apartment!"

"Are you sure?" Zoey opened one eye to stare at her. "I thought you were going to consult Jack or your mom before putting your money down."

"Nope. I want to do this all on my own."

"Wow! That's quite a statement. Maybe you should have a cup of coffee first. Don't keep me in suspense any longer."

"Hold that thought; maybe I should talk to Lyon one more time."

"Sounds like a plan. I'm going back to sleep." She rolled over and called, "Wake me up when you decide!"

Pacing back and forth on the balcony, glancing over the Arno, Rose took the plunge and texted Lyon, asking him to call her. Since it was so early in the morning, she didn't expect to hear back from him so quickly. Her phone immediately rang.

"I was hoping you could meet me to talk about my house decision," Rose said.

"Happy to help. When and where?"

"Are you available now? I totally understand if it doesn't work. Would it be possible to see one or two of the apartments one more time?"

"I'll see what I can do. I can meet you in the lobby of your hotel in, say, thirty minutes. Does that work?"

"Perfect! *Ciao*."

Rose wrote Zoey a note saying she was meeting Lyon. She put her blond hair into a makeshift bun and threw on a pair of black jeans and a T-shirt. Grabbing her purse and sunglasses, she raced downstairs.

It was Saturday and the hotel was quiet. Sunlight streamed through the lobby windows, casting a glow on a bookcase with old leather-bound volumes of Italian and French books, a white bust of a Roman soldier and Egyptian marble bookends. Another glorious summer day lay ahead. Anticipation hung in the air, and she was alive with excitement over moving here. Would this feeling fade with time? Possibly, but Rose doubted it.

Rose spotted Lyon waiting. He wore faded jeans, a black shirt and brown leather cord around his neck; her heart skipped as their eyes met. Maybe she hadn't been willing to process how much she liked his soulful blue eyes and laid-back personality.

"Morning," she said warmly. "No suit?"

"I'm technically off duty today."

"Are you sure this is okay? This is a big decision and I want to get it right."

"Rose," he said softly, "I'm happy to help you."

Their eyes locked again, and Rose realized that his smile made her feel like anything was possible. "Got it."

"So, I thought we could go grab a cup of coffee and something to eat, before we look at the apartments. Will Zoey be joining us? If so, I'll call a cab. If not, you can ride with me."

"She's asleep. I'll check in with her in an hour and see what she wants to do. She's been so helpful to me. It may be fun for her to take a break from house hunting and do something else."

"It's early yet, but I know this great little place where we can get an espresso. Do you mind hopping on the back of my Vespa?"

"Sure," said Rose, admiring the vintage bike and the Sanskrit tattoo on Lyon's left forearm. He handed her a helmet and they took off, gliding in and out of the streets of Florence with ease. It was hard not to appreciate his lean and muscular build as she held on to his hips. Noticing the Roman numeral ten on his right wrist, Rose was beyond curious. They whipped around corners and easily dodged pedestrians. Rose reveled in her surroundings, feeling so alive in the present moment. A short time later, they pulled in front of a small café with a green awning.

"A friend of mine owns this place," he explained as he took her helmet and placed it side by side with his. "Have you ever tried fresh cannoli?"

"No, I haven't. What is it?"

"So, you really haven't lived yet!" he joked. "It's a fresh Italian pastry with ricotta cheese inside. Roberto is Sicilian and he makes the best breakfast cannoli in Florence. Any coffee?"

"I'd love an espresso."

Inside the café, Rose observed silver floor-to-ceiling display cases behind the front counter, which hadn't quite been filled with customers. The place was immaculate and the row of chocolate croissants mouthwatering. Rose's stomach rumbled as she ogled some cinnamon buns, greedily inhaling the scent of toasted nuts, woody coffee and fresh bread. A bearded man in a chef's hat stopped what he was doing to greet Lyon and speak to him in torrents of Italian. Rose decided then and there that she needed to work harder to understand the language because they spoke so quickly. Lyon made the introductions, and Roberto smiled warmly at her, respectfully addressing her in English.

"Hello, Rose. Such a pleasure to meet you. Lyon says that you are thinking of buying a place here. Please excuse my poor English."

"Your English is far better than my Italian. I have much to learn."

"You'll catch on quickly. You'll find we're a welcoming group.

Lyon says that you've never had cannoli before. I am honored to have you taste mine."

Rose offered to pay for her breakfast, but Lyon refused. A short while later, Roberto handed him two white bags filled to the brim. Lyon gingerly placed their breakfast in the pouch on the bike.

"Do you mind holding the coffee?"

"Sure. Where are we going?"

"There's a park not far from here that has a wonderful view of the city. I'm intrigued to hear your decision."

"You really gave me some great options and—"

"Hold that thought. Let's go."

Rose held the bag with her right arm as Lyon weaved them around several street corners. She eyed the bag, thinking their coffee was perilously close to spilling everywhere. Fortunately, he slowed to park in an alley. Armed with two bags, they headed up a steep staircase to one of the prettiest parks Rose had ever seen. It was lush and green with a bed of wildflowers to the right.

"Where are we?"

"*Giardino Bardini*. This is a gem of a place which has some of the best views of the city without all the tourists."

After a short walk, they picked a grassy knoll with a breathtaking view. Lyon handed her a wrapped cannoli and Rose savored her first bite. "This is unbelievable!"

"I told you so."

"And the coffee made it." She eagerly sipped the hot brew.

"You passed my test."

Rose took another bite. "I'm such the multi-tasking teacher. Useful skill."

"I'm impressed."

"You must tell Roberto that this is the best breakfast I've ever had."

"He'll be so pleased. He thrives on compliments."

"Well," she said, taking another sip of her coffee. "Let's get down to business. I've easily eliminated one of the three options that you've given me."

His eyes lit up. "That was smart. Which one?"

"I think Machiavelli's Mansion isn't right for me."

"I'm a little surprised by your decision because it has the most colorful history of the three places."

"I know, I know, but it's also way above my budget and the floor plan doesn't work for my lifestyle."

"I had kind of guessed that," Lyon conceded. "I could see you were uncomfortable. So, you have two choices left. Which one are you considering?"

"As much as I liked the Master Chef's loft, it doesn't have location and, frankly, I don't need an over-the-top kitchen. So, I think I want to buy apartment number two, Balcony View!"

"That's great news! The second option is very Florentine in character and the location is practically unbeatable. You'll also have a bonus room to act as a guest bedroom or studio."

"I really like having extra space for work or entertaining. Do you think I could see it just one more time before I put my money down?"

"You're not going to believe this, but I suspected you may want to see this one." He reached in his pocket for the key. "I've made arrangements for us to go back and take a look this morning."

"Are you really this good at your job?"

"Absolutely." He paused with a wicked grin. "No, seriously, I just got lucky."

"Does your family get over here to see you much? This is a huge life change for me."

"Rose, you may find that you have more company than you really want. My parents and sister relocated to Tuscany, and I have a brother who lives in New York; he gets to Rome regularly on business. We see each other fairly often as well."

"That works."

"This could be an exciting day for you."

"Actually, I don't need to see it again," said Rose as she recalled the spectacular view of the city. "Will you write up the contract? I'm sure this is what I want." They embraced, which seemed like the most natural thing in the world.

"Excellent," said Lyon, breaking away. "I'm going to have to move quickly because I do think this place is special."

"Oh no! I hope there aren't any other offers."

"It hasn't come up on the market yet. I think the official listing is scheduled for Monday, so let me get to work. It was my understanding the seller wants a clean cash deal with no contingencies, so I think your situation is perfect. We can put in an all-cash offer with a quick closing, which would be attractive to the seller." Lyon smiled warmly. "I think you're going to love Florence, Rose."

"I'll bet you say that to all your clients."

"Actually, you're the first." His blue eyes with slight crinkles at the corners hinted at an adventurous spirit.

"Let's get this locked down. I'll call the office and have my assistant draw up the paperwork. It'll probably take the better part of the day to negotiate. Don't worry, I'll keep you posted."

"Sounds great. I'm so excited!"

"I'd really like to make this happen for you, so I need to drop you back at your place and call the seller's agent."

"Thank you for everything!"

"Don't thank me yet. I've got to get the deal done first."

Rose knew her decision would set the stage for what came next in her life. She was ready yet on edge. Questions swirled in her head about whether she could make this journey on her own. It was hard to drown out the voice of Doris, but she told herself that she had to try something new. That it was better to try and fail than get stuck in a routine. *I can do this,* she thought.

For the rest of the weekend, Rose was tied to her iPhone waiting for updates on whether her offer had been accepted. Lyon sent a series of cryptic texts that he was working on the deal but there was nothing conclusive.

***

By Monday afternoon, Rose and Zoey were tired of waiting around for news, so they decided to tour the Boboli Gardens located directly behind the Pitti Palace, which was once the home of the ruling Medici family in Florence. The vast green spaces were perfectly landscaped and encircled by stunning views of the city. In the hillside above an amphitheater, they saw the Fountain of Neptune.

"Come on, let's get a selfie in front of the King of the Sea so I can send it to Stan!"

They posed for the camera with Neptune in the background holding a large trident.

"I think Neptune is symbolically springing forth life into the city," Zoey said.

"Well, I wish he'd breathe some life into my house purchase. I'm trying not to feel like I'm drowning in a sea of anxiety. Why has there been no news? You head home in two days and I really want that apartment!"

"He'll get back to you as soon as he knows something."

They walked along the neatly manicured garden paths until Rose's phone buzzed. It was Lyon. She held her breath and listened. When she hung up, she nearly screamed.

"Well?"

"I got it!" she exclaimed. "The seller accepted my offer immediately and I've got a thirty-day close because he's relocating to Dubai and wants out."

"Oh, that's great news!" exclaimed Zoey, who gave Rose a hug.

"I need to get to Lyon's office and sign the contract right now."

"Okay, great. I'll let you head on. I'm incredibly happy for you!"

"I love it! Thank you for helping me through this process. I couldn't have done it without you. I don't even want to think about telling my mom."

"One thing at a time. The Balcony View apartment is amazing!"

Chapter 5

LYON'S OFFICE WAS ADORNED with a mahogany desk and large windows. A black-and-white family photograph on his desk caught Rose's eye. She looked at the stunning African American woman and serious-looking man in glasses. Also in the photo were two boys nearly the same age, one with brown hair and the other blond hair, along with a pretty young girl wearing a white bow.

"Great picture."

"Thanks. I'm the kid in the picture that doesn't look like his parents. My mom is from Namibia and my dad is an English poet."

"Interesting," she said, studying the photograph. "But, more importantly, I actually think you do look like the best of both your parents."

"I love your optimism. It's refreshing." He laughed again. "I'll bet there aren't a lot of half-black Brits in Charlottesville."

"Actually, you might be pleasantly surprised. Charlottesville has become much more cosmopolitan than it used to be."

"Good to know," he said, picking up a stack of papers; he guided her to a nearby chair so that he could carefully explain the details of the contract. Rose asked several questions but felt she could trust Lyon. Afterwards, he brought in a notary, and Rose felt like she was initialing and signing her life away. At the end of the meeting, she surveyed her final signature on all of the paperwork and paused to look out the large bay window in his office.

"What's the next step?"

"I'll need a good-faith deposit, so you'll need to wire the money in tomorrow morning once your bank reopens. You'll pay the rest at closing. I'm meeting the seller on Wednesday and I'll set up an inspection. Our firm can handle that for you."

"Sounds perfect. Just email me the dates because I'm sending the rest of my belongings over here once I take possession."

***

A short time later, they were walking down the street when Lyon stopped.

"Oh, I almost forgot! I have something I want to show you before we head to the restaurant to celebrate." He paused to get his bearings. "Do you mind if we take a detour?"

"Sure, no problem," said Rose. "So, where are we going?"

"*Santo Spirito Basilica.*"

"Now I am intrigued."

Rose crossed crowded streets and hurried along in anticipation; Lyon took her hand and guided her along the narrow sidewalk next to him. The dull-looking exterior of the church caught Rose off guard as she studied the plain white facade. It was the type of building that one could pass by each day and not even notice. Her curiosity piqued, she eyed Lyon warily, wondering what he had in store for her. When they stepped inside, the beauty of the interior took her breath away as she looked around the peaceful Renaissance sanctuary.

"Brunelleschi designed the interior."

"This is stunning. Look at all of the little chapels."

"When Lorenzo de Medici died in 1492, Michelangelo moved out of his palace and into a community of Augustine monks who were associated with this basilica. These monks allowed him to study anatomy in the hospital adjacent to the church."

"You know, I taught a class on Michelangelo's study of anatomy just last week. My students were horrified yet amazed at the concept. Needless to say, it was a lively discussion."

"Michelangelo was a true genius. His study of anatomy was the only way for him to create such lifelike sculptures. Thanks to the monks, Michelangelo sculpted this rendition of a nude Jesus Christ on the cross. It's recently been restored and brought here."

Rose was awestruck by the four-and-a-half-foot Renaissance masterpiece that appeared nearly lifelike in the nave. The carving was exquisite, and the proportions of the saint's nude body were perfection.

"They suspended the sculpture above the church's old sacristy in a way that allows us to see it from every angle."

The moment was unlike anything Rose had ever known.

"Lyon, this is so special. I can't believe I've actually just purchased a home in Florence and I'm now standing a few feet away from a Renaissance masterpiece. This all seems almost surreal."

They walked around the wooden crucifix several times, observing the serene and sublime Christ.

"I thought you'd like it. The crucifix was lost for centuries and they found it, I think, in the 1960s. It's recently been restored and put back here, which was its original home." He paused. "Zoey told me the way to your heart is through Michelangelo, so I thought I'd try to impress you."

"You have. I didn't even know this existed."

"It really is spectacular and off the beaten path. How about a glass of red wine to celebrate the day?"

"Yes! Let me call Zoey."

Zoey told Rose that her husband, Stan, had run into some guy named Ben Pierce the other night at a bar downtown. They got to talking and Stan mentioned that his wife taught at Bellfield.

"This Ben guy started asking a million questions about you," Zoey said.

"Ancient history," Rose said. "We dated way back in high school. I bumped into him a few weeks ago."

As Rose spoke to Zoey she glanced over at Lyon and realized that he had just shown her something far deeper than any experience she had ever had with Ben.

"Talk to you later," she said to Zoey, somewhat somberly.

"Everything okay?" asked Lyon.

"Yes," said Rose. "All good. Zoey is going to meet us at the restaurant in an hour."

Lyon led them out the door and took her hand as they walked in companionable silence for the next few blocks. Rose looked over at Lyon's profile, wondering why she felt as if she had always known him.

"So, what happens when we're neighbors?"

"Neighbors?" she asked.

"I live a few blocks away from your new place. Sounds like you're seeing someone in the States?"

"No," Rose said. "Not involved with anyone at the moment. How about you?"

"There was someone, but we recently split. It's complicated. I'm not sure that now is the time to go over it."

"Then don't. Today, I made the only commitment I really care about for a while. I want to live in the present and not overthink things the way I always have. The next month is going to be exciting. I'm ready to move in now."

"That's the spirit," Lyon said.

The restaurant was on a side street and appeared to be a local hangout. Rose eyed the amber walls, colorful array of landscape paintings and strategically placed steel spice racks. They made their way through the crowd and found seats at the end of the bar. Lyon ordered them a bottle of pinot noir in Italian, and judging by the bartender's expressive gestures, Rose surmised that it was an expensive bottle. Lyon dismissed her desire to split the tab. For the next hour, the conversation and the wine flowed easily.

"Someday, I'd love to take you to Tuscany to see my family's vineyard."

"I thought you said you're from South Africa."

"My parents bought a winery here about seven or eight years ago. They decided that they love the food and culture in Italy better than anywhere else."

"So, you're a vintner too?"

"Actually, I have several businesses, but that's not what we're here to talk about."

Rose smiled and sipped her red wine. "What's with the ten tattooed on your right wrist?"

"I'm celebrating ten years of sobriety." They both laughed. "Actually, it's my lucky number."

"Not buying it."

"Okay, I almost died ten years ago in a climbing accident and I vowed to change the way I approached life."

"And did you? Change, I mean."

"Yes. And the Sanskrit represents my commitment to all things ethereal."

"As seen in poetry."

He nodded and smiled. "My father is a poet who taught at Oxford for twenty years. Do you believe in fate?"

"I love that he was a teacher, and, frankly, right now, I believe in staying present and not questioning things too much. If my mom had her way, my whole life would have been planned out. I was given a promotion to be a dean at the private school where I teach. My mother is extremely upset that I gave up a good job and security to move here with no real plan. It's the first time in my life that I don't have a set of goals. I really just want to explore life here and paint . . . but also, not to answer to anyone."

"So, you've always been an overachiever and maybe even a bit of a people pleaser?"

"Kind of vanilla, huh?"

"I wouldn't say that, but I'm curious about your interest in painting."

"Do you know you're the first person to ask me that?"

"Really? Why hasn't anyone encouraged your art?"

"Well, Zoey has been very supportive. Unfortunately, my mom thinks artists are these bohemian crazy people with no values," she laughed. "Seriously, I have no idea why."

He pondered her comments. Rose admired his hands but quickly shifted her gaze when Zoey walked in and waved to them from across the bar, weaving through the crowd.

"Hey, guys."

Lyon spoke to the waiter, and they were soon seated in a nearby booth. Once her friend was settled, Rose told her all about their visit to the basilica.

"You told me the way to her heart was through Michelangelo, so I figured I'd show her something off the beaten path."

"Oh, Zoey, I've got to take you tomorrow. It's such a beautiful masterpiece in a church that looks nondescript from the outside."

Suddenly, Lyon's phone buzzed, and he excused himself from the table for a few minutes.

"You two were looking very cozy when I walked in," said Zoey as she studied her friend.

"I like him. He's so interesting."

"Well, looks like he's got some competition."

"What are you talking about?"

"It sounds like Ben is really interested in you."

"That's ridiculous. I just ran into him at a coffee shop. We were together in high school. No big deal."

"Hmm. This is all very entertaining."

Rose took a sip of her red wine. "I'm glad you're amused, but I'm a free agent who's about to become a homeowner."

"We'll have to fast-forward three months from now and see how you're doing. I predict there may be some romance in your life."

"Well, I'm certainly in love with Florence and my new apartment."

"I'll drink to that," said Zoey, clinking glasses.

Lyon returned to the table looking upset. "I'm so sorry. I've got to take care of some business. I'm going to need to head on for an hour or so." He stared at Rose. "I'll find you later. *Ciao.*"

After he departed, Zoey said, "He's so charming."

"He said he's married to his businesses."

"That's okay. What else does he do?"

"I have no idea, but his parents own a winery."

***

Rose ordered the chicken Bolognese, and Zoey decided upon a flaky white fish over linguine in clam sauce. Rose looked around at the young, hip crowd and admired a lanky woman's impossibly high heels. "On to more weighty matters. Did you buy any boots today?"

"You should see them; they're black over-the-knee wedges. They cost a fortune, so I'm probably done with my shopping."

"I'm certainly done with mine too! I can't believe I just bought a house. It's so crazy that this is all happening. I sent Jack some pictures and he wrote that he and Nicky are spending summers here."

"Wait a minute. He's going to have to stand in line behind Stan and me!" Zoey winked. "Just kidding. Have you told Doris yet?"

"Not yet. I'm still trying to figure out my approach. What would she think of Lyon?"

"Now that's a good one," said Zoey, trying to suppress a laugh. "Well, he's not Southern."

"Nope. He's half black and half English. His father taught poetry at Oxford. Just saw the family picture on his desk."

"So that's how he's got those sexy soulful eyes. The plot thickens."

"Do you think he's married, or maybe was? I don't see a ring."

"There's got to be an ex somewhere," Zoey said. "He's way too good looking to be living alone."

The waiter set down steaming hot plates artfully arranged with rosemary and wildflower garnishes. Rose sampled the chicken, which melted in her mouth as the taste of fresh garlic lingered.

"No wonder this place is so crowded." Zoey gave her fish a thumbs-up as they debated how they were going to spend their last two days. "Let's go to the Laurentian Medici Library for a visit. Michelangelo designed it."

"I thought you'd never ask," Rose said.

Just as they were finishing up, Lyon reappeared, smiling and at ease again.

"Hey, glad I caught you. All is well. Anyone want to go dancing? I know this great little club a few blocks from here. A couple of my friends are going. I can introduce you."

"Yes!" exclaimed Zoey, who looked at Rose. "Sure. I'd love it. Let me do a quick change at the hotel and I can be ready in about forty-five minutes. Will that work?"

"I think you look lovely the way you are, but I understand. I'll pick you up in an hour. You'll love this club, I promise."

***

Once back in the hotel room, Rose raced to get ready, quickly throwing off her jeans and digging into her suitcase for something suitable to wear.

"I'm going to email Stan so that he has a love note when he wakes up tomorrow morning."

"You guys are so adorable. I wish—"

"You'll figure it out. In the meantime, you're going to wear some non-sensible shoes, girlfriend." Zoey rummaged in her suitcase and pulled out a pair of black stilettos. "Try these on."

"I don't think I can even walk in those things, let alone dance in them." Rose looked at the label. "These are Prada. Where did you get them?"

"A second-hand designer website. You know how I love my heels."

"Smart . . . How high are these?"

"Five inches. Give them a try. They're gorgeous."

"Maybe you should stop teaching English and start your own fashion blog."

"That could be dangerous."

Rose used Zoey's straightener to redo her hair, adding some corkscrew curls on the ends. Zoey insisted on doing her eye makeup and added a layer of black liner to emphasize her blue eyes.

"Try this black halter top. I think it would look great on you," she said, rummaging through her bag. "You've got some black skinny jeans somewhere in that bag of yours."

A short time later, Rose looked at her black outfit in the mirror and smiled; she felt confident and happy. The heels were stunning. She and Zoey, who wore a black floral-print dress, posed together for a selfie, which Zoey posted on Instagram with the caption *Girls Night Out #funinflorence #teacherscandance*.

Lyon was waiting for them outside with a black town car and a driver.

"I could get used to this," said Zoey. He greeted them warmly with a European peck on both cheeks. A short time later, they arrived at what looked like a stone townhouse, and Lyon ushered them to a side door to a back courtyard filled with partygoers. A band was playing under a tent, and Lyon greeted several of his friends.

"This is Dominique and her brother, Jean-Paul. These are my American friends, Rose and Zoey. Rose just bought her first place here."

Rose greeted them and shook their hands; Dominique's red fingernails and silk neck scarf made her glad that she had allowed Zoey to dress her. Next, he introduced them to Giovanni and Salvatore, who produced their own line of women's shoes. Zoey was thrilled to make their acquaintance and immediately launched into a series of probing questions that made Giovanni embrace her.

"What a delightful and discerning young woman," he exclaimed as he noticed her shoes, "with impeccable taste."

Lyon took Rose over to a side terrace with leafy green urns. "I think Zoey will be thoroughly entertained. Giovanni is a master of his craft and he's a great storyteller." Lyon paused and locked eyes with Rose. "You look amazing tonight."

"Thank you."

Suddenly, the band began playing a disco beat with American words. "Perfect timing!" Lyon said. The crowd cheered and came to life when the DJ took the stage.

"Who is it?" asked Rose, standing on her toes trying to see through the crowd.

"It's Zedd, one of the most popular DJs in the world. Ready?"

Lyon easily led her out to the dance floor, and their bodies touched momentarily as he held her close; her head fit directly under his chin. Rose regretted that he broke away to swivel in tandem with the pulsating beat. His movements were graceful yet calculated, as he effortlessly pulled her to him and let her go. He held out his right hand, which she took as he dipped her to the right and to the left. Somewhere she sensed that a few other dancers gave them a bit more room. Rose was only focused on him and felt safe in his presence.

Lyon was different than anyone she'd ever known before—completely unpredictable. When he reached for her, she melted into his arms. Several songs passed by as they danced, their bodies just inches apart. Reluctantly, they separated when the DJ announced a short break. Feeling the sweat dripping down the back of her shirt, Rose said, "I think I need a cold drink."

Lyon took her over to find Zoey, who was still chatting with Giovanni; he promised to get them some champagne. Dominique reappeared, still looking perfectly coiffed. She gave Rose's sweaty form a once-over. "I should like to tell you that Lyon is extremely complex and you seem, well, rather out of your league."

"Excuse me?" said Rose.

"Lyon is very worldly, so I wouldn't want you to misunderstand his interest in you, which is purely professional."

"What difference does it make to you?"

"We've been together for seven years, so I'd say I know him quite well. I wouldn't want you to get any false ideas."

"Really?" said Rose sarcastically.

"You Americans think you can do whatever you want. You'll never belong here," retorted Dominique as she glided away to whisper something in her brother's ear.

Rose calmly returned her stare, refusing to be intimidated. Zoey came up and whispered, "That woman doesn't like you. Makes me appreciate Southern hospitality."

"Cheers to that!" Rose said. "I think I just met Lyon's girlfriend."

"She doesn't have a chance against you, and besides, he's barely talked to her. I thought he said they broke up?"

"I have no idea, but she's clearly still into him."

Rose wondered why Lyon had felt the need to bring her here to meet his current or former love interest. His situation was definitely complicated. "I can handle it. There's nothing close to Doris on a rampage."

"When are you going to tell her?"

"I haven't decided yet. I'm enjoying my freedom." She paused. "The hardest thing I'm going to do is say goodbye to you tomorrow. Thank you for everything, dear friend."

"I'm going to miss you."

"Me too."

"I'm so proud of you; I have no doubt that the next chapter is going to be filled with excitement."

"I can't wait for the adventure to begin!"

Zoey winked. "It already has."

Chapter 6

ROSE AWOKE EARLY EACH morning anxious to escape her one-bedroom efficiency to explore Florence and use the time to draw and work on learning to converse in Italian. The days seemed to melt into one another as she immersed herself in Florence's vibrant history.

In the fifteenth century, Lorenzo Medici was Michelangelo's patron, and his influence could be recognized in places like the Pitti Palace, the palazzos and the art galleries. Rose walked everywhere, drinking in the culture and sketching.

Another week went by and then another; she still hadn't told Doris that she had bought a place. It was ridiculous, but in her heart she didn't want to be disappointed by her response, again. She took herself to the Uffizi often, spending hours studying the treasures inside. At night, she did her best to copy some of the pictures.

Being on her own, Rose discovered a sense of freedom for the first time ever. There was no structure. She wandered the streets of Florence, taking in the sights and sounds as if she were a college student again, discovering the beauty of a historical city and reveling in its many treasures.

This experience was empowering and liberating.

The text caught her by surprise:

Hi Rose: Great to see you a few weeks ago. I'm in Florence doing some research. Would love to take you to dinner on Saturday night and catch up. Would that work? Ben

Rose couldn't believe her eyes. Ben Pierce was in Florence and had just asked her out! "Really," she said aloud, as she read the note again. Her brother, Jack, must have given him her cell number. *What is he doing in Florence?* Her surprise and excitement were palpable. She had thought about him way too much over the years, and she was sure he had forgotten all about her. She told herself repeatedly that Ben had been her first love and was part of the tapestry of her life.

Her palms began to sweat as she recalled how devastated she felt when she had heard the news of his impending nuptials five years ago. It was splashed all over the society pages that this young, handsome entrepreneur was marrying some Victoria Secret model. The woman was stunning, and Rose felt woefully inadequate. She inadvertently glanced at her athletic thighs. With a groan, she willed herself not to feel anything. Telling herself to not overanalyze as usual, Rose pushed her fears aside and decided that they would have a great catch-up no matter what. Besides, a familiar face from home would be great right now.

Rose texted back an hour later so as not to look too eager.

So glad you got in touch. I'd love to get together. When and where?
He replied: *There's a place called Notre Bene in Santa Croce. Have you heard of it?*
Yes. I could meet you there around 7 o'clock, she texted.
Perfect. See u then.
Looking forward to it.
Me too.

***

By Saturday morning, female vanity won out, and Rose made a trip to a boutique called Bella. Rose eyed the racks of gorgeous clothes, thinking that she didn't want to try too hard. A white sundress caught her eye.

"This is gorgeous!" she exclaimed, holding the dress up to her.

"Very simple and elegant. I'm sure it will look beautiful on you; such pretty blond hair and blue eyes," said the salesperson, taking hold of it and putting it in the dressing room.

"I like that," said Rose, turning her attention to a ruffled black blouse that would go with everything.

Of course, the dress fit perfectly and so did the black shoulder-baring blouse, and then she spied a fabulous pair of big earrings. *You need to leave this store now*, said a small voice in her head.

"I could never work here," said Rose, handing over her credit card. "I'd have to buy everything."

"Thank you. The white dress is perfect for summer and can go anywhere. You've got good taste."

Her hair took forever to style that evening. *High school was a long time ago,* Rose reminded herself, yet she couldn't contain her excitement; the night held the promise of summertime. Well, Ben was really handsome and he was taking her out to dinner. *Life is good,* she concluded, getting frustrated as she brushed out her elegantly arranged ponytail.

Rose's composure nearly crumbled when saw Ben standing out front of Notre Bene in a button-down, tailored khaki pants, and loafers with no socks.

"I'm so glad this worked," he said as she approached. "You look gorgeous."

"Thank you," she replied anxiously; his steely-eyed gaze knocked her off balance. She looked away and quickly adjusted the sleeve of her new dress.

"Shall we?" he said, holding the door open for her.

The restaurant was small and romantic, filled with baskets, intricate Mediterranean tiles and the scent of garlic. They were escorted to their table in the back corner of the restaurant, and Rose was glad she had chosen a classic white dress and heels. A black-clad waiter appeared soon after they sat down and took their drink order. Ben asked if she liked champagne and ordered up two sparkling glasses, which came minutes later.

"It's great to see you again, Rose," he said.

Rose blushed. "You too. I'm glad you're here."

"You know, I always thought you were absolutely adorable."

"You mean, Jack's bratty little sister? Say it isn't so. You guys used to torment me. Remember the time Jack bounced a basketball on my head when I followed you to the park. He wanted nothing to do with me."

"And who defended you?"

"Hmmm," she replied. "I'd forgotten you walked me home."

"Remember when your brother and I refused to include you in our lacrosse warm-ups? You had the most wicked temper tantrum and your mom practically dragged you inside."

"I was only ten," she laughed.

"You were a little spitfire and awfully cute in those pigtails trying to chase after us."

"I still have a temper, so be forewarned." She winked.

"I'm not worried. I've had years of experience dealing with ballistic clients after a market crash."

Anticipation hung in the air, mingling with a feeling of familiarity.

"I'm so surprised you're here."

"I was researching Jefferson's travel abroad for my book, and he loved Italy. Suddenly, it seemed like a perfect plan to visit Florence and tie it in with a trip to see you."

Rose swallowed hard. "I'm so glad you did. It's wonderful to see you too."

"I feel the same way."

Rose felt the intensity of his gaze. Moments later, a waiter came to take their order and talk about the specials of the night. Rose managed to use her conversational Italian to select her meal; she couldn't resist the grilled salmon, and Ben chose a pasta chicken dish.

For hours, they talked nonstop throughout dinner as Ben shared his tales of mountain climbing, Wall Street and his obsession with the Seattle Seahawks. Rose hung on his every word. She shared how she missed her students, purposely avoiding mention of her mom. She regaled him with some of the ridiculous moments with helicopter parents who didn't take no for an answer.

"There was this one dad who I'll call him Mr. Smith who texted me regularly to check on his daughter's test scores."

"What did you do?"

"I told him that his daughter was not a number and to get a life, in so many words. The pressure that parents put on their kids is awful. I could always tell which students really wanted to learn and those who only cared about the grade."

"I was told by a reliable source that you were voted best teacher by your students."

"Oh," said Rose. "I taught great kids."

"Clearly, you care and you're always willing to listen. That's a wonderful quality."

"Thanks," said Rose. "That means a lot to me."

"Okay, my turn. I'm going to address the elephant in the room," Ben said, dabbing his mouth with a napkin and then taking a breath. "I was married to Angelique for three long years and I've been divorced for over a year. We met through friends at a party in New York. I guess I was young and shallow, but I fell for the whole supermodel thing. Turns out, we fought all the time but managed to produce a beautiful little girl named Emily. We're still ironing out custody, but I keep a place in the city to see my daughter every other weekend. It's not perfect, but this arrangement has been working just fine."

"So, your life is complicated with an ex and a young daughter."

"Yup, but I'm still the same fun-loving guy that you knew in high school." He winked. "I never forgot about you."

"Me either, but high school was a long time ago, Ben. We grew apart and led separate lives. When my dad died, it was really, really hard on all of us. Those college years are kind of a blur now, but I have no regrets about staying close to home. And it was all I could do to keep moving forward with my life. I lost my hero," she said quietly, swallowing hard. "And it took me a long time to recover, and then I had to deal with Doris and her new boyfriends, then she got remarried, and then Jack got married, and I don't know . . . What I wanted got lost somewhere in doing what I thought was the right thing for my family. That being said, I didn't make as rash a decision as you may think."

"You were always the responsible one."

"I tried to be the perfect daughter Doris wanted me to be, and then, well, I just couldn't do it anymore. I had to get away and start a new life here on my own terms."

"Thanks for being so honest, Rose. I understand."

"I appreciate that."

She swallowed hard and their eyes locked, and then they sat quietly, absorbing the waves of truth and emotion that had washed over them.

After dinner they stepped back into the cool summer evening.

"Hey," he said. "I'd hate for you to think this evening is predictable. You know, a little wine, a nice dinner and then back to my place."

"Who says I'd go back to your place?"

"Well, I can only hope, but, in the meantime, I want to show you something I stumbled upon yesterday." He shot her a mischievous grin.

"Aha!" exclaimed Rose. "Now, I'm completely intrigued."

"That was my goal, Miss Maning."

They continued to chat easily as he led her down several blocks. Rose relaxed and shared how her dad had always encouraged her to live abroad; Ben recalled that it was her dad who taught him to play tennis and how much he had admired his intellect. The conversation was relaxed. Suddenly looking around, she asked, "Will you give me a hint as to where we're going?"

"*Gallerie Art Moderne.*"

"I didn't know you were interested in art."

"Well, actually I've got an art dealer friend at Christie's. He's guided me in my collecting over the years."

"You've acquired art? I'd love to hear about it."

"Rose, you're probably the only woman I know who's more interested in the type of art I bought than its value."

"Thanks," she said as they listened to the sounds of violin music coming from a small corner band. College students were hanging out in clusters, their laughter and clapping adding to the air of excitement. "How fun! I'd read there was some festival going on down here tonight."

"It's only ten o'clock." He paused to get his bearings. "There it is!" He grabbed her hand and they ran across the street.

When they walked inside, the manager welcomed them and kissed Rose soundly on both cheeks. "*Bella donna,*" he exclaimed. "I'm Matteo and I am delighted that you have graced us with your presence." He looked over at Ben. "And you too, sir."

Ben laughed. "Thanks."

Rose liked his curly dark hair and colorful striped shirt; he ushered them to the bar area, which consisted of a long rectangular table complete with a white linen tablecloth. Clustered groups of art lovers were peering at various wall-sized oil paintings.

"Thank you," said Rose, taking a sip of her wine as she observed several modern landscape paintings with varying shades of purple and green.

"You are free to wander around. There's a master list by the front door that gives the artist's name and the price. Please let me know if you have any questions. Okay?"

As she eyed the exhibit, she gravitated to a large oil painting in the far right corner with splashes of terra-cotta and gold. She said it reminded her of Tuscany.

"Well, you're right," said Ben, who read the description, then led her up a concrete staircase. She eagerly followed him down a short hallway to a large, well-lit room. Rose couldn't believe her eyes. It was a nine-foot rendering of Michelangelo's *The Creation of Adam*. She gasped and clapped her hands. "What in the world!" she exclaimed, moving closer to the masterpiece to see the colors. "This is absolutely fantastic! Who did it?"

"Exchange students have been copying it for weeks as a final project. The kids scanned the painting onto a board and got creative with the colors. The manager said the gallery has been crazy and two of them have slept here in sleeping bags. Coffee cups and bagels have littered these floors, and they listen to American pop and jazz."

Rose walked forward to study their rendition. "I love how they used florescent colors. This Adam in neon green is awesome. Very creative!"

"How about God over there in purple?"

"This is really fun and clever. I'm surprised that they did a scan and didn't try to draw any of it themselves."

Ben studied her. "Don't tell me you're an artist too."

Rose took a large swallow of her wine and coughed. "I shouldn't have said anything. I love it."

He leaned in closer. "Don't change the subject. Rose?"

"Um," she said. "It's a long story but, yes, I can draw pretty well, and I am passionate about Michelangelo, as you know. That's it."

"Wait a minute. That's why you moved here! And if I know Doris Maning, she'd never let you pursue anything to do with painting and drawing."

"It's a dream, and I know it's crazy, but I needed to explore this part of myself."

Ben leaned in and gave her a kiss on the forehead. "I get it. We don't need to talk about it anymore until you're good and ready." They were nose to nose, and just as Ben was about to kiss her, a loud coughing noise interrupted.

"Okay, you two," said the manager. "You're supposed to be looking at this exhibit and exchanging pithy thoughts on mankind."

"Well," said Rose. "I think Michelangelo was one of the greatest artists of all time. *The Creation of Adam* on the Sistine Chapel is the most famous panel of the masterpiece and the cornerstone of Renaissance art."

"*Prego*! You've got to be a teacher," exclaimed Matteo.

"You're right. I couldn't help myself; I used to teach art history at a private school in the States."

He raised one eyebrow and stared at Ben. "Beauty and brains. Such an irresistible combination."

Ignoring his remark, Ben looked again at the exhibit. "So, what's with the cape behind God?"

"Actually," said Rose, "some scholars believe that it is a depiction of the brain. Michelangelo used to dissect corpses so he could get his figures more lifelike."

"That's disgusting," said Matteo.

"You sound like one of my students."

"I'm not sure I could sit through that discussion," he joked.

"Me either," said Ben.

"I forgot to ask you how your dad's doing," Rose said after Matteo had wandered off to interact with other visitors. "I've heard that your parents were thrilled you decided to spend more time in Charlottesville."

"Thanks for asking. Dad's hanging in there. The prognosis is good. I'm glad to help my parents out after all they did for me. Charlottesville has changed a lot in the past fifteen years."

Downstairs, they said goodbye to Matteo and headed out the door into the warm summer night with chords of violin filling the air. Wandering along the street, they saw everything from colorful pottery to leather goods.

"I've loved the evening, Ben. Thank you so much. It was really fun to see you again."

"I had a great time," said Ben as he put his arm around her to walk her back to her place. "I hope you enjoyed seeing the college art student rendition of Michelangelo's work."

"It was wonderful. Everything was perfect."

They stopped in front of her rental apartment, and Ben took her into his arms. The kiss was electric and left Rose a bit shaken.

"How long are you here for?" she asked nervously.

"I'm heading out tomorrow morning. When do you get your new place?"

"Two more weeks. I'm really excited."

"Keep in touch," he said, placing his hand under her chin. "I'd love an update on how you are doing. Your new apartment sounds fantastic."

"It's a new beginning."

"Speaking of new beginnings, I would really like to hear from you."

"I'll check in from time to time," promised Rose. "And thanks again."

She turned away and headed upstairs, wondering if she had dreamed their whole evening.

Chapter 7

WITH A MESSENGER BAG filled with drawing paper and new charcoal pencils, Rose arrived at the Vatican around eight on a hot, July Saturday morning. She stood in line for two hours to see the Sistine Chapel, which was the main chapel of the palace. The chapel walls were frescoed by some of the greatest artists of the fifteenth and sixteenth centuries, including Ghirlandaio, Botticelli, Perugino and Signorelli, all of whom she had studied.

The rich reds and blues of the subjects' robes caught her eyes as she made her way through a throng of tourists. The sounds of German, French, Japanese and Chinese all mingled together to form a steady hum in her ears. For a moment, she had a pang of homesickness at hearing so many languages other than English, but she reminded herself that this was why she had moved abroad. It renewed her determination to savor the present and deepen her own personal connection to these great artists.

Parallel episodes of the life of Moses and Christ decorated the walls, but Rose diligently went to find a seat so she could gaze up at the chapel ceiling, which was frescoed by the one and only Michelangelo from 1508 to 1512. The main panels charted the creation of the world and the fall of man. These panels were then surrounded by subjects from the New and Old Testaments. Her mind wandered as she recalled the opening paragraph of the first research paper she had written in college on Michelangelo, which detailed how he received a commission from Pope Julius II for five hundred ducats to paint the Sistine Chapel.

Rose had always been fascinated by the depth and breadth

of how Michelangelo conceived and ultimately created this masterpiece. After all, the irreverent Michelangelo considered himself a sculptor and really wanted to create the pope's immortal tomb, which was the higher-paying assignment requiring more skill. The art of fresco demanded that he conquer an expanse of twelve thousand square feet of wall space. Fresco was notoriously difficult to master as it required that the artist paint quickly on wet plaster. An artist's design was usually transferred on this wet plaster from a *cartoon*, otherwise known as the artist's template of the figure or scene that he would be painting.

Based on her research, Rose knew that Michelangelo had to execute the demolition of the existing starry heaven fresco done by Piermatteo d'Amelia, which had been damaged. Michelangelo gave the assignment to a thirty-four-year-old sculptor and artist named Piero Rosselli, a fellow Florentine whom he considered a friend. Rosselli engineered a suspended scaffolding system approximately sixty feet high so that his team could reach the ceiling without interfering with services below. The aisles also needed to be clear so that the priests could continue holding services in this sanctuary.

Pope Julius originally asked the famed architect Donato Bramante, Michelangelo's nemesis, to come up with a scaffolding design. Bramante presented a design suspending wooden platforms from ropes that were anchored in the vault but that would create large holes in the ceiling. Michelangelo convinced the pope that this design was not workable. Michelangelo created rows of bridges across the chapel that started at the windows. Through a network of brackets, stepped arches allowed his team of assistants to link the bridges. The painters and plasterers had access to every part of the ceiling.

Rose recalled that artists really didn't have the power to conceive and create their own work. They were at the mercy of their patrons, who would tell them what to paint, often dictating the size and color of a specific project. In Michelangelo's case, he was relentless in his complaints to the pope, who ultimately granted this gifted genius far more freedom than even the greatest artists of his time. Michelangelo was charged with creating a complete pictorial program of the single most important chapel in all of Christendom. A master of Latin, Michelangelo ultimately chose nine episodes from the Book of Genesis that included such stories as the "Creation of Adam and Eve," and the "Drunkenness of Noah." His design was the most ambitious of its time and would involve 150 pictorial units and more than 300 individual figures.

As she marveled at the beauty of the chapel, the memory of her recent encounter with Doris surfaced like an unwanted swarm of mosquitos at the beach. She flinched as she recalled the scene from a week ago, right after Rose had signed the paperwork to take possession of her beautiful new apartment. Doris regularly watched HGTV, so Rose thought she would have been hanging on every detail of her story. The Facetime call didn't exactly go as she had planned.

"You're making the biggest mistake of your life!" Doris had screamed as she paced back and forth in the kitchen. The muscles of her face contorted and her pink lipstick smeared. "How could you give up an excellent job to move abroad with no connections or family anywhere in sight? It would have been so much smarter to have rented a place, but you couldn't do that. And what about Ben?"

Rose had remained resolute and unintimidated. "Mother, I'm twenty-seven years old and have a right to choose my own path. It's my life, damnit. When are you going to support me in my dreams?"

"I'll support good decisions, not reckless, thoughtless ones."

"I hardly consider it reckless to relocate to Florence."

"You have no job and no family there."

"I'll figure it out."

"Cindy says that Ben cares for you. Are you just going to throw away your one chance at happiness?"

"This isn't about Ben. Besides, there are planes and computers. The world has changed, and you can't expect me to want to spend my whole life living in the place where I was born and raised. I needed something different."

"So, you're saying Charlottesville isn't good enough for you? That your stepfather and I aren't interesting enough for you. Is that it?" she said, unable to hide the hurt.

"That's not what I'm saying. You know, you can come and visit me."

"I don't like to fly. The airports are a mess these days and you hear about terrorist attacks all the time now. It's just not safe to travel." Doris had adjusted the collar of her pink Lily Pulitzer blouse.

"I've made my decision. I thought you'd be happy for me."

"You really shouldn't treat me this way. I'm your mother; you should respect me."

"Why is this about you? It's my life, not yours! I'm not a child anymore!"

Doris had placed her palm on her chest to feel her racing heart. "So, what are you going to do all day in Florence?"

"Nothing, Mother, absolutely nothing! You can tell all of your friends at the next cocktail party that your daughter has ruined her future."

"Well, you know people will talk around here," said Doris, her eyes narrowing.

"I don't care what anyone there thinks of me. I am going to do what I want."

"Oh, so all that money we spent on your education and all of the years of scrimping and saving are going to come to *nothing* because my brilliant daughter—and I do emphasize brilliant—is going to throw it all away to become a painter, or better yet, marry some Italian stallion guy that we don't like."

"It's not your life, Doris!" yelled Rose, feeling breathless from the force of her anger.

"Well," said Doris, visibly stung by her daughter's insult. "You should feel lucky that you have parents that care about you!"

"Care?" said Rose. "You don't know what caring is. You're a control freak and that's the entire problem. And, unfortunately, all you really care about is the next cocktail party and whether I can make a suitable match so you can plan a country club wedding."

"Clearly, that's not going to happen."

"Excuse me?"

"You heard me."

"I've had enough of this. Goodbye, Doris." She switched off the computer, shaken and angry.

***

The buzz of her iPhone brought Rose's focus back to the present. She peered around at the dwindling crowds; it was impossible to hear inside the chapel. She had received several texts from her contractor. She had successfully escaped the dust and mess of her new home for the weekend and assumed that they could carry on for a morning's work without her. After confirming that she had signed a liability form to remove a section of wall, she put her phone back in her pocket.

"Are you alright?" said a well-dressed woman as she eyed Rose glaring at her iPhone. With a gray pixie cut and bright blue eyes, she had a welcoming demeanor that immediately put Rose at ease.

"Oh, yes," Rose replied. "I'm renovating a new apartment in Florence and there are so many decisions. I came to Rome to escape the mess for the weekend. I really could sit here all day every day. This ceiling takes my breath away."

"It's remarkable. I never get tired of seeing it. My daughter lives here, so I love to tour the Vatican whenever I visit." She extended her hand. "Elsa von der Layman."

"Rose Maning, but my friends call me Rose."

"Are you traveling alone?" she asked.

"Yes," said Rose. "It's all been a bit overwhelming. I moved to Italy by myself. I didn't realize how hard it would be to start over in a new place."

Rose felt tears well at the admission, and she was embarrassed by the rush of emotion.

Elsa sat beside her and handed her a handkerchief. "You should be so proud of yourself, my dear. That is a big undertaking. Where are you from?"

"The States. Charlottesville, Virginia, which is in the South."

"I've always heard that it's a beautiful historic city, but I've never been," Elsa said. "We live in Switzerland but keep an apartment in Rome so we can spend time with our daughter. So, tell me what you did back in the States."

"I was an art history teacher, and I'm passionate about the life and works of Michelangelo."

"Well, you came to the right place." Elsa smiled. "You'll be glad to know that the Vatican has eight laboratories and over 150 employees that conserve its treasures. My daughter, Beatrice, is one of them."

"That has to be fascinating work. How did she do it?"

"She received her degree in conservation at New York University graduate school and finished her studies here in Rome. It was a lot of hard work, but nothing compared to Michelangelo, who worked on scaffolding sixty feet aboveground to paint these frescoes."

"I'm looking up and trying to imagine him straining his neck each day to paint. It's simply awe inspiring!"

They talked nonstop for the next few hours, sharing a cup of coffee at a nearby local café.

"You know, Beatrice and I are planning on going on a Roman food tour tomorrow evening. Her good friend, Jess, is the leader of the tour and it's a wonderful way to meet people and learn the

Prati neighborhood through its food. She wants us to give her feedback on some new places she's decided to visit. I can give you the information. Would you like to join us?"

"What a lovely offer!" Rose realized that she would be returning to dust and debris in her new home and there was no schedule. "I've never been on a food tour. How does it work?"

Elsa gave her the information, and Rose promised to follow up online and hoped to meet them tomorrow. There were so many new experiences waiting for her; it was all she could do not to skip back to her hotel. She checked the train schedule and realized that she could easily return to Florence on Monday afternoon to check on the small construction project. After all, cutting a hole in a wall couldn't be that complicated. A vision of a support beam falling in the middle of her living room came to mind, but she quickly banished the thought.

Thanks to Lyon, Rose had received a full list of contractors, painters and various other vendor suggestions. He checked on her periodically, and they had plans to connect as soon as he returned from a business trip, which had allowed her time to begin the process of settling into this new life.

***

Rose set out the following morning to St. Peter's Basilica in Vatican City to attend church services and, once again, visit Michelangelo's *Pietà*. As she walked toward the dome of the basilica, Rose had a fleeting image of Thomas Jefferson's dome at Monticello. She snapped several photos and texted them to Ben, adding a few sentences about her weekend and how Jefferson's views on architecture must have been influenced by his time in Rome. He immediately wrote back, *Enjoy*, with a smiley face. She realized that she missed him a lot more than she was willing to admit.

Incense burned as she stood reverently staring at the masterpiece, which nearly brought tears to her eyes. Restrained sadness emanated from the marble, underscored by a quiet, constant love. Time was suspended as she marveled at this sculpture, which was so much more alive in person. Rose believed that Michelangelo's rendering of Christ allowed mankind to feel sympathy for the reposed figure, and it seemed as if he infused the figures with his own religious faith.

Michelangelo was revolutionary in depicting Christ on the lap of his mother, Mary. The composition was complex because there were two full-sized bodies. Mary held the full body of her deceased son on her lap, cradling his head as if Jesus were still an infant. Mary's face looked eternally youthful, while Christ was depicted in a quieter repose that gave no evidence of the violence that had just occurred; the moment in time made him seem both human and divine. Chills ran up Rose's spine as she gazed at the sublime masterpiece.

The day passed by in a flash, and before long she found herself standing outside a subway station, which was the designated meeting location for the Prati food tour. A friendly, dark-haired woman with luminous brown eyes approached.

"Hi, I'm Jess. Are you waiting for the food tour?"

Rose's nerves quelled the moment they shook hands. Jess was dressed casually in jeans, comfortable flats and a bright top. They launched into an easy conversation about Rose's amazing weekend in Vatican City.

"I've never done a food tour before, but I met a friend of yours yesterday, Elsa, at the Sistine Chapel and she suggested I sign up."

"Oh, I absolutely love Elsa, and Beatrice is our age. We're going to have a fabulous time."

"Your English is perfect."

"I was born and raised in Tampa but moved to Rome five years ago with my boyfriend."

In the next ten minutes, Elsa arrived with a flourish and

gave Rose a big hug. She introduced Rose to Beatrice, who had the same sparkly blue eyes as her mother. Their warmth and enthusiasm were infectious. A gentleman joined the group who had rather thick, white hair, a bowtie, and sported a tailored navy jacket with gold buttons.

"My real name is Leonard," he joked, "but tonight you can call me Leonardo."

Everyone laughed.

Soon after, a very attractive Asian couple introduced themselves as Annie and Ichario.

"We're from New York and just got married a week ago," Annie said.

"Oh my goodness, we need champagne! I'm so honored that you're sharing your honeymoon with us! This is going to be a great night."

Everyone started talking at once, sharing bits and pieces of information about themselves while Jess stepped away with her cell phone; her secret smile convinced Rose that she was probably ordering up something special for the night.

Rose asked Annie and Ichario where they lived in New York.

"We just bought a loft in SoHo, which is where we both work. I'm an aspiring fashion designer."

"She's more than aspiring," said Ichario. "She's just landed her own label."

"Are you kidding me?" said Rose. "That's amazing! I was about to say that I love your jacket."

"It's one of my designs," she replied modestly. "And Ichario handles the business end of things. We're here checking out those boutiques by the Spanish Steps and dreaming of owning our own fashion empire. How about you?"

"I just bought my first home in Florence and moved there two weeks ago. I taught art history at a private girls' school in Charlottesville and now I'm here to explore my interest in painting."

"You live in Florence? We're heading there on Monday."

Leonard joined them. "I get to Florence regularly on business myself. Where are you located?"

"The Santa Croce neighborhood. I've been wandering the streets figuring it all out."

"Aha! I know it well."

"I'm impressed," said Annie. "I'm not sure I could move abroad on my own."

Rose gazed longingly at Ichario and Annie, observing their clasped hands. To be in the presence of two people who were so clearly in love infused Rose with a renewed sense of optimism.

"I'm so glad you met my mom at the Sistine Chapel," Beatrice said. "It sounds like you both really hit it off."

"Your mom is so lovely. I was on my own and suddenly felt overwhelmed. I can't tell you how much I appreciate your invitation! I've never done anything like this before."

"You're going to love Jess. She knows this neighborhood inside and out and is going to teach you more than you can imagine about mozzarella, balsamic vinegar and gelati. Mom says you taught art history. Did she tell you that I work at the Vatican as a conservator?"

"She did. I can't imagine what it's like to restore and maintain all of the treasures in the world's most famous museum."

"You'd be surprised how innovative our approach to conservation has become."

"It sounds fascinating. I'd love to learn more."

"It is endlessly fascinating. I like connecting to the past."

"Then we have that in common. It's hard to believe that I actually live in proximity to so many historical treasures in Florence."

"Yes, you'll love living in Florence; it's such a manageable city. I'd relocate there, but I have, how do you say, a dream job. Every day is new, and we are always making new discoveries. Recently, we've been doing some restoration work on the Hall of Constantine where Raphael painted some glorious frescoes. As you know, he died prematurely in 1520. Turns out two of the allegorical figures in the painting *Justice and Friendship* originally attributed to other artists were done by the master himself."

"When I come back to Rome, I'll definitely pay another visit to the Vatican to see that fresco in person."

"Absolutely!" Beatrice said with a smile. "Let me know ahead of time so I can try to break away and show it to you myself."

"That would be lovely!"

Jess called the group to order and announced the ground rules. No one had to eat everything, and it was okay to take small bites because they would likely make six stops on the evening's tour.

"And I'm excited to take you to my favorite Roman pizzeria called Bonchi." She looked directly at Rose. "Our art history scholar here, Rose, will love that Bonchi is known as the Michelangelo of pizza!"

"I've gotta see this," said Annie. "You mean, taste this," added Ichario.

"Remember, they weigh the pizza, so pace yourselves."

***

A summer breeze kicked in as they made their way to the first stop on the tour. The crowd was daunting, so they waited to get inside and order. Jess told them that Bonchi used only the freshest of ingredients and made new flavors each day depending upon what fruits and vegetables were in season. His creations totaled up to 1,500 artisanal pizzas per year.

"They're delicious," said Beatrice, who recommended that Rose try a slice of the potato, which was their bestseller.

"Are they really weighing the pizza and cutting it with scissors?"

Jess overheard her. "You're going to love it."

The fresh crust and warm potato melted in her mouth. It was

all so delicious, and Rose managed to try a red onion and sausage sample along with a vegetable pizza topped with yellow and red beets covered in goat cheese.

The next stop involved sampling 150-year-old balsamic vinegar and learning about the origins of parmesan cheese. After tasting imported meats and salami at a local market, they ended up in a cozy restaurant which featured homemade pasta. Rose was sandwiched between Leonard and Elsa, who debated whether either of them would ever spend more than thirty euros on a jar of balsamic vinegar. The tour concluded with a tasting of various flavored gelati; Rose loved the chocolate and coffee flavors. Jess unearthed a bottle of prosecco from her bag along with plastic cups, and they went into a nearby park to toast the happy couple.

"To life and new beginnings," she said. They all clapped, and Annie and Ichario kissed tenderly.

"I'll drink to that," said Leonard, taking a hearty sip.

"And new friendships!" announced Elsa, clinking her glass with Rose's.

"Yes, let's all keep in touch," said Beatrice. "We should make Jess take us on food tours all over Italy."

"I'd love to."

They exchanged emails and cell phone numbers, promising to meet again. Everyone wanted to come to Florence, and Rose felt a warmth spread through her. She was delighted to connect with such a wonderful and diverse new group of people; this weekend had far exceeded her expectations. It was bittersweet saying goodbye to her new friends, and she tucked away the list of new numbers in her bag, promising herself to take the time on the train home to enter them into her iPhone.

Her visit to the Vatican inspired her, and she was excited to paint when she got home. It was amazing to see Michelangelo's depiction of the creation of Adam from the Book of Genesis.

Meeting Elsa and Beatrice made her think that a dream job was possible. If nothing else, she was proud of herself for traveling on her own to Rome, meeting new people and putting herself out there in a way that she had never done before. It was her own personal renaissance.

Chapter 8

ROSE'S APARTMENT WAS A disaster. The white sheets she used to cover the living room furniture looked gray. Dust and debris were all over the floor next to the new opening. It looked like the workers had left in a hurry on Saturday afternoon because a half-filled soda can was still on the countertop. Taking her eyes away from the mess, Rose surveyed the new opening, which made the space brighter and airier. The workmanship was outstanding, and the mess would only take an hour to clean.

Rose immediately threw herself into scouring the apartment. Her belongings had arrived, and she decided to unpack two of the boxes filled with her personal keepsakes: a photograph of her father, her favorite coffee table books and a pretty black box that Zoey had given her for Christmas a year ago. The beamed ceiling gave the living room such incredible charm. With gusto, she pulled off the sheets and threw them into her new stackable washer and dryer.

Having found some pretty decorative pillows while in Rome, she had fun placing the gray-washed velvet squares on her new white side chairs and arranging some patterned plates on a bookcase. Hopefully, the workers would be more mindful when they returned. *It's all coming together,* she thought proudly, as she admired her new apartment. The pictures made it look like she lived here.

Rose studied the new opening in the wall, which integrated the kitchen with the living and dining room area. The carpenter needed to add wood crown and floor molding to cover the seams created by the wall's removal. He also needed to patch a few deep cracks near the base of the wall presumably caused by the demolition.

Rose ran her hand along the cracks and wondered whether to paint the new trim white or stain it to match the beams in the ceiling. As she did, a section of plaster about the size of her hand fell to the floor.

"Damn," she said aloud.

Rose looked into the small hole and spotted something odd. Wedged inside was what looked like leather or parchment. Rose reached in to grasp the moldy object and gingerly pulled it into the afternoon light. The edges were caked with dust, which she carefully wiped away.

She stared at the dusty tube dented in two places and covered with particles of fine, dry powder. Rose went to the sink to wash her hands before touching it any further. She looked at the aged tube and stared at her new apartment, somehow feeling like an intrepid explorer in her own space. *This is my home,* she reminded herself. *Therefore I own everything in it.*

Grabbing a towel from the bathroom, she gently removed a layer of grime from the tube and continued to wipe it clean, anxious to peer inside. But she wanted to be cautious. She carefully pulled open the top of the container and tugged on the rolled paper inside. It took several tries to pry the papers free.

As if in slow motion, she unrolled the parchment and peered at a small, roughly eight-by-ten-inch charcoal drawing that took her breath away. She gently blew white powder from the rolled paper and stared at a depiction of a baby boy on some sort of cloth. The curved lines of the body were beautifully executed, and the cloth gently covered one of the baby's legs. Each detail was finely drawn, and the baby's rounded arms and face were distinct, giving him an ethereal look. Rose's hands trembled as she wondered who the child was, and who sketched him. She thought of her own sketchbook upstairs filled with copies of pictures and scenes around Florence. This aged drawing was outstanding in its simplicity and yet so incredibly exquisite.

Rose meticulously peeled the sketch of the child away from a second, larger drawing. She held her breath as she stared at the next drawing, the face of a young boy, handsome with angular features. *Is it the same person?* His high cheekbones and prominent nose made him look like a member of the ruling class. The young man was depicted staring directly at her. It was surreal. Rose felt as if she were looking directly into the past at a man who had been hidden for perhaps generations. From the jaunty angle of his plumed hat to the confident expression, Rose was captivated. *Who's the boy?* He looked to be around twelve years old, she guessed. *Is it a portrait that this artist had completed?*

Her breathing came short and fast as the enormity of the discovery struck her. All of her senses were alive. Carefully, she unfurled a third drawing, which was about the same size as the second one. It depicted intertwined hands, the side of a reclining figure on the left and a partial rendering of God surrounded by several figures on the right. A chill ran up her spine because she knew the scene intimately; yet, there was something different about it.

The drawings were fascinating in their intensity, and it was abundantly clear they had been in the wall for some time. Her hands trembled at the age and beauty of the work before her. The third drawing captured her imagination, and she thought about the beginning of time; she was surprised, scared and excited all at once. Her heart pounded in her chest as she reverently touched the edges to bring a sense of reality to this moment. It felt as if she were dreaming as she studied the images on the moldy paper. Running into the living room, she grabbed several books to secure the edges of the drawings so she could study them more and take pictures.

Who's the artist? How long have these drawings been encased in the wall? Rose had so many questions. Taking a breath to calm herself, she concluded that someone had deliberately hidden the sketches long ago given the amount of dust and debris that had covered them. *Could the drawings be related?* She wondered if the baby was a depiction of Jesus Christ because it looked like he was wrapped in a cloth. Certainly, Florence was filled with paintings, sculptures and statues of the saint, but this baby had a different look. Perhaps more earthly than divine.

The second drawing seemed so portrait-like and almost out of place with the other two. The young boy's face had an angular jaw, sharp nose and wide forehead. His eyes looked so real; it felt as if he could jump off the paper and into the room. The details of his hat and clothing suggested someone who lived in a different era, but which one?

Rose was mesmerized and for hours examined the three drawings with the intensity of a police detective at a murder scene looking for clues. The third drawing looked like a thoughtful study of *The Creation of Adam,* which she had just witnessed at the Sistine Chapel in Rome. That idea seemed so preposterous to her. Perhaps an artist had studied Michelangelo's body of work and these were copies. Rose wondered if these drawings had been stolen and then hidden.

Rose paced the floor of her new kitchen pondering how the clasped hands fused God with Adam in a special way that seemed unbreakable. It was such an exquisite rendering that the spiritual message seemed irrefutable. She considered the quality of the paper along with its dusty and moldy edges, which added a level of authenticity worthy of further research on her part. *This is so weird,* she told herself, trying to come to terms with the contents of the historic papers in front of her.

Fear took over. *Were they stolen? What if they belonged to a previous owner and he planned to come back for them? Would I be incriminated?* Given the hiding place, the previous owners may not have known about them. Calming herself, she quickly went in search of something to hide the treasure. She wrapped one of her scarves around the drawings and gingerly placed them in a leather tote bag for protection. She opened the door of her new wardrobe and put the tote gently in a corner. Rose began pacing the floor, not sure who to call or what to do. She suddenly felt incredibly alone, but decided not to tell anyone about her discovery until she had figured out her options.

Rose's mind raced. *What century are they from? Was this house once owned by an aspiring artist like me who worked on copying this theme?* Perhaps the answers could be determined by testing the age of the paper.

As she paced back and forth, she contemplated the current scholarly interpretation of Michelangelo's *Creation of Adam*. In the Sistine Chapel, the two hands reached toward each other. Adam had always appeared somewhat relaxed, and many historians believed that this symbolized the moment that God infused Adam with life. But this drawing was different. The hands were clasped tightly, seeming to connect mankind with the very spirit of God. Perhaps the two worlds were closer than anyone realized. Rose's head began to pound. She knew that she would need to consult someone with far greater knowledge than her own to decipher the meaning.

What should I do? thought Rose, wandering around her new home and finally sitting quietly on her new balcony. The city was lit up. Shivering slightly despite the summer breeze, Rose tried to formulate a plan to research and understand what she had found. She was excited to have discovered such beautiful drawings, and yet an inner voice warned her to proceed with caution.

A text message from Ben was a welcome diversion.

Hey. What's up? I'm still writing. Kind of crazy but I couldn't sleep. I miss you.

*Me too. I'm sitting here on my new balcony looking at
the stars.*
B: *I wish I were beside you.*
*I can't wait to show you my new place. It's heavenly
over here.*
B: *Maybe I'll hop on a plane again. New York is hot and
I've thought about you way too much.*
That would be lovely, but I can't ask you to do that.
B: *Yes, you can.*
Okay, I'd love to see you again.
B: *I am thinking of you on a balcony in the moonlight.*
That's sounds very romantic.
B: *It sure does and far more interesting than Jeffersonian
architecture. I've been working around the clock lately.*
Okay, night night sweetheart.
Night

Had Ben just called her his *sweetheart*? Rose felt like she was dreaming. It was Ben, her first love, and they had reconnected. A feeling of warmth spread through her. Charlottesville felt suddenly closer. With a smile, Rose calmed down about the drawings and decided that it was all going to be okay. And Rose thought about her mother and how much she adored Ben. He was part of the fabric of her life, and she decided that she was okay with the fact that he had been married and had a child. It was messy and complicated, but he had ended things and was clearly ready for a fresh start, which might include her. Excitement filled her being. *This has been quite a day*, Rose thought happily, as she put on her silk nightshirt and got ready for bed.

That night, curling up in her fabulous bedroom, Rose peered at the light pouring in from the balcony. This was her new home and her new life. The bed was soft and warm, yet she felt a bit overwhelmed.

Rose was exhausted and fell into a deep sleep. She dreamed of being in darkness and of chaos erupting. She felt frightened and alone. As she swirled into the night, she couldn't breathe, and the world spun at an alarming rate. She screamed, and then out of the darkness a voice called to her, and she could see a strong hand reaching down from above to take hers. Rose grabbed it and heard the words, *"Trust the Lord Jesus Christ."*

With the hand came light and a calmness. Rose awoke as the sun streamed through her window. The image in her dream, those clasped hands between Adam and God, pervaded her consciousness, and she believed that the meaning would be revealed.

Chapter 9

THE SUNSHINE DANCED ON the terra-cotta rooftops, captivating Rose as she sipped her morning coffee. It was surreal watching the city come alive from her new balcony with the spectacular view. A calmness descended upon her as she contemplated the beauty of her surroundings. Still, the past twenty-four hours crept into her mind as she tried to figure out what to do about her discovery.

Rose wanted to talk to someone she could trust for advice. Her brother, Jack, came to mind first. He was smart and she trusted him completely. On the other hand, Beatrice, who worked at the Vatican, could, in fact, be helpful, and Rose laughed aloud as she contemplated a conversation:

"Hi, Beatrice. Remember me? We met on Jess's food tour."

"Yes, sure, you were the art history teacher. How are you?"

"Well, you're not going to believe this, but I found three old drawings last night hidden in the wall that the contractors cut open. Well, I think they, uh, contain a mystery. There's a portrait of a baby, a young boy and, well, a scene from the Sistine Chapel. This may sound kind of odd, but the third drawing could be a preliminary study of the Creation of Adam. And I think this because I had a dream last night about the clasped hands between God and Adam. You know I'm passionate about Michelangelo, so I swear I didn't make any of this up. Really, I'm not crazy because I have the drawings and they are clearly old. Would you like to see them?"

There was no rush to do anything, Rose decided. She

needed to take her time and think through what was best. In the meantime, it made perfect sense to get on with her life and continue pursuing her art. She had never felt so energized and creative as she selected various spots in the city to draw.

Later that week, Rose ran into Lyon on her way to sketch in the Boboli Gardens. He seemed genuinely pleased to see her.

"Hi," he said warmly.

"Hi," she replied.

"I've been meaning to get in touch but have been out of town on business."

"Got it. No worries. I've been settling into my life here. So far, so good."

"Glad to hear it. I'd love to get together sometime," he said casually.

"Sure," she replied easily. "You know where to find me," she shot back with a smile.

He returned the smile and their eyes met. "I sure do. It's hard for a simple guy like me to ask out such a beautiful American girl."

"Ahh," said Rose sweetly. "I don't buy it, Lyon. Nice try." She laughed. "I don't believe for a minute that you aren't a professional at asking women out."

"Me? That's ridiculous."

"I do believe that you're blushing."

He reached for her hand and grinned as she passed by him. "See you soon."

"You can count on it, Rose," he said with a chuckle.

***

It was a rainy Friday, so Rose headed to the Uffizi Gallery, which opened at ten. Her plan was to wander through it, looking at the myriad paintings for inspiration of her own. She would shoot Jack an email and try to catch him after work, which would put her about lunchtime.

That morning, Rose lost herself gazing at Sandro Botticelli's

The Birth of Venus painted around 1480 as she studied the lines of the Renaissance masterpiece. The painting, probably one of the most famous in the world, took her breath away with its mastery of color, form and shape. It depicted the goddess Venus standing at the shore on a large seashell after her birth, but she was portrayed fully grown. The size and grandeur of the painting were extraordinary, and the classic scene from Greek antiquity reminded her of both earthly and divine love. Rose could have gazed at the painting for hours, but her phone vibrated with an incoming text message.

Thinking it was Jack, she found a quiet corner to see what he wanted.

Surprise! I'm here.
What? Ben?
B: *I just got to Florence.*
Really? Are you kidding me?
B: *Nope. Where are you?*
The Uffizi staring at the Birth of Venus. Where are you?
B: *Standing in your apartment. Your realtor came by to check on your reno project, so he kindly let me in.*
OMG. I'll be there as fast as I can!
B: *Good. Mind if I shower?*
Rose paused. *Perfect!*

A thousand questions coursed through her brain. Had Ben actually hopped a plane to be with her? She wished she had put on some makeup or something this morning. Looking down at her flip-flops and jean shorts, she realized Ben would appreciate her casual attire. She wound her way through the burgeoning crowd to the exit. Fortunately, there wasn't time to think about anything but the present and the fact that Ben was back in Florence and at her house.

As she walked, she pictured his handsome face, the dimple on his cheek and that ready smile. *At least my apartment is habitable*, she thought. Her palms sweaty and heart racing, she turned down a cobblestone path thinking that she should have worn sneakers so she could move faster.

"Hi," she said breathlessly as she walked into her apartment. "So, you're really here."

"Hi," he replied, getting up to greet her. "I was in the neighborhood." He pulled her close to him, and Rose molded right to his muscular form as he kissed her passionately. "I missed you."

"I missed you too."

"So, I beat out Botticelli for the day, huh?"

They both laughed and flopped on the couch with their legs intertwined. "Oh, Ben, it was so amazing to see Venus rising in person. So many treasures, so little time!"

"You look happy and well," he said, running his hand over her tanned legs. "Should I take it personally that you don't seem to have missed me as much as I missed you?"

"Not true! But I do love it here . . . " Her words hung in the air.

He was quiet for a moment and then said, "I can't wait to get the official tour of your new home. It's really impressive. You did well."

"Thanks! I was able to buy all of the existing furniture from the previous owner, so it made everything so easy on that front. You're lucky you didn't come last week because I recently opened up this wall and it was a mess in here." It was on the tip of her tongue to tell him about her discovery, but she decided to wait. "I have so much to tell you! I went to Rome for the weekend to escape the mess."

"You went by yourself?"

"Yes! This is my new normal. Seems crazy that I'm just getting comfortable exploring. I met this wonderful Swiss woman named Elsa in the Sistine Chapel and her daughter, Beatrice, who works for the Vatican."

"That's awesome, Rose. I'm proud of you for exposing

yourself to new things."

"Dare I ask if you've seen Doris?"

"I have."

"And?"

"She's still very upset that you left Charlottesville and committed to a life in Italy without your family, but you knew that," he said softly.

"Come on, there are lots of ways to keep in touch. If she was that worried about me, she could get down off her high horse and actually visit." Rose caught the note of bitterness in her own voice.

"For what it's worth, your mother lost the love of her life way too young. She was never the same after that, even though she remarried. Jack used to talk to me about that a lot. We both know that she clung too tightly to you. Anyway, she's just not in a place to be happy for you."

They paused for a moment in silent understanding.

"Fair enough," said Rose, considering his words. To fill the sudden quiet, she added, "So, I love all of the Old World features here, from the original iron handrails to the beamed ceiling. But the best is yet to come." She took his hand and led him upstairs.

"Well," he joked. "I thought we'd have a romantic dinner first."

Rose laughed and watched as Ben admired the decor and all the modern conveniences. "Check this out. I put a stackable washer and dryer up there."

He looked around him. "This place is huge," he exclaimed. "You could do cartwheels across the floor."

"Yup. And check out the renovated bath."

He stuck his head in the door and peered at the spacious shower and double sinks. "I think I forgot my toothbrush."

"I'll find you an extra. I'm still getting organized. But you've just won the award as my first guest. Jack won't like that." Rose pulled back the curtain to open the sliding glass door.

"Wow! This is spectacular! Look at this view."

The sun shone on the terra-cotta rooftops as they walked outside. The morning rain had yielded to the sunny summer afternoon.

"I had my coffee up here this morning," Rose said. "It's amazing. I'm still pinching myself that I did it."

"Well, seems like we could take in the sunset and enjoy a glass of wine up here tonight."

"That sounds great. I may have to run to the market to grab some dinner for us. Do you want to take a nap?"

"I know I'm not supposed to be tired, but I've never slept well on any transatlantic flight. Would you mind?"

"Not at all."

"Hey," he said. "I want you to be comfortable. I don't have to stay here."

"Really?" she said playfully, pushing him down on the bed. They kissed passionately, and she fit perfectly in the crook of his arm. "Let me go out and grab some dinner and wine for tonight while you sleep for a bit."

"I'd love that. Are you sure you don't want me to come with you?" At her resistance, he said, "Well, at least let me pay for everything. You're a starving artist."

"You know, that would be true," she replied with a giggle. "Except I don't even qualify as an artist. I'm an ex-teacher with a crazy dream."

"Rose, you're entitled to your dreams! Here," he said, handing her his VISA card.

"Thanks!" she said, artfully plucking his credit card from his fingertips.

"Angie used to be able to do that as well," he said.

As if hit by a bucket of cold water, Rose backed away and threw the card at him.

"Rose, wait. I didn't mean it. I'm tired and shouldn't have said that."

"I'm going to grab us some dinner and we'll talk when I get back."

"I'm sorry."

"Are you?"

Rose left and wondered if Ben's visit would make or break them.

***

Walking out along the streets of Santa Croce calmed her nerves as she made her way to the market. Dinner would consist of some fresh bread, salads, penne pasta in meat sauce and some Ruffino Chianti. The preparation was simple, and she grabbed some extra garlic.

Ben's slip had irritated her. She wasn't quite sure what ended his marriage, but it very well could have been money. She thought about how deeply she and Ben were connected. She had enjoyed other relationships over the years, but no one had ever captivated her the way he did. Ben knew her family, her childhood, her school; he had even lived on the same street where she grew up. And he had gotten along with her father. The familiarity felt so incredibly good, and, well, she was just plain delighted to see him.

A vision of the drawings loomed, and she decided she needed to talk to him about them. He wouldn't think her dream was crazy, and she was sure he would have some good advice about the discovery. Ben was sound asleep on the sofa when she returned home. He was really way too handsome for her peace of mind.

As she placed her items on the countertop, she eyed the opening in the wall, reminding herself to leave a message for the contractor to finish up the last odds and ends in her apartment. She wondered whether Lyon was jealous of Ben, or even really cared.

The new wooden salad bowl she had purchased last week was christened as Rose washed and threw in some arugula and pine nuts. She chopped a bit of onion and red pepper. The homemade penne looked divine, and Rose decided she would never tire of pizza or pasta in this lifetime; they would always be her favorites. As she added extra garlic to the red sauce simmering on the stovetop, she felt Ben wrap his arms around her, kissing the side of her neck.

"I'm so sorry," he said softly. "I was wrong and, frankly, I'm embarrassed I said that."

"Thanks," she replied, turning to face him. "Apology accepted, but you can't ever, ever compare me to your ex. I'm a completely different person, and if anything is going to work at all, we need not to go there."

"Understood," he said solemnly. "I really do feel terrible about what I said. You're nothing like her and I don't know why I snapped."

"I really don't want to rehash the past while you're here."

"That's a relief because it wasn't a particularly great time in my life." The room went silent as they both got lost in their own thoughts. "This apartment is fantastic," he exclaimed.

"Thanks. I love it. I couldn't be happier with things right now and I'm so glad you're here." She looked into his hazel eyes. "For how long?"

"I fly back to New York on Monday."

"That's not much time," she said, turning back to stir the red sauce and place it on simmer.

"Well," he replied, "Ben Franklin once said, 'Guests, like fish, begin to smell after three days.'"

"On that note, how is the Jefferson book coming along?"

"Very well. I've been back and forth to Monticello a fair amount doing research. I'm thinking I may look for a place in Charlottesville while I'm writing. Dad seems to be doing well and I want easy access to Jefferson's world."

"That sounds like a good plan."

"On a lighter note, did you know Jefferson loved pasta, and when he was ambassador to Paris he ordered his secretary to buy a pasta machine so he could make spaghetti when he was back in America?"

"Smart man," said Rose.

A short time later, she finished organizing dinner, and they left her apartment to walk hand in hand through the streets so Ben could get a feel for her new neighborhood.

"What do you say we climb to the top of the Duomo tomorrow morning?" she suggested. "And then have a picnic lunch in the Boboli Gardens?"

"Great idea," he replied. "I know you'll want me to see Michelangelo's *David* too."

"Of course! Speaking of Michelangelo, I want to talk to you about something later, okay?"

He eyed her. "You look suddenly serious. Everything alright?"

"Oh gosh, yes. I just need your help on something that's come up."

"Don't tell me," he exclaimed. "You want me to pose nude for you in your studio. If that's the question, then I would be happy to be your muse."

"Ben Pierce! So you think your body is that good, huh?"

"Well," he replied, "you're just going to have to evaluate my candidacy this evening."

"And what if I decide that your form isn't quite what I'm looking for?"

"Oh, I think I can get the job." He smiled.

"We'll see," she laughed as he put his arm around her and kissed her affectionately. Rose felt so incredibly happy in this moment as they exchanged smiles and paused to kiss again on the street. Before long, they made their way back to the apartment.

***

Rose took a quick shower and put her hair up in a bun. She changed up her jean shorts for a cool sundress and flat sandals. Ben uncorked the Chianti and poured them each a glass as they made their way outside to her balcony to watch the sunset. Splashes of yellow, orange and pink filled the evening sky and Rose sighed in contentment.

"This is an outstanding view," Ben commented as he reached for her hand.

"I'm so glad you came," Rose said sweetly. "It means a lot to me that you made the effort."

"I'm glad I came too," he said, taking a sip of his wine. "Hey, you seem to have something on your mind."

Rose took a deep breath and recounted her visit to the Sistine Chapel and how she met Elsa and Beatrice. Then she talked about how she came home to find her apartment a mess and then uncovered the drawings in the wall. And, most importantly, the dream she had about the intertwined hands in the drawing.

"That's unbelievable! Have you told anyone yet?"

"Well, I had planned to call Jack at lunch today and then you arrived. I'm still in a state of shock and have no idea what I've found and why I had that dream."

"Where are the drawings now?"

"I've hidden them here."

"Well, let's check them out!"

"Sure," Rose replied, heading inside to retrieve them.

The parchment was still dusty, and she wiped it off before handing it to him. Ben looked intently at the package, commenting on the authenticity and age of the moldy paper. He said nothing for several minutes as he studied the three images.

"Do you think they were drawn by a Renaissance artist?" She wasn't going to dare suggest that they were drawn by a master.

Ben looked at the three drawings quietly and placed them on the edge of the bed in the same way she had to study their integrity. They both peered thoughtfully at the images of a baby, a young boy and the intertwined hands.

"I've seen rough drawing like these in galleries," Ben said.

"They appear to be very high quality. I'd guess that whoever did them was a master."

"That's what I thought."

"And you know the scene in the third drawing all too well. Are there any children depicted in the *Creation of Adam*?"

"Yes, there is a figure of the baby, but not at this angle or looking anything like the one shown here. In the current *Creation of Adam*, scholars always believed that the baby shown may be Christ."

"And the young boy in the second drawing?"

"I have no idea! It seems more like a portrait than part of a larger religious rendering," said Rose.

"My first instinct would be to photograph this parchment and send them to an art historian at Christie's in New York. You know about that lost Leonardo da Vinci that someone found last fall? It sold for roughly $450 million. It made national news."

"That's crazy," said Rose. "Okay, works for me."

"There's no harm in photographing these drawings and sending out an email. You may want to safeguard them and put them in a lockbox at a bank. It wouldn't be a bad idea while you go through this process."

"Do you really think they're legitimate?"

"I have no idea. I mean, they could be well-executed copies for all we know."

"I wonder who put them in the wall. I have the strangest feeling about them."

"Like what?"

"Like I was chosen to safeguard them."

"Why?"

"I don't know. They mean something, and I'm no biblical scholar."

"My Christie's contact will know the right person to evaluate this work. I'll make some calls in the morning and help with a plan."

"I'd really appreciate that," she said, putting the drawings back in the cabinets. She looked over to see the sun setting in the night sky. "How about a drink while I prepare dinner?"

"Great idea!"

It didn't take long to put the salads and steaming hot plates of pasta on the table, light some candles and pour two ice-cold glasses of water. She opened a window to get some fresh air, and she sighed thinking that it was so great to have Ben there. Dinner was delicious and the conversation was easy and relaxed. They washed the dishes together and headed back upstairs to look at the stars in the night sky from Rose's balcony. The silence was both beautiful and powerful, and Rose felt really connected to him.

"My life is here now, and yours is still back home. I mean, you have a job there and your daughter . . . . Do we really have a chance?" Rose asked quietly.

"I hope so," said Ben, putting his arms around her.

"Me too," said Rose. "But no pressure. I have a long way to go in figuring out my plan, and finding those drawings has certainly complicated things."

"They could be worth a considerable sum of money, you realize."

The talk of money bothered her. She wasn't a greedy person, and she was mostly interested in their historical significance rather than trying to make easy cash. She had a feeling that the Christie's representative shouldn't be the first to see her discovery. It occurred to her, again, that Beatrice could be very helpful in getting her to the right person. "I'm very private as you know; I'd never want to be anywhere near the press or part of some sordid story."

"Been there, done that. Having my divorce all over the newspapers was literally one of the worst periods of my life."

"I'm sorry," she said softly.

"I've gotta tell you, Rose. I'm really embarrassed I fell for that whole New York social scene and everything else that went with it. I don't know what happened to me. All of a sudden, all that mattered was power and money and keeping up my image. Too much alcohol, too many drugs to stay competitive. And, well, Angie was arm candy and fit my vision of success. Such a dark period of time that's still kind of a blur."

"What made you change?"

"Angie isn't a bad person, but she's more interested in partying than being a good mother to our daughter. We fought way too much, which is no way to raise a kid. The divorce was costly and we still don't have custody ironed out. I want a joint plan. The bar is high because I had the best mom ever."

"You did luck out on the mom front. Cindy is amazing."

"I do have a beautiful daughter, which I will never regret. I can't wait for you to meet her."

Rose pondered meeting Ben's baby girl and she smiled, wondering how any of this could work. "Sure," she replied. "I'll look forward to it."

"I'm sorry if I've been rambling. I just wanted you to know that I never forgot about us."

"Neither did I."

A new warmth seeped into her heart along with the promise of something more.

The stars lit up the night sky around them. When he took her in his arms, the moment felt magical. It all seemed so beautiful and right. His movements were tender, and she could feel that something had changed between them. There was a shift in the way he was touching her, almost reverently like she was the most important person in the world to him. A whisper of times past flashed through her mind as she remembered the two of them together when they were teenagers. Long-forgotten memories and a sweet tenderness invaded her heart as she inched closer to her first love. The years seemed to melt away, and Rose knew she would never forget this night, no matter what the future held.

"It was always you," he whispered in the heat of the summer night.

His words danced as their bodies molded together almost too easily. *It was always you,* she thought, as she touched him tenderly.

"Hopefully, you won't forget about me," he whispered.

"That's not possible."

Chapter 10

THE NEXT MORNING, THEY returned to the bright sunshine of the balcony, enjoying coffee and making plans.

"Let's climb to the top of the Duomo!" Rose said. "I've been dying to go and this is the perfect day to do it."

Ben smiled at her. "Okay, you win. And I'm sure you'll want me to say hello to the *David* and meander around the Piazzale Michelangelo."

"Of course."

He looked down to check his phone for messages and raised an eyebrow. "Looks like my friend has already alerted his colleague about the drawings. He wants to see them immediately. What do you want me to tell him?"

"Oh no! We don't have much time together. The last thing I want to do is fall into the whims of some art dealer."

"Okay, I'll tell him that you can't discuss the drawings until early next week. Sound good?"

"Perfect. I'm going to put on sneakers and turn my phone off," announced Rose.

"Me too. But," he said.

"But what?"

"I really think you should put the drawings in a lockbox at the bank."

"How long will that take?"

"Hopefully, it won't be too long, but I think you should be cautious."

"Fine, you're right. I'll grab my ID and let's go."

The bank trip took several hours, and Rose did her best to contain her annoyance at losing part of a beautiful morning. With a key lodged safely in her pocket, they made their way to the Duomo lined with eager tourists.

***

Soon after, Rose began climbing the narrow steps in the darkened corridors to the top of the Duomo. She breathed in the musty air and reminded herself that the view was worth it as she hiked up the endless stone steps. A vision of the intertwined hands in the third drawing came to mind. The drawings felt almost sacred, and Rose thought that the best place to search for answers would be within the walls of the Vatican. Pope Julius II commissioned Michelangelo to do the Sistine Chapel, so the Vatican archives might contain more information on the artists who helped him, Rose reasoned. Her thoughts circled around the idea that the hands were some sort of preliminary study by an artist. Cool air greeted her when she reached the top; the panoramic view of the city was breathtaking.

"I love this!" she exclaimed.

"Amazing," Ben replied. A breeze ruffled his hair. Rose turned on her cell phone so that they could get a few pictures. Tapping a German girl on the shoulder, she asked her to snap a shot with the terra-cotta wallpaper of rooftops, sunny sky and hills in the distance. As Rose deleted a picture where her eyes were closed, Ben looked over at her.

"Turns out the appraiser has been in Rome on business; he can get to Florence tonight and really wants to meet with you tomorrow morning."

"I thought you told him to wait until next week."

"He's insisting on seeing them. Remember that Leonardo sold for $450 million last fall. No one thought it could happen. You found three drawings that could be hundreds of years old."

"I really don't want to talk about money."

"Don't be so naive! You may be sitting on a fortune. Look, not to state the obvious, but everything comes down to money."

"When did you become so cynical?"

"I'm a realist, not a cynic."

"Well, I'm a historian and an optimist. Maybe those drawings are about faith and mankind's relationship to God. They don't really belong to me. I want to safeguard them."

"You need to consider how this could change your life and secure your future. I mean, what are the chances of you making a living as a painter?"

"You sound like Doris." Rose paused, reining in her anger. "For the record, I'm a highly qualified teacher and know I can always go back to that profession. I haven't taken time for myself since my father died, so the painting thing works for me right now."

"Hey," he said, putting his arms around her. "I get it. I didn't mean to upset you."

"No, I'm sorry for the rant."

"Let's get another picture."

"Sure," she replied.

Ben persisted throughout the day, convincing Rose that she should allow professionals to view her discovery first, which would give her the necessary information to come up with a plan. Rose finally capitulated and agreed to show the drawings to the Christie's representative the following morning. The young boy's portrait with the intelligent eyes, thin face and prominent nose haunted her. And pondering the meaning of the intertwined hands was giving her a headache, so hopefully the appraiser could shed some light on the images. Her dream hovered on the edge of consciousness, and for a moment, she thought about her faith, which had all but disappeared since her father's death.

"Rose, you're absolutely right. I want to enjoy our time together," said Ben, gently taking her hand. "I can put him off."

"No, no, it's okay. Why stay in suspense?" She paused for a moment. "I'm going to ask my realtor where I can find the property records. I wonder who owned the home before me. That may shed some light on things. They could very well be of no value."

"Is that what you really think?"

"Well, I believe in doing all of my homework. You know what a good student I was."

"Now that's an understatement," said Ben, kissing her on the forehead. "You were always so responsible and diligent. I admired you for that. Your dad used to brag about you all the time. 'My little Rose; she's so smart.'"

"Why didn't you come to his funeral?" she asked quietly.

"You know, I regret it. I was working for a very difficult employer and had to finish a deal."

"Got it," she said, recalling her brother's disappointment in not having his best friend there. "It doesn't matter anymore. I was just curious."

Ben said the best fish restaurant in Florence was Fuor D'Acqua, which was a twenty-minute walk from Rose's house. The summer heat had abated, and a cool breeze tantalized her senses. As they walked hand in hand, Rose felt wrapped in the moment with Ben, who looked impossibly handsome in his crisp white shirt and linen pants.

"You look beautiful," he said as he ran his gaze over her bare legs. Her white sleeveless dress kept her cool, and her hair was piled on her head in a loose bun.

The restaurant boasted clean white tablecloths, arched doorways and artfully arranged fresh seafood on a bed of ice in the front entrance.

"You're not going to see that in the States," quipped Ben.

Rose eyed the large shrimp with their bulging eyes and several large gray finned fish.

"Our fish is brought in fresh daily from Tuscany," explained the manager, who shared that the restaurant was once an old chariot house. He pointed to the massive vaulted ceiling. Rose thought once again that there was something magical about history. A hot-pink azalea bush adorning a black pot caught her attention as she admired the sleek white decor.

As they were seated, Rose glanced over the room and caught sight of Lyon, who was dining with an attractive woman. She felt a stab of betrayal, but quickly dismissed the feeling. She waved to him and he smiled at her. The woman turned around and Rose recognized Dominique, who she had met at that party. *Well,* she thought, *no wonder the woman warned me off.*

"Who's that?" asked Ben.

"My realtor, Lyon Walker, and his friend Dominique. He's the one who let you in."

"Right," said Ben thoughtfully as he followed her to their table. Lyon made the introductions, and Rose felt Dominique's glare.

"How are you enjoying your new home, Rose?"

"It's absolutely fantastic. I'll be glad when the renovations are complete. Anyway, I was going to call you tomorrow to see if you could help me find the records to my property. Maybe figure out the previous owners."

"How far back?"

"I don't know, say the 15th century perhaps."

"You're kidding, right?"

"Not really. You know how I love history. Where are the city records?"

"There's a city office not far from the center of town. The records only go back a hundred years or so, but I'll see what I can do."

"That would be wonderful. Thank you so much."

They were seated in a cozy corner by the maître d', who offered to select a menu for them. Without hesitation, they both agreed to follow his suggestions, and their decision proved to be brilliant. Their first course was an artfully arranged tasting platter. The poached white fish practically melted in her mouth, and she picked up a piece of fresh lobster dripping in butter. "This is absolutely decadent. Everything is so fresh," Rose said.

"They know what they're doing, and I love it when the waiter makes a winning wine selection that doesn't cost a fortune," Ben said.

"The wine is perfect," said Rose as she looked around the room at all of the elegantly dressed men and women. Laughter filled the air and she took Ben's hand.

"You're going to pose for me tomorrow morning, right?"

"Excuse me?"

"I thought you volunteered to be my muse. I'm trying to come up with some samples of my work."

"Only for you, darling," he said with a wink. His eyes seemed to skim the sheer fabric of her dress.

"Thank you. I hope Lyon can help me out."

"Hmmm. I wonder what he'll find. You said the last owner was a businessman."

"That's right, but I feel certain he had no idea they were there. Given the mold and dust we found on the drawings, they must have been put there a long time ago. I wonder if there's a connection between the child in the first drawing and the young boy's portrait."

"Maybe Michelangelo fathered a child and covered it up?" Ben laughed.

"That's actually a possibility."

"I was kidding."

"He may have been in love with Contessina de' Medici when he lived as a young man in Lorenzo's palace." She paused. "Seriously."

"Maybe they hooked up somewhere along the way."

"It could have happened, you know. It's not so farfetched. Contessina had an arranged marriage and ended up with several children. Who knows? Maybe one of them belonged to Michelangelo. It's not that crazy of an idea. Love can change things." They looked at each other until Rose felt her cheek burn. She swallowed hard and continued. "Maybe the drawings were preserved and passed down by her or a trusted friend."

"Okay, now we're going into uncharted territory. So, let's assume that these drawings are 500 years old and they really were by your hero Michelangelo. And you've uncovered a mystery behind an iconic artist and his masterpiece."

"Wouldn't that be so cool? I mean, think about it. It would change the whole story if it's true."

"How so?"

"First of all, it would mean that Michelangelo had this other life that no one knew about, and maybe that influenced his art. He was perceived as a genius and a bit of a loner."

"It would also mean those drawings would be worth a fortune."

"I told you it's not about money for me. If it's true, then it's a piece of history that I've had the privilege to safeguard."

The tinkling sound of Dominique's laughter grated on Rose. She could see that they were holding hands under the table, and she eyed the woman's five-inch heels. The waiter placed a chocolate soufflé with two spoons on the table. The artistic confection had white powdered sugar decorating the top.

"This is a work of art," said Rose, eyeing the dessert.

They each took several bites as they lingered to chat over coffee. The conversation turned to Ben as he talked about his research and writing and then, rather awkwardly, brought up his daughter.

"Now, this is my pride and joy," said Ben as he took out his iPhone to show her pictures of Emily. The little blond girl was precious in her white smocked dress and hair bow. There were multiple pictures of her in the bathtub, or in her bouncy seat, or smiling in the arms of her mother. The reality of Ben being a father suddenly hit Rose. This little girl was his prize, and it felt strange to be jumping in on this part of his family story.

"I can't wait for you to meet her," Ben said, taking Rose's hand. "I know she'll love you."

"Ben, this is all moving a little fast for me. I mean I just moved here and—"

His expression changed. "I'm sorry. I didn't mean to overwhelm you. It's just that— We connect and always have. You've always been a special person. You spoiled me in that regard. I understand that we're both in different places in our lives right now, so I'll try to respect that."

"Thanks. I'd love to meet Emily when the time is right."

"Absolutely."

Ben kissed her sweetly, which made Rose suddenly feel self-conscious. Pulling away, she looked over at Lyon, and their eyes locked for a moment before she looked away.

***

The next morning, a specialist in Renaissance art who did appraisals for Christie's greeted them with a firm handshake. He reminded them how lucky they were that he was already in Rome on business and took the train to Florence. He stared at the drawings, reviewing and directing his questions to Ben, which Rose found annoying. He introduced himself as Paul Klonadis, a bald man with oversized glasses; he seemed to be evaluating every inch of the paper: the first eight-by-ten-inch drawing, and then the two larger images that were roughly twelve by fourteen inches. The conference room at the bank was quiet for the better part of an hour while Paul studied the quality of paper, the extent of the mold damage, the authenticity and the possible meanings of each picture.

"These drawings are old, as you can see. They were done on high-quality parchment, but the mold and dust would take months for us to remove and cost a bloody fortune."

"They seem to tell a story," offered Rose.

"I'm not sure what you mean by that," said Paul.

"Well," explained Rose, "there's a picture of a baby that does not appear to be a depiction of Jesus. The young boy could possibly be the baby in the first picture, and the intertwined hands seem like some sort of study."

"First of all, it's hard to see all of these pictures given the age and deterioration. That being said, it's also nearly impossible to distinguish any kind of likeness from the first two drawings. As for the hands, Leonardo da Vinci did many studies of hands, but this is definitely not his work." He breathed in sharply. "Are you aware that my team was involved with the original discovery of the secret drawings done by Leonardo?"

"No, I have no idea what you are talking about. Which ones are you referring to?" asked Rose.

"There were some drawings bound into a single album by sculptor Pompeo Leoni around 1590, and they entered the Royal Collection during the reign of Charles II." He paused. "There were some blank pages in the collection, which were known to scholars, but nobody could figure it out. Then, one of the scholars noticed the indentation marks on the pages."

"Go on," said Ben.

"These works were finally examined under ultraviolet light and revealed a series of drawings of hands. So, I can see how you thought they were done by a master. Anyway, it was not until one of the sheets was examined by the UK's national synchrotron that we saw the truth. Because of the high copper content in the stylus Leonardo used, his drawings were invisible to the naked eye. The copper had become a transparent copper salt, thus making the hands disappear."

"That's fascinating," said Rose, trying to mask her disdain for the pompous man.

"That is the kind of find that makes national news," Paul

continued. "The sheets that we uncovered were studies of hands for the *Adoration of the Magi* around 1481."

It was on the tip of Rose's tongue to suggest that her drawings could have been a study as well, done by Michelangelo, but she refrained for fear of his contempt.

"Indeed, Ben told me that you are passionate about the life and works of Michelangelo and I think, Miss Maning, you let your imagination run away with you. These pictures could have been done by a Florentine artist who was practicing his craft. That's what it looks like to me."

"I see," said Rose, feeling incredibly embarrassed and a bit miffed.

"Well, Ben. I wish that we had better news. Thanks for contacting me."

"I'm very sorry, Paul. I thought they could be valuable."

"Highly doubtful. The restoration process alone would cost a fortune, as I said, and I don't think it's advisable to invest in this project. So, if you'll excuse me, I have another appointment. Good day." He gave her a snippy stare and a definite lackluster goodbye.

"Well, I guess that's that," said Rose, rolling the sketches up.

"I could always take them back to the States and get a second opinion."

"Why would you do that?"

"I was trying to be helpful."

Rose eyed Ben, feeling decidedly uncomfortable with his helpfulness. "I see. Clearly, they were damaged after being in the wall after so many years, but I know someone I met here two years ago who does restoration work. Maybe I could work with him to clean them up. It would be an interesting project."

"That's a good idea," said Ben. "You're always thinking." He glanced at the lockbox. "I guess you don't need it anymore."

"You're right. It's a waste of money," said Rose. "I'll just stick these moldy old drawings in my tote bag and bring 'em home. Do you mind talking to the manager here and cancelling the lockbox?"

"Sounds like a plan," said Ben. "Happy to help you."

"I'm going to head to the market to grab us some dinner tonight before it gets too crowded at lunchtime. What are you in the mood for?"

"You," he said with a salacious grin.

"Seriously?" She blushed.

"Surprise me."

Rose kissed him and headed out the door of the conference room. Once outside, she sent a text to Lyon and asked if he could meet her at his office immediately.

Everything okay? he texted back.
Not really. I need a favor.
See you in ten.
You're the best.

***

Rose raced to the market, bought a chicken and some vegetables and kept moving. Checking her watch, she realized that fifteen minutes had passed. She looked over and saw a leather stand and bartered to buy a tan leather tote for twenty euros. Practically jogging to Lyon's office, she was out of breath when she got there. Lyon rose from his desk and hugged her.

"Are you alright?"

"Yes and no. Can you do me a huge favor?"

"Sure. Anything."

"I need something, anything that I can roll. I'll explain later."

Lyon opened up his filing cabinet and pulled out some old documents, sifting through them quickly.

"Would this work?"

"Not really. What else do you have?"

Rose spotted some older, darker-looking prints of architectural plans. Hopefully, the age spots would be the first thing anyone noticed. The bag switch idea was something she wasn't proud of, but her instincts demanded that she protect the drawings. "How about I borrow those from you? How soon do you need them back?"

"You can have them as long as you wish. They belonged to my predecessor here and I never got around to throwing them away."

He handed the scaled drawings to her, and she immediately rolled them up and placed them in her bag. Then, she quickly handed Lyon her tote bag.

"Can you hang on to this for me? It would be really helpful."

"Should I ask why?"

"Not really," she replied. "Just keep them in a safe place."

He raised one eyebrow, but asked no questions.

"Thanks!" she said breathlessly, gathering her groceries and heading back to meet Ben at her apartment. "I'll be in touch."

"I'm here if you need me."

"I really appreciate that."

"I was hoping to take you to Fuor D'Acqua before your American friend came to visit," he said.

"He leaves in a few days."

"Good," said Lyon. "And now I have something of yours."

"Yes, you do, and your help means the world to me," said Rose, studying his handsome face. She knew instinctively that she could trust him.

"Very good then. You can come and get your tote bag anytime!"

Rose tried to tamp down her disappointment in Ben. He seemed to care only about the value of the drawings instead of their artistic significance. Had Wall Street changed him? Rose decided to follow her instincts. Something troubled her about Paul and his assessment. He seemed too flippant and dismissive. *Ben may trust Paul's expertise, but I don't*, she thought. The man seemed too sure of himself.

When she got a free moment, Rose decided that she would

send Beatrice a picture of the drawing of intertwined hands. Perhaps she could offer some guidance. In the meantime, Rose would spend the next twenty-four hours focusing on Ben and their relationship. The time ticked by in a haze of passion.

***

"You have no idea how much I'm going to miss you," Ben said, taking her into his arms.

"I feel like you just got here!"

"Me too. This has been an amazing few days. I've loved every minute of it, and I love—"

"Don't say anymore," said Rose as they held each other close.

Ben held her in his arms, scanning the apartment once more. "This place is great. You really did well. The view and the location are outstanding. I wish I didn't have to go."

"Me either," said Rose, kissing him again.

Ben's iPhone buzzed, indicating that the driver he had hired to take him to the airport had arrived. A feeling of sadness swept over Rose as she kissed him goodbye.

"Please let me know when you land safely back in the States."

"Will do," he said as he pulled away, throwing his bag over his shoulder.

Hours later, Rose couldn't stand it anymore. She walked to the wardrobe where she had hidden the drawings to peer inside for her lookalike tote bag. It was gone. *Ben, Ben, Ben. Why?*

Chapter 11

RIGHT AFTER SHE HIT send on her email to Beatrice, Rose received an enthusiastic response, which was the surge of optimism she needed to hear. She was still devastated that Ben had stolen the decoy drawings she'd borrowed from Lyon. Before another round of anger took hold, Rose gave Beatrice a call.

"I'd be happy to show them to you. They would need a lot of work, but I'm convinced they tell a story."

"Based on your photographs, they look interesting and, frankly, very few artists could draw such an accurate representation of Michelangelo's the *Creation of Adam*; I can use new technology in the lab to see through the mold. We could use some modern technology to test the paper and try to determine its age, then work through the mold. Hard to believe that you found a piece of history in the walls of your new home!"

"I agree. I'm still trying to understand what happened. I wonder if I could be so bold as to ask to be part of this process? I mean, I would love to learn more about what you do."

"I'd have to get permission but, after all, you found them, so I think it should be fine. We do have contacts in Florence, but I wonder if you would allow me to show these to Cardinal Baglioni, who is a close friend. I trust him completely."

"Please do, and let me know how you want to proceed."

"Will do."

Ben sent her a text that evening when he had landed in New York. He signed it, *Yours forever, Ben*. Rose's heart skipped a beat, and suddenly she felt physically sick. Clearly, he hadn't checked inside the tote bag yet to find that she had switched the drawings. A part of her wondered if his intent had been positive. What if she had made the biggest mistake of her life? Would he ever forgive her for not trusting him? After all, he had come to Florence to see her before he knew the drawings existed. Perhaps he took them to have further research done.

Ben may be a businessman and profit oriented, but is he really a thief?

After a series of emails back and forth, Beatrice asked Rose to come to Rome to show the cardinal the drawings before the week was out.

The workers should finish up in a couple days. When they do, I'll make the trip, Rose wrote.

In the meantime, Rose figured she better get working on her painting, which was the reason why, or so she thought, she had come to Florence. Soon after the workers arrived to finish up her kitchen, she grabbed her sketchbook and headed back to the Uffizi to find inspiration. Signs and symbols of the powerful Medici family surrounded her as she made her way there.

At the forefront of the Renaissance in Florence was Italian statesman Lorenzo de' Medici, who was also a major collector and patron of the arts. Many of his contemporaries called him Lorenzo the Magnificent because of his power and influence on the politics, art, culture, trade and essentially all aspects of Florentine culture. Studying the museum map, Rose took the stairs two at a time as she went in search of a Medici portrait by Agnolo Bronzino that had been one of her favorites. It was of Bea Medici, whose intricately woven gown and earrings were stunning. There was an almost mythical quality to the portrait that made Rose want to try to recreate the precise lines of this work. She was consumed by the gold braid in the front and the elegant jewels she wore.

She opened her sketchbook and her breath caught in her throat. On the page was a drawing she had done of Ben's profile as he looked out at the view from her balcony. Her rendering had caught the tiny lines by his eyes, his strong intelligent forehead and hint of a smile. Tears stung her eyes as she thought about him. The past few days had been magical, and she had dared hope that they had a future together. *It's all so strange*, she thought, as she caught sight of the Medici princess in front of her. Bea's beautiful angular face seemed to jump off the canvas.

Rose spent the next few hours trying to capture the essence of the painting but make it her own. She shaded and drew until the museum closed. Her flurry of drawing and painting continued on for the next few days, proving cathartic.

***

Before heading to Rome, Rose met Lyon at his office to fetch her tote bag with the sketches.

"Are you going to tell me what's going on?" he asked as he unlocked the file cabinet and handed her the tote.

"You're not going to believe this, but I found these drawings in the wall during my renovations last week and they are rather mysterious. I'm heading to the Vatican tomorrow to see a conservator friend. She knows a cardinal there who can help. I hope they might tell me something about them. A representative from Christie's looked at them and said they are too moldy and dirty to salvage. But I disagree."

"That's so fantastic, Rose. May I see them?"

"Sure," she said, unrolling the parchment to reveal the three images.

"Why would anyone not want to salvage them? At the very least, they are part of history."

"That's what I think," she said. "I knew I liked you."

"And I like you too."

"What about Dominique? You seemed to *like* her too."

"It's complicated. We've been together for years, but it's definitely over. I don't want her to divorce her husband for me."

"She's married?"

"She is. And your American boyfriend?"

"Divorced. He has an ex and a two-year-old daughter." She paused. "We grew up together, but I'm afraid that he has changed too much."

"That's great news for me," Lyon said, looking down at the drawings. "I think the baby and the boy are the same. Look at the shape of the eyes and the hand. There's a ring on the boy's finger, which is a sign that his family is part of the ruling class."

"Oh my goodness, I never picked up on that. Could he possibly be related to the Medici family?"

"Hard to see with all that mold."

"But the ring could give a clue as to his identity."

"Absolutely," said Lyon. "And what have we here? It's the most iconic image in Italy drawn a different way. Now, that's really interesting."

Rose felt a surge of excitement. "I thought so too. I mean, could it be his?"

"Anything's possible," said Lyon. "How'd would you like some company tomorrow on your way to the Vatican? I don't think you should take these drawings on public transportation. They're potentially too valuable."

"But that expert from Christie's told me they weren't worth their time." She paused. "Regardless of the outcome, I think this is an incredibly cool experience!"

"Well, they were either deliberately misleading you or incompetent. Well?"

"Oh, I'd love a ride to Rome tomorrow. Are you sure?"

"I'll reschedule a couple of appointments and pick you up in the morning."

"You have no idea how relieved I am right now. Thank you so much for helping me."

"Ah, Rose, it would be my pleasure to spend the day with you."

No word from Ben, Rose mused, as she tried to imagine his anger when he realized that she had switched the drawings. Fortunately, exhaustion won out and she fell into a deep, dreamless sleep.

***

The next morning Lyon showed up as planned.

"Nice car," she said, eyeing his red Tesla. "I thought all you had was a scooter."

"It belongs to one of my clients. He said I could borrow it to impress you. Is it working?"

"I'll bet Cardinal Baglioni will love it," joked Rose.

"Come on, it's fast, so he'll appreciate that I'll have you to your meeting early."

He weaved his way through the winding streets of Florence and onto the highway where they made record time to the Holy City. Rose held the tote bag close to her body and hoped that some answers would be forthcoming. She felt strangely calm as she looked over at Lyon's profile in the driver's seat. His long, lean hands maneuvered the car with precision, and he had this inner confidence that she liked. As much as she enjoyed his adventurous spirit, Rose knew she could trust him. A small voice warned her that she was nothing like Dominique.

Rose's heart raced as they were led to the cardinal's office, adorned with a circular Renaissance painting of the Madonna and child; Rose surmised it was a portrait done by Raphael. The image was striking in its intensity, and the blue of Mother Mary's robes practically leapt off of the canvas. Rose held the drawings tightly in one hand and gripped Lyon's hand in the other as they were told to be seated. A short time later, Beatrice arrived with Cardinal Baglioni, who was a tall, elegant man with white hair and a crimson robe.

"Good morning, Miss Maning," he said, shaking her hand. She introduced him to Lyon and then got down to the business of explaining that she had just relocated to Florence and bought her first home in the Santa Croce neighborhood, and how she discovered the hidden sketches.

"I spent several years teaching art history at a private girls school in Charlottesville, Virginia, so I am very familiar with the artists who were shaping this part of Italy's history."

"Well, Rose, if I may, don't keep us in suspense any longer. Let me see what you've uncovered."

Beatrice helped her unroll the parchments and put them on the table; she had small table weights to hold down the curled edges. She also produced a large magnifying glass with a light so that her hand could highlight each section. The cardinal leaned in to study them beside her, and Rose saw the look of surprise on his face.

"And you found these drawings in the wall?" he asked. "This is incredible!"

He studied the three drawings for several more minutes.

"You may have provided proof to a story that's been whispered about for centuries." He looked at Lyon and then Rose. "Who else knows about these?"

"I showed them to a friend who contacted representatives from Christie's. The man who saw them was unimpressed and said the sketches weren't worth restoring."

Cardinal Baglioni shook his head. "They had no idea what they were looking at," he said. "These renderings are fascinating."

"Don't keep *me* in suspense any longer!"

"Well." He paused. "I would say at first glance the child in this drawing is the same individual as the boy. And with the fact that they are together with a third drawing, which looks like a scene from the Sistine Chapel, I'm guessing—and this is just a *possibility*—that these drawings could be associated with a Renaissance artist like our own Michelangelo. But, again, I shouldn't speculate without proper lab work."

Beatrice chimed in. "We would use X-rays to determine the

type and quality of the parchment paper, do a cleaning process and see what is underneath some of these spots." She moved her hand to the right. "See the tape on the right side. We've had some good luck using a particular gel to dissolve it, which may lead to more answers."

Cardinal Baglioni stared further at the drawing. "Look at the boy's ring. He's definitely of the ruling class. We would have to test the age of the paper to know for sure."

"Do you think the drawings are connected in some way?"

"I do," he replied. "I think that the child and the boy are one and the same." He directed the light and pointed to the brow line and nose.

"So, what about the third drawing?" asked Rose.

"If the parchment is indeed the right age, then, as I said at the outset, there's a possibility that this could be attributed to a Renaissance artist."

Rose touched the parchment reverently. "That would be quite a discovery . . . but I won't get my hopes up." She studied the three drawings together. "I had a dream about the third drawing, which is why I brought them to you, Cardinal. I felt like they need to be safeguarded."

"I completely agree with you, Miss Maning, which is why I don't feel you should share any information with anyone, and especially do not post anything on social media at this time."

Lyon, who had been quietly observing the exchange, asked, "Why not?"

"You never know how these things can be construed," the cardinal said.

"There's a story here and something you're not telling us," Lyon said.

The room was silent for several minutes as the cardinal pondered and rubbed his chin.

"Cardinal," said Lyon. "Rose is trying to do the right thing and she came to you for answers. You can at least give her the courtesy of your initial thoughts."

"Given the condition and age of these parchments, I would allow for a level of authenticity here. They've been hidden in a wall for a considerable period of time, so I agree with Rose that they seem to tell a story. And one that comes to mind is that the artist gave them to a trusted family member or friend to safeguard."

"Go on."

"There have always been rumors that Michelangelo fathered a son who worked for him as an apprentice, but these claims have never been substantiated. Some people have whispered that he fell in love with his patron Lorenzo de Medici's daughter Contessina when he lived and studied in the palace as a young man. Again, we've never heard of anything that would validate such a claim but . . . " He looked at the first two drawings. "The ring on the boy's hand is very compelling, but again, we can't be sure of a relationship that could have led to an illegitimate son. At this point, it's all conjecture."

"But perhaps when the material is cleaned and the tape removed we may see some sort of signature."

"So, these drawings could be the key to a mystery about the great Michelangelo? This is all fascinating and extremely important," said Rose, trying to contain her excitement. "Think of the historical value!"

"Indeed, that is true," Cardinal Baglioni said. "But it also could place a negative light on one of the most iconic artists in Italy's history."

"How so?" questioned Lyon.

"Scholars have been debating the meaning of the Sistine Chapel for generations. This find challenges years of academic study."

"But that's possibly been conducted with partial information. She's found a new piece of evidence."

"Indeed, you may have," he said, turning his gaze to Rose. "And you will be rewarded for bringing this find to us."

"But—"

"I need to consult with my peers on these drawings." The cardinal looked at Rose and Lyon. "You have my word that they will be safe in my care and we will come up with an adequate way to compensate you."

"I want to be part of the conservation process. I found them," Rose pleaded.

"But you have no formal training. That would be impossible."

"Why couldn't I be an apprentice and learn?"

"I would be willing to supervise her," said Beatrice. "She could work with me in the laboratory and observe."

"We will give this idea every consideration."

Beatrice gingerly took the parchments and rolled them up. The cardinal approached Rose.

"You have done the right thing by bringing this part of history back where it belongs."

"Thank you," said Rose, who felt uneasy. Did the cardinal have an agenda? "We will plan to stay in Rome, in close proximity to the Vatican, until you make a decision on them."

Cardinal Baglioni nodded his consent.

***

As they headed outside into the sunshine, Rose felt a sense of calm.

"Cardinal Baglioni will compensate you for your discovery," said Beatrice.

"But if they are authentic, I get the impression that he isn't going to tell anyone that they exist?"

"I think we would need to go through the restoration process first before a decision is made on that front. Things don't just happen here. There's a governing board, and they would have to debate the merits of the find. It's my understanding that he's quite close with Cardinal Rothsay, who is a biblical scholar; I bet the two of them will debate the meaning of the intertwined hands forever," she said with a laugh.

"What do you think the hands mean?" she asked Beatrice.

"I think they're a symbol of mankind's ultimate relationship with God. That they are one."

"And your opinion?"

Lyon paused for a moment. "I'd like to think the same thing. That we're all from the same God and we need to respect each other despite earthly differences."

"What would happen if we lived in a world governed by the laws of love? I wonder why Michelangelo painted it with God's fingers touching Adam rather than the intertwined hands? It's also a beautiful message. In my opinion, he made a distinction between the earthly and the divine."

Rose paused, considering the meaning of the current panel in the Sistine Chapel and the possible ramifications of the third drawing she found.

"We also have to consider the possibility that the Master may have had the opportunity to discuss the drawing with his possible son. I can imagine a debate between them as they considered both options. I mean, what if Michelangelo had wanted the hands touching and his son argued to have them intertwined? That is a really fascinating concept." She cleared her throat. "But it may just be too farfetched to even consider. What I do know is that maybe these hands mean that God isn't just this distant being that we touch with our fingers. Maybe the divine is something we need to hold tightly and feel."

They all paused for a moment.

"That was a beautiful analysis, Rose," said Lyon. "It's probably something that I will ponder in the coming weeks. I mean, aren't we all often ruled by earthly desires? I think our spiritual side doesn't get enough attention."

"Is that a rhetorical question?" asked Beatrice.

"I think we all have a responsibility to treat our fellow man with dignity and respect," exclaimed Rose. "Wouldn't that be amazing if such a message became a cultural phenomenon? That we all need to experience God in our midst from the moment we wake up to the moment we go to sleep."

Lyon added. "Maybe, but it's certainly not going to happen if the discovery is locked away forever."

Beatrice eyed Rose. "You would be foolish not to accept the conditions offered by the cardinal. I have known him to be a very fair and generous man."

"I understand," said Rose, wanting to end the payment discussion. "On a lighter note, where can I get a cup of coffee around here? This has all been a lot to absorb in one day."

"I'll take you to the secret employee café where you can get an amazing cappuccino."

"Now, that would really make my day," joked Rose, now buoyed by her discovery, one that might confirm the intention of one of the greatest artists of all time.

Chapter 12

WAITING WAS THE HARDEST part. Lyon drove back to Florence that evening, promising to come back as soon as she heard some news. Beatrice invited Rose to stay in her apartment while a decision about Rose's involvement was being made.

The next couple of mornings, Rose commuted with Beatrice to the Vatican to spend time in the laboratory watching her newfound work, which was both exciting and eye opening.

***

Several days passed with no news until Rose received word that Cardinal Baglioni would like to meet with her. She texted Lyon for moral support and asked if he could clear his schedule to return to Rome. Her patience was frayed, but she was relieved that she might finally get some answers. When Lyon arrived, Rose was delighted to see him and rushed into his arms. He kissed her and took her hand as they entered the inner sanctum of the building.

Beatrice's words rang in her head as she nervously headed to the cardinal's office. *He's a man of his word. The cardinal is not going to let you down.*

They were directed to a conference room on the second floor where Cardinal Baglioni, dressed in crimson and white, immediately invited them in and shut the door.

"After careful consideration, Ms. Maning, we are prepared to offer you the sum of $3 million dollars for your discovery," said the cardinal. "However, the proposal is only good now if you sign these legal documents that we have drawn up."

"What?!" Rose gasped. "That's a lot of money for a discovery that hasn't been authenticated yet. Any more clues?"

The cardinal did not respond.

"But it's not a lot of money," Lyon piped in, "if the drawings are authentic. They reveal information about Michelangelo and the thought process behind an iconic artwork. Not to mention that there might be a chance that he fathered a son who worked with him."

"That's true," said the cardinal. "That's why the Vatican wants control of her discovery and whether we make it public. We have specific conditions for you to follow. We don't want any information on social media or through the press by Ms. Maning."

Rose couldn't believe her ears. Three million dollars was more money than she could have ever dreamed about having in her lifetime! She willed herself to remain calm when she asked, "May I observe the conservation process? I've been shadowing Beatrice all week and I don't think I've slowed her down."

"No, I'm afraid that's not possible."

"Please. It's very important to me. I found the drawings and want to see them restored."

He reviewed the legal document at his desk.

She pushed harder. "Then I'll refuse your offer and take the drawings and my story elsewhere."

"You could do that, but we have made you a very generous offer. These drawings are a part of history and we would be most capable of guaranteeing their safety."

"I understand, but the conservation process means the world to me. This discovery has already affected my life in ways too numerous for me to talk about now. I repeat, it's important that I have access to a historical find."

He stared at her intently, pondering her request.

"Alright," he said reluctantly, "I will amend our agreement. You can work out the details of your apprenticeship with Beatrice and her superior."

"I have several ideas on how to make it work and still live in Florence the majority of the time," Rose added.

Lyon whispered that she should have easier access to the Sistine Chapel in the future.

"Cardinal, I realize that you are making me an extremely generous offer, but I would be releasing my rights to a historical find that could have a major impact on how art historians would view Michelangelo's iconic work. It could dramatically increase the number of tourists if, in fact, the drawings are authentic or even speculated to be as such. I would like to ask for VIP access to the chapel as my final part of this settlement." She took a breath. "I am passionate about the life and works of Michelangelo, and it would be my pleasure to share this love with others."

"Fair enough," said the cardinal. "I'll make that happen. There will be conditions on your request, of course."

"I understand."

My life will never be the same, thought Rose, as she signed the documents.

"And you said you had a dream about the third drawing?" asked the cardinal.

"I did. I saw the intertwined hands in my dream."

"God has a plan for all of us." The cardinal smiled. "I look forward to seeing more of you in the future, Rose."

***

Rose and Lyon immediately met with Beatrice to agree on a plan for watching her clean and restore the drawings, which was going to take several months.

"I've so enjoyed your company this week. You are welcome to stay in my apartment when you come. You could come down by train on Monday morning, stay with me and return to Florence on Tuesday afternoon. We will figure something out."

"That's so lovely. Thank you, Beatrice. That idea works for me."

Rose made her way to the Sistine Chapel to look at the ceiling one more time. She would never tire of viewing this masterpiece. With Lyon by her side, she stared at the panels that always inspired her with their timeless beauty.

On the drive back to Florence, Rose tried to process all that had happened.

"Three million dollars is a lot of money."

"You realize they could make ten times that if and when the news breaks and, of course, if it's all true that these sketches are connected to Michelangelo himself. Regardless, it's a fascinating story with a beautiful message."

"But now it's *their* story to tell, not mine."

"Fair enough. But you'll be part of whatever history is made."

Soon after, Rose dozed off in the car, and when she awoke they were on the outskirts of Florence.

"You've had quite the week, Rose."

"I know. It all seems so strange."

"It may take a while for it all to sink in."

"I still feel uneasy about accepting money to guard some centuries-old secret."

"I'm not in the art business, but I do know that a Leonardo found last year sold for $450 million dollars and yours has a far more interesting story."

"Pope Julius II originally commissioned Michelangelo to do the Sistine Chapel, and that is where the drawings belong," countered Rose, trying to justify her decision.

"Not many people would look at it that way."

"It's not about money for me," Rose said. "Three million is a lot, and I'd like to use some of it to help others."

"Perhaps you could set up some sort of scholarship fund for

students to come to Florence and learn about the Renaissance?"

"That's a great idea! But I'd want it to be for people of all ages, not just traditional students. What a gift to be able to help others explore my passion for Michelangelo! I'm a very lucky art historian."

"That you are," Lyon chuckled. "Too bad I can't advertise your find to all of my potential clients. I can imagine the billboard now: *Relocate to Italy. Discover a Hidden Treasure. Change Your Life.*"

Rose laughed. "I really can't believe what just happened today! And I've got a once-in-a-lifetime opportunity to observe firsthand the conservation and restoration process at the Vatican! That's so incredibly awesome!"

"I'll drink to that," said Lyon. "Let go out and celebrate!"

"Sounds great," said Rose. "Do you mind dropping me off at home so that I can do a quick change?"

"Only because I like you."

                                  ***

Lyon decided that he would wait for her if she promised to be quick.

"Fair enough. I'll be no more than fifteen minutes."

Lyon gave her a knowing smile as she jumped out of the car, practically walking on air as she made her way up the steps. The door to her apartment was slightly ajar, which Rose found strange. Maybe the contractors hadn't locked it properly, she decided, not wanting to relinquish her excitement over the day's events. She nudged the door open and turned on the light to see that her home had been completely ransacked. Doors were hanging open, pictures thrown on the ground, cushions slashed. She screamed and ran back downstairs.

"Lyon, somebody broke into my apartment! We need to call the police."

Lyon dialed an emergency number from his cell phone and

tried to calm her down as they waited for the authorities. Rose felt shaken and afraid, wondering if this was a random act or something more sinister. A team of police officers arrived within minutes and went upstairs to investigate.

An officer started speaking to Lyon in torrents of Italian, and Lyon answered his questions, explaining how she had been out of town for the last few days. An officer returned from her apartment and said in halting English, "It appears like someone was looking for something specific because the television and personal belongings appear to be intact. Will you confirm this, Miss Maning? Do you have any idea what someone might be looking for?"

Rose shook her head and looked over at Lyon, who explained that she had relocated to Florence a few weeks ago and only recently had work done on the apartment. The officer wrote down her name and cell number and promised to contact her if they came up with any leads.

Rose nodded, wondering at how her new life had become so dramatic.

"Hey, why don't you pack a bag? I'm thinking it would make sense to not have you stay here alone tonight. You could stay with my parents in their guest house. It would give us time to get the apartment cleaned and perhaps a better security system installed. I think we'll both sleep easier if you are there and safe."

"Thank you," said Rose, relieved.

"Absolutely. Their guest cottage is extremely private and the perfect place for you right now. I'll call and let them know that you're coming."

"That would be great. I can't thank you enough."

"Please don't thank me. I'm glad to be able to help."

"Do you think this was a random act?"

"I'm not sure yet what to think. It could be, but it seems like a strange coincidence. There are only two other people who know you found the drawings. Your American friend and the professional from Christie's. Something doesn't add up. This neighborhood is not known for its crime."

"Ben is back in New York, and I have no idea about Mr. Klonadis."

Rose raced up the stairs to her new home, feeling suddenly very vulnerable. With a speed born of fear, she managed to grab an overnight bag and place a few days' worth of clothing and toiletries in it. Remembering her sketchpad and some paints, she threw those into a tote bag so she would have something to do once she arrived at Lyon's parents' home in Tuscany.

"Ready?" he said. "My parents said they'd be delighted to have you stay as long as you like."

"I can't thank you enough for your help. You're right. I wasn't going to get any sleep here alone."

***

The traffic was light as Lyon expertly wound his way out of the city onto the highway.

"Don't think too much. I don't want you to worry."

"Thanks. I needed to hear that," said Rose thoughtfully. "The timing, and now we have two suspects, which is sad, but true." She sighed heavily, telling herself to stay calm. "I think the Christie's professional lied to me about the value if Cardinal Baglioni was willing to shell out three million dollars. I know the story and the drawings are worth far more than that on the 'open market,'" she said sarcastically.

"Would anyone believe it? It's the stuff of movies."

"I'm not sure what I think anymore," said Rose quietly, looking into the night.

They stopped for gas and headed to Tuscany, which took less than thirty minutes. Soon afterwards, they pulled up to a guarded gatehouse. Lyon spoke in Italian to the guard, who opened the massive gates. The driveway was well lit, with gorgeous cypress trees winding along a moonlit path. A grand estate loomed before them, and Rose's breath caught in her throat at the circular driveway, cascading fountain, and large stone villa.

"Are you kidding me?" she said, taking in the glorious property. "I thought you said your father was an English poet— you know, the starving artist kind."

Lyon threw back his head and laughed. "He was also kind of an English aristocrat."

"Seriously?"

"All is well, Rose," he said as a servant came down to greet them. "You are safe here."

"So, you didn't borrow the Tesla."

"Well, I borrowed it from my family, who happen to be one of my clients, so I was technically truthful. Come this way and I'll show you to the guest house. You can get some sleep and meet my parents tomorrow morning. Sound good?"

"I really appreciate your help. I'm feeling a bit overwhelmed right now."

He escorted her into a beautiful one-floor sitting and guest room, which looked more African than Tuscan with white sofas, dark hardwood floors and a series of tribal masks lining the main wall. Colorful modern landscape paintings added an open and airy feel. As Rose gazed toward the masks, Lyon reminded her that his mother was born and raised in Namibia. It was on the tip of Rose's tongue to ask who the artist was, but she was exhausted. As soon as Lyon departed, Rose looked around, taking in her elegant surroundings, and asked herself how she got here. Suddenly, this new reality made her feel anxious and scared. She checked the lock on the door and made her way to the bathroom to take a shower.

Rose sat and relaxed, minutes from falling asleep. As she began to doze off, she thought about home, her friends, and the security she felt there. The memory of the going-away party in her honor made her teary-eyed. Her thoughts turned from home to BenThe big surprise that night was Ben. He showed up and offered to drive her to the airport the next morning. Why did she always think about him? He seemed to have this power over her that she couldn't explain, not even to herself.

Chapter 13

ROSE AWOKE TO SUN streaming in the windows of her bedroom, casting a bright light on an abstract painting of yellows and oranges. The colors soothed her senses, and for a moment, she forgot where she was and looked around in confusion. Then, she recalled the series of events at the Vatican, the break-in, and felt suddenly relieved to be in Tuscany with Lyon and his family.

Rose quickly donned a sundress and sandals, ran a brush through her hair and headed outside to wander around. Checking her iPhone, she saw that Zoey had tried to reach her, but she decided a good espresso was her first order of the day. The call would have to wait.

The grass seemed to roll on forever on this property, punctuated by flowering trees and a shimmering kidney-shaped pool. Rose saw someone swimming laps and she inched closer, realizing it was Lyon. He waved her over and she obliged, smiling.

"Good morning, Rose. How'd you sleep?"

"Actually, surprisingly well." She looked around at the dreamy countryside. "This setting is absolutely beautiful."

"My parents love it here. My mother is in her studio and she said to drop in on her anytime."

"Don't tell me. Those beautiful landscape paintings in the guest cottage are hers."

"That's right. She also likes to sculpt objects from antiquity. Some of her artwork is for sale at a gallery near your place."

"Aha! I thought I had seen something like this before. What's the name of it?"

"*Area Galleria Contemporare* near the Ponte Vecchio."

Rose eyed his athletic form, thinking he was way too good looking for her peace of mind. Rose turned away. She had always thought Ben was the love of her life, and suddenly she was here in Tuscany with Lyon, feeling a definite attraction. Lyon was far more worldly than her, but he seemed to enjoy sharing his experience rather than making judgments. She averted her gaze when he jumped out of the pool naked and threw on a towel. He led her to a sunroom off the main house.

"Coffee?" he asked.

"You read my mind."

"I'll give you a private tour of the vineyard later. My father has been up since sunrise. He can't stay away. He loves every minute of the vintner's life. We also have a tasting room open to private tours on the property."

"I can't wait to see everything," said Rose, pouring an espresso from the pot on the side table, trying to avert her eyes from Lyon's nakedness. She made small talk. "In the States, hard cider has become a whole phenomenon and people love it, especially the college kids. Same with craft beer."

He seemed genuinely amused by the way she avoided his gaze.

"I think the cider idea is interesting and something I'd like to learn more about, but—" He looked down at his towel. "Let me do a quick change while you drink your coffee. I'll be back down in a few minutes to join you for breakfast."

Rose sipped her espresso and peeked in a large dining room with high ceilings, a mahogany table and stone fireplace. A silver bowl on the table sparkled in the morning light, as did the candlesticks. Lyon returned with his usual easygoing manner, making her feel comfortable in this lavish setting. He took his coffee black and they sat down at an airy table to a breakfast of eggs, crispy bacon and fruit. She cleared her throat.

"I hate to think about last night, but I do wonder how we should go about looking for who broke into my apartment."

"I'm a step ahead of you. I hired a private investigator this morning to keep tabs on Mr. Klonadis. And your American friend?"

Rose cringed at the thought. "I really don't think he had anything to do with it."

"Why not?"

"I've known Ben my whole life; he's not the type to hire criminals to break into my apartment. There's absolutely no way."

"In my opinion, there are only two people that know you found the drawings unless Ben has told others. He also attempted to steal them from you."

"There's more to the story," said Rose, feeling suddenly ill. "He's not like that."

"I beg to differ. He was the one who brought in the professionals from Christie's. Perhaps it was a setup the whole time."

"I just can't believe it," said Rose, thinking that perhaps the fates had been telling her lies.

"Well, the good news is that the drawings are in safe hands at the Vatican and they paid you very well for them."

"This all seems surreal. I'm going to check in with Zoey this afternoon and tell her how I met Beatrice. I'll say that I found some historical drawings and she is going to let me observe her work to see if I want to pursue conservation of historical paintings, which fascinates me."

"You can't tell her about the money or the deal you made. It wouldn't be prudent."

"Got it. I won't say a word."

Rose pondered her agreement, thinking it was so strange to not tell anyone about her discovery or the impact that it had already made on her life.

"Well, in the meantime, I'd like you to meet my mother and

let her show you her studio. I'll probably duck out early because I have a few appointments in the city. Will you be okay here without me?"

"I'm doing well. I really appreciate your help." She paused. "What about the investigation?"

"Don't worry. I'll inform you whenever I hear something."

After breakfast, he led her down a flowered pathway to a clearing with a small wooden cottage surrounded by yellow wildflowers and lavender. The blue French door was ajar, so Lyon called for his mother. The vibrant woman who greeted them gave Rose a European welcome with a kiss on each cheek, telling Rose to call her by her first name, Faith. She wore no makeup and had thick, long gray hair that was tied loosely in a ponytail. Thanks to perfect bone structure and luminous coffee-colored skin, she still looked amazingly young and bohemian in linen, wide-legged striped pants and a white shirt. Once Lyon had excused himself, her radiant brown eyes locked on to Rose, who felt an instant connection.

"Rose, it's so wonderful to finally meet you. Lyon has told us so many lovely things about your move here. I applaud your adventurous spirit to leave your home and family to live abroad. Your new home in Florence sounds marvelous despite the unfortunate events last night."

"I can't thank you enough for having me. It's been a hectic few days and I appreciate the solitude here in your lovely home. I was admiring your landscapes this morning. They are *bellisimo!*" Rose laughed. "That's the extent of my Italian."

"Come in, my dear, and let me show you my work-space."

Rose responded instantly to her warm and engaging manner. The studio looked worn and loved with paints everywhere and numerous half-finished canvases on the walls.

"Sometimes I work on several ideas at once," she explained. "I never know each day what is going to inspire me."

"I love that blue painting," said Rose, going over to take a closer look.

"Ahh!" she said. "I call that one *Moon River*. Isn't that an old American song?"

"I think so."

Something about the studio felt oddly comforting. Rose felt at ease with Faith, who went on to explain how she mixed colors, and they talked about brushstrokes.

"I have no formal training, but I can copy things very well. I just love to paint and draw. It's good for my soul."

"Then you are an artist."

"Oh no," said Rose. "I wouldn't go that far. It makes me happy and I guess that's what I came to Florence to explore."

"Rose, dear, I've lived long enough to know one doesn't leave their home unless they have a reason to do so."

Rose stared at Faith's *Moon River,* admiring how the blues swirled into gray abstract lines.

"My father died when I was in college and, well, I've been lost without him. He was my hero; he was born in Poland, so I feel at home in Europe."

"And your mother?"

"Doris." She thought for a minute. "There's no better way to say it, but my mother, whom I call Doris, is difficult. She wanted to control my life and I wouldn't let her."

Faith nodded and peered at her thoughtfully. "That must have been hard on you, to lose your beloved father and have a mother who didn't provide you with the nurturing that you needed."

"After my dad died, I felt like there was no one to guide me anymore. Then, I became a teacher to help others, and I realized I needed a break from that too. I needed time away to find myself again."

"Sounds to me like you've made a great decision. You need to know and love yourself first in life. That's not so easy to do." She laughed and gave her a hug. "Dear girl, you've just given me my inspiration for today's work. I'm going to paint in pinks and reds and perhaps a bit of yellow. You do know Van Gogh considered yellow the color of love."

"I knew that."

Rose liked Faith's easygoing manner. She could have stayed in her studio all day, but she didn't want to overextend her welcome too much. Reluctantly, she made her way back to the guest cottage to call Zoey. A familiar voice was exactly what she needed.

"Rose! How are you? You have no idea how much I miss you!"

"I miss you too, but the renovations and traveling have kept me crazy busy."

"And Ben!"

Rose gulped. "Yes, Ben. I can't believe he came over and surprised me!"

"I ran into Doris, who was gushing about his visit. She thinks he's very serious about you."

"Really?" said Rose.

"Uh, you don't sound so enthusiastic."

"Oh no, um, I am."

"Come on, girl. Something's going on."

"I'm in Tuscany right now with Lyon and his parents."

Zoey screamed. "I knew it! I saw the way he looked at you. You're one lucky girl."

"I don't know about that. I'm not sure about anything right now."

"Well, you better get clarity soon because your mother made it sound like Ben was ready to propose."

"Huh? It's too soon." Rose scratched her head. "That makes no sense. And it sounds like Doris is letting her fantasies get the better of her."

"I don't know, girl, but you've got a lot to figure out."

"I sure do. Now tell me about Stan and your new promotion. I hope you got my card congratulating you on your success. You'll do a fantastic job, better than I could have ever done."

"Thanks! You know you'd be great at it too. I miss you and it's only been a few weeks."

"Me too," said Rose, who missed Zoey more than she was willing to admit.

After she hung up, Rose's thoughts drifted to Ben. Why would he act like he wanted to propose? She assumed he hated her for switching the drawings. Perhaps time would reveal his true intentions, but could she ever trust him again? There was no way of knowing what was on his mind, and she wondered why she still cared so much about what he thought.

Meanwhile, there was something special about Lyon, who was so supportive and easy to be around. She really liked his positive attitude, and it was all effortless, even with the drama surrounding the drawings she found. Sighing heavily, Rose hoped that she would gain some clarity before long. In the meantime, she pictured the clasped hands in the drawing and her dream.

Taking out her sketchpad, she spent the next few hours drawing the intertwined hands from memory and placing them in various relationships—mother and child, father and son. And she changed the colors of the hands to represent different nationalities and cultures.

The idea sparked her creative energy, and she lost all track of time. When Lyon appeared at her cottage door, she was on her hands and knees on the floor sketching rapidly as an idea began to take shape.

"Hi," he said sweetly. "You've been busy!" He walked over and they kissed as if they always did so at the end of the day.

"I absolutely loved talking to your mother this morning. She insists that I call her Faith. I came back here and thought about the intertwined hands in the drawing. I decided that I could play off the beautiful message in my own work." She looked up, rubbing the back of her neck. "What do you think?"

"I think they look terrific. You are very talented, Rose."

"I don't know where I'm going with this, but I've been entertained for hours," she joked, standing.

"You're definitely onto something."

"I absolutely love to create."

"Hmm, you might be having dinner with someone who shares your passion. How about a swim and we'll visit with my parents?"

"I didn't bring a swimsuit."

"Works for me." He gave her an indulgent grin. "I'm sure my mother has extras in the pool house. No worries."

***

The cool evening water felt sublime on her skin as she stared up at the cloudless sky. She knew she should ask Lyon if there was any news on the intruder but shied away from doing so, not wanting to jump back into the drama quite yet. They lingered in the pool until Rose's skin started to shrivel. She got out and went back to the cottage to shower and get ready to meet Lyon's father.

A tall, energetic man walked into the sunroom and immediately embraced her. Rose was caught off guard by his vibrant figure and thought Joseph looked like an older version of Lyon—handsome and charismatic with a firm handshake. Something about him reminded her of her father, too. Maybe it was his European background or his energetic presence. Nevertheless, she felt completely at ease. He had just come from the tasting room and he was excited about a new Chianti that they were about to bring to market.

"Everyone must come and try it."

Faith heartily agreed, and they drove a tired-looking black sedan to a modern stone building on their property. Joseph told the story of how they had found out about the property ten years ago and had immediately fallen in love with Tuscany and the life here.

"It's warm and the colors are so beautiful. Nothing like it in the world," said Faith, who wore a gray linen tunic and white pants. Her hair was up in a messy bun.

"This is the part where he tells you about how if the wine has soul, you can taste it in a tenth of a second," explained Lyon as Joseph pointed out the stone bench he had installed for Faith to watch the sunset after a day in the studio or on the tennis courts where Lyon's sister, Katherine, loved to play and always tried to beat him. He shared how Lyon's brother, Peter, was part of the family's wine business.

"So, your siblings are named after famous Russian czars. What happened to you?" she joked.

"Smart mother. No pressure," he shot back confidently.

"He's always been quick," said Faith. "Even as a little boy. It was always a challenge keeping up with him. He's endlessly curious about everything . . . You are correct. Joseph taught a Russian literature class at Cambridge for a few years when we were young." She winked at her husband. "By the way, Lyon designed this building and the new architecture that went along with this place."

"So, you're a realtor with a degree in architecture," Rose said dryly.

"Mostly self-taught."

The reference to architecture reminded Rose of Thomas Jefferson, who was also a self-taught architect and the foundation of Ben's book. She quickly banished the thought from her mind, focusing instead on the interior of the wine-tasting room. The place was exquisite with mahogany wood beams on the ceiling, a wide stone counter for tastings and a mosaic-tile W in the center of the room.

"Very impressive," said Rose as she surveyed the floor-to-ceiling windows. "Love the incredible Palladian windows."

"You know, the original concept was from Venetian architect

Andrea Palladio in the 16th century, but of course many of his ideas came from ancient Greece and Rome," Lyon said.

"Thomas Jefferson used many of Palladio's concepts to build Monticello in Charlottesville, Virginia."

"Maybe you'll take me there sometime to see it."

"Sure," said Rose automatically, trying to picture Lyon in her world.

"Come, everyone," said Joseph, eagerly ushering the group to the counter where he had arranged for them to taste several red wines. "We are going to see which one is the favorite, and then I will know for sure that my newest Chianti is as good as I think it is."

It was a little overwhelming to think about sampling four different red wines and picking out which one was the most flavorful. Joseph was beyond enthusiastic about wine tasting, explaining how one needed to use all the senses to understand good wine.

"You must get a sense of the depth of color first," he said, holding his glass up to the light. "It's a lighter shade, which tells you what kind of grape it could be." He noted that the first glass they were tasting was clear and brilliant, which was a good sign. "I'll tell you right off that this is a pinot noir."

"So, your Chianti is hidden in the middle," joked Lyon as he leaned over to share that she could swirl her wine and didn't have to sniff it the way his father showed them.

"He's so passionate," said Rose, as she smelled a mild blackberry flavor. She offered this information and Joseph gave her an indulgent smile.

"It takes years of practice to train your nose to know the different smells as there are potentially thousands of aroma components. I think blackberry is a very good start. There's also a hint of apple."

Rose smelled her wine again and appreciated all the fruity flavors that he was pointing out, but she hadn't the slightest clue how he was able to identify them. Joseph indicated that they were sampling a vintage pinot noir, which Rose guessed was an expensive bottle of wine. The second red wine, which Rose dutifully swirled and sniffed, was a much darker red with a more herbal scent.

Joseph shared that the scents of earth, mineral and rock were aromas that could be detected in the very finest white or red wines. He also noted that toast, smoke, vanilla, chocolate, espresso, roasted nut or even caramel would be a result of the wine aging in new oak barrels.

"I had no idea that the barrel or the age of the barrel could influence the taste of the wine," said Rose.

"Then I must show you our cellar after this! You can see how this all works."

Faith chimed in. "Darling, dinner is ready back at the house. Rose can see the cellars tomorrow."

Joseph looked about to protest, but Faith's look quieted him down. "You see who's the boss of this house. As I was saying, the age of the barrels, the level of char and the way we mix and match them allows us to infuse a wide array of scents and flavors to finished wines. Have we stumbled upon my new Chianti?"

"No," said Rose, taking a sip of the rich red wine. "This is definitely cabernet sauvignon."

"Smart girl! You are correct."

Rose was enjoying the private wine tasting so much that she felt completely in the present moment. The rolling hills seen through a fifteen-foot Palladian window were as sublime as the company. Breathing for a moment in between wines, she felt a sense of belonging and almost pride that she had done this on her own.

Lyon and Rose stared at each other for a moment in silent understanding. He had been talking to his mother, and she liked the way he leaned in to listen carefully to her viewpoint.

His brown, tousled hair was a bit longer in the back, and she realized how much she liked everything about him, which was a bit dangerous for her already overloaded senses.

A black-and-white-clad waiter came over with a large silver tray filled with a large array of grapes, cheeses and fresh bread. Rose greedily helped herself to some mozzarella drizzled in balsamic vinaigrette.

"This is my favorite," she said, putting the cheese on a little white plate, grateful for the snack to cleanse her palette. She guessed that the Chianti would be last given Joseph's flair for the dramatic. Her instincts were correct as she tasted the final sample, a mildly fruity full-bodied red wine that was incredibly smooth. Clearly, the last two wines were the best, and Rose was torn between which one she liked most.

They all clapped and agreed that the fourth wine sample was by far the best, and Joseph decided that they would, of course, have it with their dinner. It was dusk by the time they returned to the main house, and they enjoyed a wonderful meal of traditional lamb crusted in herbs, roasted potatoes in garlic and olive oil, and spinach salad with pine nuts.

The new Chianti worked well with their supper, and Rose enjoyed hearing about Joseph's poetry and how he believed that there was nothing so beautiful as Mayfair Park in London after the first snowfall.

"I wrote a poem about it once, and about the prime minister, who was inept. The government didn't like my political views, so they ultimately gave me a choice to leave the country or face charges." He looked at Faith. "Those months were dark days in my life, and I decided that we must go somewhere else. It broke my heart, but it was the right thing for my family."

"I can't imagine how hard that must have been," said Rose as she pictured Lyon as a young man dealing with his father's legal issues.

Later that night, when they were alone on the terrace, Rose asked Lyon, "Where did you go after you left London?"

"To my mother's family in South Africa. They were two completely different worlds, which is putting it mildly. We went to Kenya on a safari last year and it's always so spectacular. We were in the Maasai Mara in tents for over a week around the holidays. It was rather lucky that we saw so much game. There was cheetah, lions, zebras, you name it. First time for our whole family in Kenya, since we usually go to Namibia with my mom's family."

"How extraordinary," said Rose. "And to think, I feel like I've already seen so much after a few weeks in Italy!"

"I'm proud of you for coming here. Selfishly, it was quite special for me to have the honor of helping you buy your first home."

"You have no idea how much that means to me. I'm still not quite sure what to make of all the drama. Any news today?"

"It seems that Paul Klonadis, the Christie's professional, has had some run-ins with the law and problems paying his taxes."

"Hmmm. Money problems?"

"Sounds like he has champagne tastes, as the saying goes, and lives way beyond his means."

"That might be a good enough motive to lie about the drawings and potentially have someone burglarize my apartment."

"There's still work to be done on the case, but I'll keep you informed." He looked at her and said quietly, "There's a chance your friend was involved."

Rose swallowed hard as the potential reality of Ben's actions sunk in. He was the one who brought in the professional from Christie's, maybe offering him a cut of the future profits to deliberately mislead her into believing the drawings were worthless. Then, she assumed, his plan would have been to have them restored by his people and sell them to the highest bidder.

Rose's anger surged along with a sense of relief that the drawings had revealed a side to Ben that she had no idea existed.

He had charmed everyone and was the guy who always got what he wanted.

"I'm still trying to reconcile the Ben I thought I knew with the man who set me up. It's really just crazy to me."

"Actually," said Lyon, "I have to admit, I'm not in the slightest bit upset about your American friend being gone." Their eyes met. "Well, I know you've had a lot to deal with lately, but I'm hoping that you feel comfortable with me and my family and that, well, you're willing to—"

"To?"

He came over and took her into his arms. "To see where we go. I really love just being around you."

"I feel the same way. It's so easy and relaxed. But we're from two completely different worlds. I worry about that."

"Don't."

When he kissed her, Rose practically melted in his arms. There was something about Lyon that felt so safe and familiar, yet he was completely unpredictable. She really liked that he had so many layers—his sense of family, his adventurous spirit, his intensity and his passion for living. The kiss was long, slow and seductive, and Rose knew that she was exactly where she wanted to be.

"Lyon, I'm warning you . . . my mother . . . she's difficult."

"Darling, the last thing I am worried about right now is your mother."

They both started laughing uncontrollably, and he took her hand and strolled with her along the property. She could see Faith's bench in the moonlight, and the stars were like shards of glass in a clear night sky.

"I think you're onto something with those drawings you were working on, Rose. They are quite beautiful and clever."

"Thank you! Do you always know the right thing to say to me?"

"I hope so. You're very talented."

"You think so? I don't have much formal training, but I do know the hours fly by when I'm working on a painting."

"That should tell you that you've found your passion."

"I'm still trying to figure it out. I was a really good teacher and I'm very proud of that."

"But you can teach people with your artwork."

"I never looked at it that way."

"Your message is strong and so important in our fractured world. The intertwined hands are a beautiful idea and you've already started making it your own."

"I see bright colors and a series of work that captures the human spirit."

"Great idea. You need to keep going!"

"Oh, Lyon, you have no idea how lovely it is to have someone support my dreams." A tear pricked her eye. "Ever since my dad passed away, I felt like I lost my roadmap."

He gently wiped away the moisture. "I'm curious about your mother. Why do you call her Doris?"

"We got in a fight when I was in college and I started calling her Doris and it stuck." At his questioning glance, she added, "We're just too different."

"She's your mother."

"She's not nurturing at all. It's always all about her. She doesn't know how to listen. Besides, my older brother, Jack, is her favorite. She fawns all over him."

"Don't you think calling her Doris is a bit harsh? She's your mother after all."

"I'll call her Mom when she starts acting like one."

"Fair enough." He put his arm around her, and Rose asked, "So, when were you going to tell me that you're an architect?"

"I enjoy creating and designing the same way you do. The real estate business is cyclical, so I'm someone who likes to be busy."

They walked hand in hand back to the house where Faith

was reading quietly in a corner of a soft-green sitting room in a cozy armchair. A large painting of palm leaves hung nearby, which gave the room an airy feel. She looked up from her book and smiled warmly when they walked in.

"I'm glad you're still up because you may have a visitor in your studio tomorrow if that's alright," Rose said.

"Absolutely."

"I have a new idea! I wonder if you'd be willing to show me how you create those glorious colors on your canvas."

"Oh, it would be my pleasure. Come anytime. Now, it's off to bed for me."

"I'm looking forward to it."

"Good night. Sleep well."

Soon after, Lyon walked Rose over to the guest cottage and shared that better locks were being installed on her apartment and that the cleaning people had done a masterful job.

"It's probably safe to return home," Lyon said.

To Rose the news was bittersweet. But she knew Lyon was right; she needed to return to Florence to continue with her new life and home. But first, she wanted to spend time with the artist Faith to learn her technique.

Chapter 14

ONCE INSIDE THE GUEST cottage, Rose checked her iPhone and found a text from Ben.

Where are you? I've been trying to reach you for days. We need to talk. Please Rose!

Rose felt a wave of anxiety. She was nervous, angry and annoyed. A thousand angry responses ran through her mind, and she started typing, but then refrained. Was there anything more to say? He had betrayed her; she could never forgive him for stealing the drawings from her closet.

And yet, maybe it was an innocent act, or a mistake. Could there be a logical explanation as to why he did what he did? Her heart still refused to believe that he had become so dishonest. After all, he was her first love; how could he have changed beyond recognition?

The next morning, sunlight streamed in Faith's studio as Rose placed her sketchpad and a few colored pencils on a corner table. Faith immediately embraced her, kissing her on both cheeks, which made Rose feel at home. Lyon's mother exuded warmth and kindness, and Rose felt privileged to be in the presence of an artist who was going to share her creative process.

A large color photograph of a Tuscan sunset was clipped to a wood post in the corner. A canvas was propped up beside the picture, and Faith had placed colors on a wood palette along with a palette knife and paper towels. It occurred to Rose that the last parent to show her how to do something was her father. He was patient and would explain things readily as if anticipating any question Rose might have. How she missed him.

Rolling up the sleeves of her blue shirt, Rose was excited to get going and learn from such an accomplished artist.

"I call this my Renaissance palette because it consists of four colors: white, yellow ochre, vermillion and black." Faith took the knife, scraping the yellow ochre to mix with white and a dab of black. "This is my own version of a Tuscan yellow," she added as she swirled the colors together. "I don't want it to marble up like, uh . . . " She hesitated, looking for a word. "Like *gelati*!" They both laughed. "Now you try."

The technique was trickier than it appeared. Rose's first attempt created a sickly yellow rather than Faith's golden color.

Rose pursed her lips. "This looks like Charlottesville yellow." She laughed at her poor attempt. "Actually, it looks too muddy to even have a name."

"Yellow is a notoriously difficult color to get right. And, besides, why would you expect you'd get it right the first time? I've been doing this for years!"

"I can hope, can't I?"

"An American expression?" Faith smiled. "You have to learn to walk before you can run. These things take time like everything else in life. You must be patient with yourself."

"You're so right. I'm not very good at being patient."

"I'm going to use this yellow and create the horizon line for a sunset like this. What I do is simplify the image I want to paint by putting in the main colors first." Rose watched as Faith drew a loose line across the lower portion of the canvas. Taking out a wider brush, she smoothed over the surface in wide strokes. "Would you like to try this?"

"Are you sure?"

"Of course. It's important you use the flat part of the brush to fill in some of the skyline." Rose tried to copy the back and forth motion with the wide brush while Faith stood beside her, guiding her movements. "I'd call this the first stages of a block-in where we're using main colors."

Rose handed back the brush and Faith said, "Darling, you need to feel the brushstrokes."

"I hadn't thought about it like that."

"Then, you're going to take the smaller brush and shadow this skyline with the red mixed with a hint of black. Like this." Faith shadowed each line, practically caressing the canvas with her brush. "Now, you try." Faith handed her the brush.

Rose copied Faith exactly and was rewarded with a large smile of approval.

"Very good! You're a natural!"

"Do you think so?"

"I just saw the way you took what I did and made it your own. Very interesting."

Her words meant so much to Rose, who suddenly conjured up a nasty image of Doris with her pursed pink lips carrying on about the stupidity of anyone wanting to be an artist. The contrast was sharp and real, and Rose eyed Faith's beautiful profile, wondering how she could connect so well with someone she had only known for a few days.

"What's next?"

"A hint of blue left in the skyline, which is a cooler color. See what happens on the palette if you place it next to the reds and yellows; it comes to life." Faith helped her shadow a low-lying cloud and put a streak of orange in the night sky.

The hours practically flew by, and Rose was transfixed by the canvas, the paints, Faith's patient instruction and her company. It wasn't until Lyon poked his head in the door that both women realized that it was close to dinnertime.

"Have you really been here all day?"

"We lost track of time. The beauty of the Tuscan sun was too much for us."

"It was absolutely fantastic!" gushed Rose, so appreciative of Faith's time and talent.

"We had a ball," said Faith, who embraced her son. "Now, I need to get to the kitchen and figure out our dinner immediately or your father is going to turn into a hangry British monarch!"

Rose watched as Lyon viewed the painting, trying not to notice how handsome he looked in his tan khaki pants and white shirt open at the collar.

"This painting is wonderful."

"Your mother is a natural teacher. I learned so much today."

"She's an amazing person . . . and a cancer survivor."

"Really?"

"She was very sick years ago and I promised myself I would never go more than ten days without seeing her or somehow checking in."

"Your tattoo?"

"You figured it out," he said, kissing her soundly. "It's all about Faith."

"That's so incredibly . . . loyal."

"I adore my mother."

"I wish I could say the same," said Rose with a lump in her throat.

Sensing her mood, he added, "The city was a bit steamy today. I'm so glad I made it back out here. How about a swim?"

"Lovely!"

They walked hand in hand back to the main house, and Rose ran inside with her phone ringing. It was her brother, Jack.

"Hey, I've been trying to reach you. What's going on?"

"What do you mean? Is everything okay at home? I've been staying with a friend at their place in Tuscany."

"Everything's good here." He paused. "So, what's going on with you and Ben? I just got off the phone with him and he was worried something had happened to you. He said he's been trying to reach you and you've been acting very strangely."

"I promise you, Jack, things here are really good. I've met lots of new people and I'm learning so much each day."

"What happened when he came to visit two weeks ago?"

"Why do you ask?" The phone was not the place to tell Jack about the drawings and all the drama that she had dealt with.

"He said that he came over and surprised you, but for some reason you don't trust him. I'm still not quite sure I get the whole story."

"We had an awesome visit, Jack. Nothing more, nothing less. I just moved a few weeks ago. I haven't even had time to adjust to my new life here in Italy. It's been a bit chaotic with all the changes, but please don't worry about me. I'm happy and well."

"Okay, great. Just checking on you, little sis. I'm really proud of you for going after your dreams."

"Thank you," said Rose. "That means a lot to me. Start planning your visit. I have a spare room. And more importantly, how are your girls?"

"We're heading to the beach next week. It's Laney's first time seeing the ocean. All is well."

A longing for home swept over Rose, quickly turning to despair. Jack's call seemed manipulative, but she couldn't be sure.

***

Rose returned home and decided to take the morning off to enjoy being back in Florence. She wandered around Santa Croce with no real destination. A gorgeous blush-colored wrap dress caught her eye, and she went inside the pretty boutique shop to try it on. While she browsed through the racks of silks and designer clothing, Dominique walked in and eyed her with a sneer.

"Oh, it's the little schoolteacher. I know Lyon is totally bored with you." She laughed.

"Excuse me?"

"Ask Lyon why he came to see me yesterday."

"I'm sure you'd love to tell me."

"We've been together for years; our bond is unbreakable."

"So why are you still married to someone else if you two are so deeply connected?"

"You are very naive, darling," she chuckled. "My husband won't let me go. Someone like you wouldn't understand; he's a very powerful man."

"Sounds pathetic to me," said Rose.

"You're the pathetic one," Dominque huffed. "Lyon told me he feels sorry for you. You know, a young woman with no family or friends in a new city. He has a good heart. He wanted to be helpful." She looked Rose up and down. "Besides, why would he want to be with someone like you."

"Unlike you, I'm young and free. Now, if you'll excuse me."

Rose stepped away and asked the saleswoman if she could try on the beautiful dress in the window. Her thoughts became even more jumbled and confused. Why did Lyon get in touch with Dominique? Her run-in with Dominque was a chance meeting, after all. The woman hadn't had time to formulate a story.

She must have mistaken his feelings for her or lack thereof. Maybe Dominique was telling the truth and she had completely misread the situation at Lyon's parents' house. Feeling a sudden sense of embarrassment, Rose ran through the scenes of her time with Lyon in Tuscany, wondering if she had made a fool of herself. Regardless, a kernel of doubt crept into her mind while she considered the woman's nasty comments. But what really bugged her was the fact that Lyon had a long-term relationship with an obnoxious *married* woman.

The dress needed some minor alterations but was stunning on Rose. She liked how the silk fabric draped her body. Without hesitation, Rose splurged on the outfit and a great pair of nude patent heels; she wandered around other shops, indulging in some much-needed downtime. She had a fleeting thought that she should tell Lyon of her encounter with Dominique but changed her mind; she didn't want to appear so vulnerable or naive.

Doubt about Lyon seeped into her consciousness. Was he really her type? How could he be, given his relationship and lifestyle?

She was walking home from the dress shop when she ran into Nicole, the owner of the leather shop whom she had met her first week in Florence.

"How's it going? I've been meaning to get in touch."

"So far, so good. I'm settling into my life here and painting and working on the apartment."

"Aha! So, I haven't seen you since that first date with your American friend? How'd it go?"

A wave of sadness assailed Rose and she brushed it off. "We had fun but I'm not sure the long-distance thing is going to work."

"Well, no problem. You may just find an Italian man here," she said with a laugh. "Hey, I'm in the process of redecorating my shop. Would you have any interest in helping me?"

"What exactly are you doing?"

"I don't know yet!" They both laughed. "I just think the front window could be prettier and so could our displays. We need to attract more tourists to come into the store. You get it."

"I'd love to help. Sounds very creative."

"We could work out some sort of payment."

"That sounds perfect. When and where?"

"Bright and shiny tomorrow morning. Is seven too early?"

"Not at all. I used to teach, so I'm used to starting work early."

"Wear something casual. We're cleaning and mopping too."

"Sure," said Rose. "I'll see you guys tomorrow."

***

The next morning, with a spring in her step, Rose made the twenty-minute walk to the leather store and knocked, thrilled to have a fun project. It took her mind off figuring out her life. She felt incredibly grateful and lucky. Thanks to the drawings, she had plenty of money in her bank account, so she could take her time to decide what was right for her. It was a true blessing and lessened a lot of anxiety.

Rose greeted Nicole and her assistant, Ariana, who was dressed in ripped jean shorts, heels and a T-shirt. Rose suppressed a grin as she eyed her cute shoes. Ariana reminded her of one of her students and she said as much. She poured a cup of coffee from the pot in the employee area and listened as Nicole expressed her dissatisfaction with her lackluster store window.

"What about painting the walls white, which would make it clean and fresh looking in here, and then adding separate shelves to display your colored handbags?"

"Love that idea!"

"Why not black?" said Ariana.

"Black?" said Nicole. "That doesn't seem inviting."

"It would be cooler."

Nicole shook her head. "I don't think so. I'm thinking light and bright."

Rose added, "You can't go wrong with high-gloss white. It wouldn't be hard to roll on a coat of white paint today, and perhaps, in the front window, we could do something kind of modern, like hand silhouettes holding a handbag? One of my students showed me her project once on Christian Dior, and they did something along those lines."

"Excellent," said Nicole. "Works for me. I certainly asked the right person to help!"

Ariana rolled her eyes and began texting.

"This is fun. I did tons of these kinds of projects with my high school students and I always enjoyed helping!"

Rose plunged into the painting, feeling happy and at ease. It had taken the better part of the morning to purchase the white paint and prep the tiny store for its makeover. The day practically flew by as Rose wiped down baseboards, taped certain areas to get a straight line and filled in cracks. Nicole bought sandwiches for lunch and they sat in the back room talking and laughing. Rose didn't check her phone or analyze anything, which was cathartic. As she took a break for a moment to peer outside, she looked over at a café across the street only to see Dominique and Lyon seated at a table. Her trust in him evaporated, and she wondered how she had almost fallen for him in the first place. *Men,* she thought, *make my life complicated.* She wondered about the costs of idealization.

Turning away, Rose attacked the painting with a vengeance, determined to get the first coat on the entire store. That night, Nicole insisted they all stop around ten and indulge in a pizza.

"Hey," said Nicole. "You must be exhausted from all of the painting, which you've done perfectly, by the way. This place looks fantastic."

"Oh, thanks," said Rose, gratefully accepting a glass of red wine. "I've loved the project. It's always amazing to me how much a coat of paint can change the look of a room."

"I can't believe how light and bright it is in here now. Great idea!"

"Yes," said Rose. "I think it looks so much more inviting."

Ariana, who hadn't exactly done that much, said, "I've never worked this hard."

Both Rose and Nicole suppressed a grin.

"Sweetie, I'm so sorry this has been such a long day. Thank you for everything. Do you want a glass of wine?"

"*No grazie.* I have a date with Roberto. He'll be here in five minutes."

"Perfect."

When she left, Nicole peered over at Rose. "You looked upset this afternoon. Everything okay?"

"Well, there was someone here that I liked a lot, but he's been in a relationship for years and I saw him today with her again."

"Maybe it was nothing," she said.

"Or maybe they'll always be connected."

"Well, you were certainly very excited to see your American boyfriend."

"Yes, we had a great time, but . . . " Rose sighed.

"What happened?"

"He did something that made me not trust him."

"Did he cheat on you or hurt you in some way?"

"It's a long story, but he took something that belonged to me and I've been really angry about it."

"Maybe you should forgive him and give him another chance. It sounds like your Italian friend isn't who you thought he was. But don't listen to me. I've only been dating my boyfriend for a few months."

"I'd say that makes you an authority," Rose grinned. They clinked glasses. "This place looks great."

"Thanks to you," said Nicole. "You're a hard worker. I'm impressed."

"I love being creative."

"I can tell. So, I think that purse over there has your name on it."

"Really?" said Rose. "I love it!"

"Well, thank you so much for your help. Can you come back tomorrow? I need you!"

"I'd be happy to help finish this up."

***

Rose grabbed an Uber ride home. She was feeling lonely and forlorn over seeing Lyon. So, she decided that she was ready to hear Ben's side of the story and texted.

Hi: So sorry for the delayed response. I was visiting friends in Tuscany. It was an amazing experience!

B: *I think we've had a misunderstanding and I know what you're thinking.*
Do you?
B: *Yes, I can explain. Please sweetheart.*
Sweetheart?
B: *It's not what you think. How many years have you known me? I don't want to lose you over this. I swear to you that I will do anything to earn your trust back.*
Thanks. I appreciate that you would want to do that.
B: *Why wouldn't I? I fell in love with you again and can't get you out of my mind.*
Did you just use the L word?
B: *I did and I mean it. It was always you.*
I need some time to process everything. I'm feeling overwhelmed with all of the changes in my life right now.
B: *I completely understand. I want us to work, Rose. I mean that. Do you feel the same way?*
I don't know what I think, Ben.
B: *I'm yours. Please believe in my feelings for you.*
I'll try.

His declaration of love was crazy. She was crazy. Her world felt crazy right now.

All her life she had longed for a real relationship with Ben. She couldn't let go of that part of her that still believed they were meant to be together—no matter what.

Chapter 15

HER DAY STARTED OUT with a piping-hot cup of coffee on her balcony as she savored the view of terra-cotta rooftops. She still couldn't believe that she actually bought a place and lived in this amazing city. Each day she felt an inner confidence that she had never known; everything was so new—and sometimes a bit overwhelming. Rose had to admit to herself that she was a little homesick. She rubbed her temples and realized that she had no real structure in her life. A vision of her teaching days at Bellfield crossed her mind, and she missed her morning chats with Zoey.

As she contemplated her options, Rose decided that she was ready to enroll in formal painting classes so that she could take her art to the next level. She went online and made a list of requirements, determined to figure out which program would serve her best. It seemed like she would need to complete a bigger body of work to have a chance at some of the more prestigious institutions.

As she packed her art supplies in a bag, her phone buzzed, and she saw it was a text from Ben.

Can you meet me at the entrance to the Boboli Gardens in a half hour?

What? You're here?

B: *Surprise! I think we need to talk in person! It has been ridiculous trying to communicate via text.*

Okay great, I'll see you soon.

Rose didn't understand her own racing heart or her excitement at knowing that Ben had flown to Florence, again, to see her. She didn't analyze or second-guess. It was Ben, and he never failed to captivate her. In a rush, she changed into a white blouse and sandals, thinking that looked far more presentable than her stained painting clothes. Vanity won out and she brushed her hair and left it loose and flowing the way Ben liked it.

The brisk walk to the entrance seemed suspended in time. Ben was waiting for her, and she smiled at the thought of seeing him again. Everything else was forgotten as she spied his tall, handsome form in the distance. Something made her slip into a slow jog, and he held his arms open when he saw her again, effortlessly twirling her in the air.

He kissed her passionately the same way he had the first time he came to Florence.

Moments later, they were walking hand in hand through the entrance gates into the lush expanse of gardens peppered with timeless statues and fountains. Finally, Ben stopped and turned to her, getting down on one knee. "I never thought I would say this to anyone again, but, Rose, I can't live without you. Will you marry me?"

"What?"

"I want you to be my wife, Rose. That's what I'm saying. We'll figure out a way to make things work. I've been so upset since I left Florence, and I realize that you are my everything."

"Ben, I'm overwhelmed." She gulped, feeling a desperate need for air. "Can we please sit down for a moment and talk?"

"I know what you're about to say . . . and I can explain!"

His words touched her heart and she felt a sense of relief. "Go on."

"My plan was to take them to a contact I had in New York and get another appraisal of their value."

"Why didn't you share your suspicions and ask me?"

"It's not right and I'm not proud of it, but I did everything for Angie and, well, I guess I've become a bit heavy handed. You are so smart and different than her. I made a poor assumption. I am so sorry." He continued. "When Paul Klonadis said they were worthless, I knew he was lying. So, I wanted to bring the drawings to New York and have them appraised there by the folks I know at Christie's."

"So, you knew Klonadis was lying but you didn't tell me?"

"I really am sorry, Rose. I was embarrassed and felt responsible. And I should have talked with you first about it and not decided for you . . . for us. Again, I was wrong. Please don't let this get in the way of what we have." He paused. "Don't ever forget that when I boarded that plane to come and see you, there were no drawings. It was all about you and me before we started dealing with your discovery."

"But they do exist, and it was my right to figure out how I wanted to handle the situation—not yours."

"I completely agree. I was heavy handed and I made a mistake."

Rose sat quietly for a few minutes. She wanted so much to trust Ben, and his story seemed plausible.

"I forgive you," she heard herself saying.

"I love you and I promise never to do anything to make you distrust me again." He pulled out a gorgeous diamond ring that shimmered in the Florentine sun. "Marry me?"

"Oh my God!" Her heart pounded. She felt dizzy. She thought of Lyon. "Yes!" she blurted.

They embraced, Ben hugging her tightly.

Is this really happening?

"Your parents are back at the hotel. Shall we go and tell them?"

"Wait, my mom's here? I can't believe Doris came to visit."

Ben gave her a cocky smile, and Rose raised her eyebrow

at him. "Don't say it," she said. "I already know how she feels about you."

"About us," he corrected, pulling her closer.

Rose looked again at her hand and the beautiful ring, an absolutely perfect solitaire set in gold with two baguettes on either side.

Ben kissed her passionately, and Rose forgot everything else in that moment. The drawings ceased to exist, and Lyon . . . She pictured his handsome face and realized that they were not meant to be. It was always Ben.

***

The whirlwind began at the hotel. Doris began to cry, practically clutching Rose to her.

"I'm so happy for you both. This was always meant to be. You know how much I've always adored Ben!" She paused to take a breath. "And you'll be a mom to little Emily!"

Rose gulped, realizing that she had somehow just catapulted into a whole new reality. Ben came over and took her hand. "I've made arrangements for us to head to New York in a few days so Rose can spend time with Emily."

Rose nodded, too caught up in the moment to think straight. Was she really going to leave Italy to be a mother in New York?

Doris grabbed her hand with tears in her eyes. "My beautiful girl is going to be a beautiful bride. Don't you agree, Eric?"

"Absolutely! You two make a very handsome couple!"

Doris turned to Rose. "I know we've had our differences in the past, but I want us to make a fresh start. Please, dear, I'm your mother and I love you. You and Ben are such a perfect couple and I wish you all the happiness in the world."

"Thank you," said Rose. The word "mom" lodged in her throat, but she blurted it out. "Mom."

Tears welled up in her mother's eyes. "This is the happiest day I think I've ever had! Oh, sweetheart, we can begin again!"

Rose was so touched that her mother and Eric had gotten on a plane to visit along with Ben, who had orchestrated the whole reunion. Her mother was like a different person—loving, solicitous and kind. "I'd love to take you shopping to look at dresses as soon as we get back to the States."

"That would be lovely. Ben and I have a lot to figure out!"

"Rose," said her mother, "you've made me so happy and proud. This is the best day of my life. We must celebrate, but I'm hoping that you will take Eric and me to some of your favorite places in Florence, starting with your new home. We can't wait to see it."

She and Ben walked holding hands back to the apartment where he settled in as if he had just left. The first kiss was long, slow and passionate, and Rose felt that familiar sense of belonging in his arms.

Doris plowed open the door with Eric in her wake as she surveyed the space. Rose had found a beautiful flowered blanket to cover the slash marks in the center of the sofa while she waited for its replacement. Doris scrutinized every detail and asked a blitz of questions about the neighborhood, crime, the fixtures.

Doris made her way upstairs to survey the spacious bedroom and balcony.

"This is spectacular!" she exclaimed, opening the door to look at the view. "However did you find this place!?"

"One of my students has a mother who specializes in international real estate."

"Aha! Makes sense." She looked out at the terra-cotta rooftops. "Very nice, but it is steamy out here!"

Rose reminded her that August was hot everywhere and it would cool down with nightfall. A short time later, amidst the animated conversation, Rose heard the doorbell ring and came face-to-face with Lyon, who looked shocked to see Ben and her mom and stepfather standing in her living room. His gaze immediately went to the ring on her finger.

"So, you're Rose's real estate agent," Doris said as she eyed his shaggy hair.

"Yes," said Lyon curtly.

"You did an excellent job, young man!"

"Thank you," he said. "Glad I helped you, Miss Maning; I was just coming by to check on your new alarm system. I assume it's working properly."

His chilly stare rendered Rose speechless. She had so many things she wanted to say to him, but she could only manage, "Uh, no. I'm fine. I mean, all is well."

"Good. I didn't mean to interrupt your reunion," said Lyon, who turned and left.

Rose felt her heart hammering, not sure what to say or do. She snapped back to life and told the group, "Shoot! I forgot to ask him a question about my air-conditioning. Be right back!" She chased him down the stairs and called, "Hey, Lyon!"

He just kept walking. Rose ran after him and grabbed his arm. "Lyon, I am so sorry!"

"Are you? When were you going to tell me?" he snapped.

"It all just happened!" She cried breathlessly. "I didn't mean to—"

"Well, you did. Frankly, I'm shocked. At my parents' house you said it was over between you and Ben—that he had changed . . . that you weren't sure he could be trusted—and now you're wearing an engagement ring! Maybe you're the one who can't be trusted."

"Wait a minute!" she said angrily. "You've been with Dominique, so why are you judging me?"

"What are you talking about?"

"I saw you together . . . at the café? And when I saw her, she told me that I bored you and that the only reason you have been kind is because you feel sorry for me."

"Dominique contacted me because she was thinking about selling a family property. Our personal relationship has been over for months. She wanted my advice, and if you were so concerned, why didn't you ask me about it?" He held up his hand. "Never mind. It's too late now. But for the record, I was always honest with you, and unfortunately, you didn't return the courtesy." He added, "I really thought you were different!"

Rose stood shell-shocked.

"I hope you know what you're doing, Rose," he said, shaking off her arm. "Any questions or concerns you have will be directed to my assistant. I wish you the best."

"But—"

Rose watched him walk away with a lump in her throat. Ben came downstairs and told her what a great life they were going to have together. He looked at Lyon's departing form with a smirk.

***

"Why would I want to stand in line for hours to see a marble statue named David?" said Doris, pushing her sunglasses back from her nose.

"It's a Renaissance masterpiece and Michelangelo was a genius and one of the most amazing artists of that time."

"You sound just like your father!"

"I'll take that as a compliment, right?" said Rose as she escorted her mother to the Galleria dell'Accademia.

"I don't know much about art history, Rose, and I'm not sure it really interests me."

"What would you like to do"—she took a breath—"Mom?"

"Go shopping! I'd like to find a nice leather handbag to bring back to Charlottesville."

"How about a compromise? I'll take you to the leather school in Florence, otherwise known as the *Scuola del Cuoio,* which has every leather item that you could ever imagine. We'll grab lunch, and on the way back to my apartment, we can stop into the Basilica Santa Croce where Michelangelo, Galileo and Machiavelli are buried."

"I guess," she said with about as much enthusiasm as might be elicited by a trip to the dentist.

Doris was like a lioness with a juicy steak the moment she entered the leather school with its wide array of jackets, purses, wallets, and notebooks along with a selection of shoes. She shoved her way to the coat section, sideswiping a young girl in yellow to get her hands on a black leather asymmetrical zippered creation.

"That's so cool," she said.

Rose flinched. "That's not your usual look," she replied. "Are you sure you'd wear it when you get back to Charlottesville?"

"I can tell by your expression that you don't like it."

"Uh, no, it's very nice. Just a bit unexpected." A pretty dark-haired sales associate approached and told Doris that it was a one of a kind and then quoted a large number with multiples zeros.

"Maybe you should think about it?"

Doris went back to the rack and found a bright-red leather long coat that Rose thought would look absolutely ridiculous in the South. Then, she tried a blue snakeskin-patterned blazer, and Rose prayed for moral support from somewhere . . . anywhere. Suddenly, the black jacket looked vastly more appealing and she said as much.

"Will you look at that ice-skating rink on your finger," exclaimed Doris, grabbing Rose's hand and holding it up for any and all to see. "You're a very lucky girl," she announced proudly.

The comment touched a nerve. Rose took a deep breath and replied, "I think he's lucky to have me."

"Of course, dear. I know that, but don't forget, he was married to a supermodel and, well, he's extremely successful and so handsome." She turned to the salesgirl. "My soon-to-be son-in-law is hot!"

"Did you just call Ben hot, Mother?"

"I did and he is," she shot back, walking over to ogle a hot-pink wallet.

Doris asked the salesperson to hold the black leather jacket so that she could explore the next room, which contained a beautiful selection of handmade leather pocketbooks. Doris wanted to thoroughly check out every single one, which Rose knew could take forever. While waiting, she clicked on an email from Beatrice, which made her hand tremble.

Rose,
Ciao! I have begun the process of cleaning the parchment and found some interesting things! I can't wait to show you my work so far. There appears to be a signature on the drawings, and it may take a few weeks, but I intend to reveal it! When can you return to the laboratory?

***

That night, Ben took Rose in his arms and the world felt right. They talked about the possibility of getting married in Charlottesville at his friend's winery and honeymooning in Europe. It all sounded so wonderful, and she still hadn't quite come to terms with the fact that she would be Mrs. Benjamin Pierce after all these years.

"So, dare I ask, how do we plan to work out living arrangements? You know how much I love living in Florence." She paused. "And, really, I just got here."

"I understand. Maybe we figure out how to live part of the year here and maybe rent the place for extra income if we're in the States."

"I like that idea. I'm happy here and I don't want to give it up."

"I understand," he said sweetly. "I told you, Rose. It's our future together, and we'll make plans that work for both of us. I've got an apartment in New York on the Upper East Side. I bought us plane tickets. I can't wait for you to see it."

They would leave the next day.

Chapter 16

LUXURY APARTMENT IS AN understatement, thought Rose, walking into Ben's lavish three-bedroom New York abode, which boasted a separate study and state-of-the-art kitchen. White marble and sleek, it lacked the traditional elements that Rose liked. In many ways, it was too magazine-ready and sterile.

Rose contrasted it to Faith's cluttered art studio, with its worn countertops, oils paints everywhere and breezy windows. Rose tried to block thoughts of Lyon as her fiancé showed her around, highlighting some of his museum-quality abstract artwork in carefully chosen blacks and grays.

"Where does Emily stay when she comes over?"

He took her to a very adult-looking bedroom with a twin bed along with a crib. Everything was a crisp white. Mirrored shelves were lined with meticulously chosen silver julep cups, probably baby gifts, and crystal animal ornaments arranged with military precision. There was one doll on the bed, which was made up with more pillows than anyone could need in a lifetime.

"Would you mind if I added a few things before she spends the night with us tomorrow night?"

"Absolutely," said Ben, who looked thrilled and kissed her on the forehead. "You're the kind of mother Emily needs in her life. She's lucky to have you."

Rose thought about how to be helpful but not overstep her boundaries as a new mom.

"I know it's going to take time and practice to learn to be a good mother to your daughter, but you know I'll give you my best."

"Oh, Rose, she'll be our daughter before long. I can't wait to officially start our life together. I love you so much."

"I love you too," she said as she nestled into his arms.

Rose hit the ground running the following morning on her mission to add some homey touches to Ben's place. *Our place,* she corrected herself. It was too sterile for her at this point, and she made her way up Madison Avenue looking for a cozy throw, some stuffed animals and games for Emily. The shops were beyond gorgeous, but the prices made Rose pause to consider each purchase. As she made her way up the street, she came upon a window display with several mannequins wearing white silk gowns. Looking up, she saw the name *Vera Wang.* Filled with excitement, she looked down at her sundress and sandals, wondering if she had the nerve to go inside. Suddenly, she took the plunge and opened the heavy door to step inside a sanctuary of elegance, from the matching blush suede chairs and caramel-paneled walls, to the rows of elegant white gowns.

"Can I help you?" asked the saleswoman dressed in a crisp linen skirt.

"I'm just looking," she replied, spying a row of silk and taffeta.

"When's the big day?"

"We haven't set a date yet, but I've always wanted to be a June bride."

"How lovely. I can show you several options from our collection if you'd like."

Feeling a bit guilty because she was supposed to be shopping for Emily, Rose nearly refused but decided that she could maybe just look at one option.

"I'd like something very simple and strapless."

"I've got just the thing."

She brought out two dresses, which were both every girl's dream. Rose surprised herself by liking the gown with a lace bodice and spaghetti straps. She decided to try it on just for fun.

No one would have to know, and it seemed more than appropriate now that she was officially engaged. The sumptuous silk gown fit perfectly, and she stood in front of the mirror seeing herself for the first time as a bride.

"I love it!" she exclaimed, not daring to look at the price tag. Then it occurred to her that she had money from the sale of the drawings, so she could afford it. Suddenly, her heart sank as if she'd been hit by a bucket of cold water.

Ben had no idea that she had sold the drawings, and frankly she dreaded telling him. But it was a fact that they were hers to do with as she pleased. She cringed at the thought of the discussion that needed to happen. She hoped he would understand why she sold them to Cardinal Baglioni. *Of course he will.* Feeling slightly ill, she removed the silk confection and took the woman's card, promising that she would be in touch before long. With a pretend smile, she gathered up her packages and returned to the apartment where a precious Emily had just arrived in the arms of a nanny dressed in black pants and a collared shirt. Ben introduced her as Rose, his best childhood friend in the world, which seemed a bit odd to Rose.

"Hello, sweetheart," she said, taking out a stuffed pink dog from her shopping bag.

Emily smiled broadly, pleased with the gift. When Ben handed her to Rose to hold for a moment, a wave of panic momentarily swept through her, but she overcame her fears and swooped the little girl into her arms.

"I can't wait to spend more time with you!"

Emily's big blue eyes studied Rose. "Hi," the little girl said shyly. Then Emily immediately put her head on Rose's shoulder in solidarity.

"That didn't take long. I knew you'd be a natural." He dismissed the nanny and told her to take the evening off, which brought a wide smile to the woman's face.

Rose recognized that familiar look of female adoration as the nanny looked up at her employer. Turning her attention to Emily, Rose said, "She's absolutely precious, Ben. Really a lovely little girl!"

Rose walked with Emily back to her bedroom so she could show her some of the things that she had purchased to warm up the white space: a cozy pale-pink blanket, a small fuzzy dog and a learn-and-play soft tea set. Ben leaned against the door as Rose sat on the floor to show Emily that she could entertain her fuzzy new dog with tea or make cookies or add sugar and cream. Delighted with her toys, Emily clapped her hands, and Ben soon wandered away, leaving the two of them to their game.

That night, with Emily safely tucked in bed with her new fuzzy pink blanket, Rose found Ben working on his book in the study. She looked at his handsome profile, still in a state of disbelief that this man was going to be her husband and she was soon to be a mother to a beautiful little girl.

"How's it going?" she asked casually.

"Very well, actually. I'm at the part where Thomas Jefferson redesigned Monticello to include many of the modern conveniences he enjoyed while ambassador to France. You know, like indoor toilets, and of course that includes his penchant for octagonal rooms to make the most of his space." He smiled. "I need to head down to Monticello in a week or so. I'd love for you to you come with me and I'll show you around. You know what an amazing historical property it is."

"Great! I'd like to really see Indian Hall again with some of the artifacts from the Lewis and Clarke expedition, or even some of his inventions again. I remember the weather station in the front hall and the clocks he made on the pulley system. But it's been a while."

"Don't forget my favorite contraption—that dumbwaiter in the dining room." He flashed his sexy smile. "And if you're really nice to me, I'll take you upstairs to the secret Dome Room that was really never used. It's bright yellow now with a stunning Palladian window." He paused. "I've got special access," he joked, holding up his badge.

At the mention of a Palladian window, Rose recalled the winery in Tuscany that Lyon had designed, and the memory felt bittersweet.

"I'd love to come."

"Did you know that they've restored the Rotunda at the University of Virginia? I've heard it's spectacular." He paused. "Maybe we should consider the chapel there?"

"I hadn't thought of that."

"There are lots of great options for a reception in Charlottesville."

"These are good problems to have," she joked. "I'll leave you to your writing and get started on dinner."

Rose was eager to learn her way around Ben's gorgeous kitchen, which looked like it hadn't had much use. She had purchased some fresh halibut that afternoon and put it in a Pyrex with Dijon mustard, olive oil, salt and pepper and a dash of lemon. Popping the fish in the oven, she washed some arugula, sliced several tomatoes, grated some parmesan cheese and stirred in a mixture of balsamic vinegar and pepper. As she waited for the fish to cook, she set the kitchen table and filled up two large glasses with sparkling water and a lime.

Ben lavished tons of praise on her supper. "Come on," she said after he thanked her for the tenth time. "You're making more of this than it is."

"Nope, I'm just crazy about the future, Mrs. Pierce. We're going to have a great life together." After dinner, he helped her with the dishes and kissed her passionately.

***

The inevitable confrontation came the following morning

when Angelique, Emily's mother, appeared in a flowery navy dress, sandals, perfect hair and a resting bitch face. Clearly, she had cajoled the doorman to let her up without alerting them first.

"Where's my daughter?" she snapped, brushing past as if Rose were of no consequence.

Rose stepped aside to follow her into the living room where she and Emily had been playing with the tea set she had purchased earlier.

"My baby!" Angelique cooed, grabbing the little girl as if she were a package she had just purchased on Madison Avenue. "Where's Ben?"

"He's gone out to run an errand. Can I help you?"

It was at that moment that she spied the ring on Rose's finger. "Are you the new nanny Ben's been talking about?"

"Excuse me? My name is Rose Maning and I'm Ben's fiancée."

"You can't be serious! Is this some sort of joke?" She gave her a once-over. "You look so, so . . . ordinary."

Rose wanted to say something like, *At least there's no plastic and my boobs are real.* But after years of dealing with Doris, she bit her tongue.

"I think what you meant to say is 'Hello, Rose. How can we work together for Emily's sake?'"

But Ben's ex wanted no part of a truce. "Sorry, honey, you're crazy if you think you're going to have anything to do with my daughter." Angelique sneered at her and left the room.

Ben walked in the door, and she brushed by him with Emily whimpering in her arms. "Angie, stop it! Can't you see you're upsetting her?"

"Why did you assume it was me? Ask the new nanny." She laughed. "Rosie the Nanny."

"Now that was clever," said Rose dryly. "Maybe you can have a second career as a poet." Rose eyed both of them. "I'm going to let the two of you work out the details of Emily's next visit."

"Thanks, Rosie," Angelique said smugly, inching closer to Ben.

Rose excused herself to the bedroom and went in search of her phone to call Zoey. She really needed a friend. Much to her delight, Zoey agreed to hop a train to visit the city the following week when Ben planned to leave. Easy enough to skip the trip to Charlottesville and let him go alone.

Listening to the voices in the other room, Rose reached for her sketchpad, realizing she hadn't drawn anything since Tuscany. With a few fluid strokes, she began drawing a cloud formation and a sunset from memory. Faith's painting of *Moon River* came to mind while she shadowed a swirl in the body of water. Raised voices interrupted her, so Rose delved deeper into her drawing, hoping that Ben and his ex would figure out how to be civil for Emily's sake.

When he came back to find her, Rose noticed that he seemed flustered. She asked firmly, "What are we going to do about Angelique? She snapped when she saw the ring on my finger."

Ben ran a hand through his hair. He replied, "We'll figure it out later."

***

Angelique's "Rosie the Nanny" dig still stung, making Rose feel inadequate. Determined to hold her own, Rose recalled that the mother of one of her students used to go to SoHo to get her hair done. Rose decided to pay more attention to her appearance and freshen up her look. Checking her face in the mirror, she thought some makeup would help too. She did feel rather provincial in the big city, so a change would hopefully boost her self-confidence.

The hours of preening and hair coloring and application of seriously expensive makeup were worthwhile given Ben's response.

"Wow! You look amazing!" he said, staring at her elegantly coiffed hair. "And your timing is impeccable! Turns out my friends Dan and Tina are having a small group of us over for drinks and apps tonight. I'd love for you to meet them. Dan's a hedge fund manager and Liz has her own accessories business. Linda and Ron are also going to try to make it; they're both art dealers. I'm sure you'll have a lot to talk about with all of them. Does that suit you?"

"Sure!" she said, trying to quell her anxiety. "Sounds great."

"Okay, I'll let Dan know we're coming." He leaned over and kissed her. "I can't wait to show you off."

His words made her heart sing. Ben Pierce had just made her feel beautiful.

***

They grabbed a cab downtown to an amazing loft with a pristine view of the city. Rose swallowed hard, wondering how she would fit in with Ben's friends, who all seemed very confident and successful. As it turned out, their welcome was warm, and Rose loved that Dan gave her a big hug and kiss.

"Finally! It's so great to meet you, Rose. Ben's told me so many wonderful things about you. I can't believe you guys reconnected after all these years. What a great story!"

"Sometimes I can't believe it," she replied, turning to greet Tina, who also gave her a big hug.

"I love your necklace! It's gorgeous," said Tina sweetly.

Rose wasn't going to admit that she had just removed the tags after an afternoon spent on Madison Avenue.

"Thanks! That's quite a compliment coming from you. I checked out your company's website and it looks amazing. It's so well done!"

"Oh, thank you! I really appreciate your kind words; we just changed our marketing strategy not too long ago, so I'm eager for all feedback."

"What can I get you?" asked Dan. He turned to Tina. "Linda and Ron are on the way. They said about fifteen minutes."

"A glass of pinot grigio would be wonderful."

The men left the room, and Tina showed her around the apartment, which had gorgeous views of the skyline. "We gutted this place and took two apartments to create a bigger space for our family."

"Oh, how old are your children?"

"Maddox is six and my Laura just turned three."

"I'd love to meet them."

"Boy, are you the antithesis of Angelique. She always thought kids should be seen and not heard."

"That's too bad. I love kids. I was an art history teacher for years in Charlottesville."

"That's terrific. Okay, I'm just going to be rude and tell you I've got to see the ring." She grabbed Rose's hand and nearly gasped. "Wow. That is just stunning. Ben did well." Tina immediately embraced her. "I hope you guys are so happy together."

"Me too," said Rose, feeling her cheeks burn.

Dan and Ben walked back in the room talking numbers. Tina rolled her eyes. "I've told him not to bombard Ben with stock tips now that he's retired, which we never thought he would do."

"Why not? It's a tough business."

"Well, Ben may not like to brag, but he was one of the most respected hedge fund managers in the country. He was at the top of his game when he got out. But I really don't think he'll stay away from the financial business forever. He's too competitive."

"He seems pretty happy these days researching and writing about Thomas Jefferson."

"It's just a phase. I promise you, he's got that killer instinct. He'll get back in the game before long."

Her words were not unexpected or surprising, but Rose realized that she had no idea what made Ben tick. He was handsome and charming, and he seemed to know how to maneuver every situation to his advantage. She looked down at the massive diamond ring on her finger.

Linda and Ron arrived a short time later and Tina made the introductions. They were thrilled to hear the news that Ben was engaged, and Linda hit Rose with a barrage of questions about her life in Charlottesville, the move to Florence and wedding plans.

As soon as Rose thought she had successfully dodged any mention of her interest in Renaissance art, Ron came over and took her aside.

"So, Ben tells me you're passionate about the life and works of Michelangelo."

"Absolutely," she replied innocently enough, feeling her stomach tighten.

"You know, we buy and sell art all over the world."

"Really?" she replied. "How fascinating." Rose looked over at Ben, giving him a wink like she was hanging on Ron's every word. He was certainly knowledgeable and talked all about his gallery's recent sale of a Van Eyck and his company's high level of expertise in Renaissance portraiture and, of course, their professionalism.

"Can I give you my card?"

"Why would you want to do that?"

"Well," he said, "just in case you ever need a confidential and expert opinion on a piece of Renaissance art."

"I'm not sure where you got your information, Ron, but I was a teacher and certainly don't have the budget to be buying or selling high-dollar art."

"I see," he said thoughtfully. "Take it anyway. I'm confident I can be helpful."

"Thank you so much," she said politely. "I've really appreciated learning about your firm." Rose stuffed the card into the pocket of her breezy white linen pants, making eye contact with Ben as if she had enjoyed making the connection. The timing of the gathering was not lost on Rose, who told herself to stay calm and not jump to conclusions, again. Fortunately, Ben was heading to Charlottesville in the morning, and he'd been very gracious about her change of plans to invite Zoey and not accompany him.

In the cab on the way home, Ben asked casually, "So, what'd you think of everyone?"

"Oh, I adored meeting your friends and especially learning about Ron's firm. You know how I love Renaissance art."

"Great," said Ben, smiling warmly. "Ron is a highly respected art dealer and so's his wife."

"I look forward to getting together with them again."

That night, sleep came slowly for Rose, who tossed and turned for hours. She made Ben scrambled eggs and coffee in the morning and sent him on his way, promising that she would try to meet him in Charlottesville in a few days.

Chapter 17

THE DOOR FLEW OPEN and the women embraced. Zoey broke free to study Rose's coiffed blond hair, stylish black ankle pants and chic sandals.

"Wow! You look amazing but—" She studied her again. "Is this the Rose Maning, carefree art teacher, that I used to know?'

Rose smiled and curtseyed.

"How long are you here for?"

"Maybe another week. I need to get back to Florence and check on my apartment."

Rose walked her to a sleek white guest room with navy accents and told her to make herself at home.

"Honey, this is more like a luxury hotel. It's gorgeous."

"I must admit Ben's ex has great taste, despite her obnoxious personality."

"Oh! We've got *sooo* much to talk about. But I'm kind of confused. I mean, you were with Lyon in Tuscany last month and now you're engaged to Ben and planning a wedding. It all seems like a whirlwind."

"If you only knew the half of it."

Zoey dropped her bags on the bed and took a seat on the white sofa in the room. "Come on, out with it. You've been so cryptic on the phone that I can't figure out what's going on."

Rose was relieved to finally share the truth with someone she trusted. "I don't know where to begin."

"Take it from the top," said Zoey.

"After you left, I hired contractors to come in and take out that section of wall between the kitchen and the living room. The mess and noise all day drove me crazy, so I went to Rome for the weekend. When I was visiting the Sistine Chapel, I met a woman named Elsa and then her daughter, Beatrice, who works as a conservator for the Vatican."

"I'm sure that was an instant connection," joked Zoey.

"Of course," said Rose, relaxing a bit. "Anyway, I came home and there was this hole in the wall since the contractors hadn't installed the molding yet. The edges looked unfinished, so I went over to examine their work. Then, a piece of plaster fell off and I saw something stuck in the wall. When I reached in, I found this old dusty tube. It was the most incredible moment of my life!"

"Seriously? What was in it?"

"It had three moldy drawings of a baby, a young boy and a scene from the Sistine Chapel, only it was a different version with the hands clasped rather than the fingers touching."

Zoey covered her mouth. "That's amazing!"

"It gets better. I knew the drawings were special, so I hid them in my new wardrobe upstairs by my bed until I could figure out what to do."

"Smart, as always."

"Well, it was all surreal and then I had this dream. It was almost a vision, and I knew I needed to safeguard them. That I was meant to find them. I know it sounds crazy, but that's what happened."

"Okay, so how does Ben fit into all of this?"

"He came to visit me in Florence and spent a few days, and, well, when he left, he took the tote bag with the drawings."

"Wait a minute. Back up a second. Say that again."

"I showed Ben the drawings and he recommended that this contact in Italy that does appraisals for Christie's take a look at them. The appraiser said they were worthless, but I didn't believe him, so I went to Lyon's office and put them there for safekeeping. Then I hid some parchments in a tote bag and put them back in my wardrobe."

"You say Ben took them from you?"

"Well, he explained that he took them to have another appraisal done by people he knows in New York. He said he knew the Italian appraiser was lying. Anyway, I've forgiven him, but there's more."

"This is unbelievable. Go on."

"I got in touch with Beatrice, and Lyon took me to Rome to show them to a cardinal there to see if there were authentic."

"And? Hurry up, girl, and tell the story! This is wild."

"And they paid me $3 million for them."

"No way! That's insane."

"Yup. But when I got back to my apartment, there was a break-in, so Lyon took me to stay with his parents in Tuscany. I absolutely loved—" She paused and looked down at her engagement ring.

"So, back to Ben. What is his part in all of this?"

"He doesn't know I sold them."

"*What?* . . . Why haven't you told him?"

"I want to figure out how to do some sort of scholarship fund for kids with it."

"Can I apply? I'd love to study abroad," Zoey chuckled.

"I haven't told him because Ben and I have differing opinions on how the situation should have been handled. He was all about selling them to the highest bidder. I cared more about their historic significance. There is a possibility they were actual sketches by Michelangelo or his son."

"What? That's huge," Zoey said. "Maybe Ben doesn't know you very well. You'd never let money get in the way of your principle."

Rose suddenly looked forlorn, so Zoey changed the subject.

"Since when do you use a gallon of hair spray?"

Rose burst out laughing. "That bad?"

"Sweetie, you're so naturally beautiful. You don't need fake hair and eyelashes."

"But—" She gulped, feeling a tear prick her eyes. "I want to fit in Ben's world. And, well, Doris and I made up. She's actually acting like my mother, and she's so thrilled that I'm marrying Ben."

"Hold on! You're going to let Doris dictate anything in your life? Whew! I'm glad I came to see you. This is all crazy, Rose. Doris has always been self-absorbed. You know that." Zoey paced the room. "Okay, I'm not sure where to start."

"Help!" exclaimed Rose. "I feel like I'm drowning."

"You mentioned you stayed at Lyon's parents' home. Where is Lyon in all of this?"

"He hates me. He walked in right after Ben proposed. Ben flew in with Doris and Eric. After I accepted his proposal, they all came to my apartment. Then, Lyon dropped by, supposedly to check my new alarm system."

"Oh no!" Zoey looked deeply into the eyes of her friend. "You don't really love Ben, do you? You're in love with Lyon."

"Of course I love Ben. I agreed to marry him. What kind of question is that?"

"Let me rephrase the question. Do you love the old Ben or the current Ben?"

Rose froze and her hands shook. She would have done anything in the world for the Ben she grew up with; she had worshipped him.

"He was my first love. I dreamt about him for years. It's all so perfect now."

"Well, if it's so perfect, why are you shaking?"

"Because I'm so happy and so scared all at once. I always dreamed this was meant to be."

"Unless it's not. You can't sell your soul for what you think you should do! What about you? Your goals? Your desire to pursue painting? And what about Lyon?"

"It was a stupid mistake to quit teaching and pursue some childish ideal of becoming an artist and living in Florence. And it was stupid to become infatuated with that Italian playboy."

"It didn't seem farfetched or stupid to me," Zoey scolded. "Clearly, you wanted to take this time for yourself and grow as a person. You were so excited and so adamant."

"I changed my mind. It's all been a mistake. Doris was right. Can we stop talking about this? My head hurts."

"I'm surprised you can move your head with all of that product on it."

Rose threw back her head and laughed. "Let me take a shower and let's explore the city."

"I need to go to the budget side of town to find some new dresses to start work this year."

"Oh! We're going to ZARA, one of my favorite stores in Italy. The clothing is great looking. They have one in midtown."

Rose scanned her email inbox and saw a message from Beatrice. Rose sighed when she read the news; Beatrice's team had uncovered another layer of dirt and there was a strong possibility that the drawings were, in fact, signed. She shared the news with Zoey.

"When are you going to tell Ben?" Zoey asked. "You can't put this off forever."

"I don't know."

"Come on, Rose, you're too smart for that answer. How do you think he'll respond?"

"I'm sure he'll be furious."

"Wait a minute, didn't you say that Lyon was with you when you made the deal with the cardinal?"

"Yes," Rose replied, recalling his thoughtful expression.

"Why was he there?"

"Because I knew instinctively he had my best interests at

heart and he'd never want me to do anything that made me uncomfortable."

"Bingo!"

Rose gulped and looked down at the ring on her finger.

***

A trip to the Whitney Museum of Art capped off a perfect day in New York with her bestie. The setting was spectacular, and they looked at a range of photographs and Calder sculptures. As they headed to the fifth floor, Rose's phone rang with a New York number she didn't recognize. She motioned Zoey to head in to the exhibition.

"Hey, Rose. Glad I caught you. It's Ron. I got your number from Ben. Hope I'm not interrupting anything."

"Not at all, Ron. What can I do for you?"

"I'm not one to the beat around the bush, so I'll get straight to the point. Ben told me that you made some sort of discovery of Renaissance work in Florence. Is that correct?"

"Um, I'm sorry, Ron. I'm at the Whitney with a friend and it's hard to carry on a private conversation."

"Okay, okay," he said, sounding annoyed. "Let me be clear. There's a lot of money at stake here if your find is legit. Any chance you can bring me the drawings so I can take a look? You could end up becoming a very wealthy woman."

"I'll have to get back to you, Ron. Thanks!"

Rose hung up, overwhelmed with anger. She paced back and forth trying to rein in her disgust. Once calm, she found Zoey enjoying the Calder sculptures.

"Everything okay?" Zoey asked.

"Not really," replied Rose.

"Want to talk about it?"

They headed upstairs and stared at an installation of ten pairs of solid gold sneakers. Rose joked, "I could use some of those right now."

"What's going on?"

"That was Ben's friend, and I do emphasize the word *friend*. He wants to evaluate the drawings for me. Says I could become very wealthy."

"You need to talk to Ben and tell him the drawings are sold. It seems kind of manipulative that he gave this guy your cell phone. Why didn't he just ask you directly about them? I mean, Rose, you're always so incredibly forthright."

"Do you think this is a deal breaker?" Her words hung in the air.

"That's for you to decide. It's your life, but I don't think you're the type of person who could settle for a marriage without complete trust. Let's cut to the chase. Ben obviously has made enough money. Why does he want more? I mean, seriously?"

"Maybe it's never enough for someone like him." She paused. "Did I just say that?"

"You did. And by the way, what does he do for others? What else is important to Ben besides money?"

Rose looked at the gigantic diamond ring on her finger and suddenly found it very ostentatious.

"When I was in high school, he was my everything!"

"Honey, in case you haven't noticed, high school was a long time ago."

"Oh, Zoey, what do I do now? If I break off the engagement, Doris will have a heart attack."

***

Rose returned to the apartment and immediately booked a flight to Rome. She was dying to see Beatrice and discover what was happening with the conservation process at the Vatican. She suddenly missed her apartment and all that surrounded it. She studied the diamond on her hand, slipping it off and on, off and on.

"Rose, I don't think you should just leave New York without talking to Ben face-to-face. You need to tell him that you're disappointed that he gave Ron your cell number. You need to be honest about how conflicted you are."

"I know," was all Rose could muster. "You're right. I need to be honest, for both our sakes."

When Zoey left, Rose's newfound courage disappeared as she contemplated how to approach Ben. Rose checked her phone and saw a text from Ben saying he was returning to New York, cutting his trip short. Rose reasoned that Ron must have called Ben.

Rose packed her bags, then unpacked them, telling herself she was being foolish. One minute she was completely sure that Ben was not right for her and the next she wavered, thinking that they could have a great life together. She packed her suitcase for the second time and waited at the glass kitchen table for Ben to arrive. Her heart started pounding when she heard the door slam. He seemed disheveled, and she wondered if he'd been drinking.

"What's going on?" he snapped. "Why were you so curt with Ron? He was just trying to do you—I mean *us*—a favor."

"I'm not sure why you felt compelled to talk to him before consulting me."

"Are you kidding me?"

Rose cringed at his temper. "Ben, I sold the drawings."

He sneered. "You did what?"

"I did what I thought was right."

"How much?"

"The Vatican bought them. Three million dollars."

"Were they legitimate?"

"I don't know yet. They're still in the restoration phase of the process. These may be important pieces of art history and I felt they should be properly preserved."

"You made a huge mistake, Rose. You'll regret not listening to me."

"Why?"

"I'm a businessman. I succeeded by doing multimillion-dollar deals, and you let some fluffy, naive, idealistic notion drive a major financial decision. That was stupid. I knew you were going to pass up a great opportunity; I just knew it. You're such a dumb—"

"So, it's all about the money? That's all that matters to you."

"Why are you so idealistic?" he shot back. "I'm glad you got some money out of the equation, because you didn't have a prayer of making it as an artist."

"You sound just like Doris," said Rose, swallowing hard, feeling her breath come in small gasps. "No wonder she adores you." Rose stood. "You know what, Ben, I think you got it right the first time with Angie."

"What's that supposed to mean?"

"She's shallow and materialistic like you. I'm heading back home to Florence. I think we're done here." Rose slapped her diamond ring on the table.

"Keep it," he said. "It's worth a lot of money."

"Money, it's always about money with you. I don't really like the ring, anyway. It's ostentatious, just like this apartment." She picked the ring back up and put it on her finger.

"You're not being rational. I think you're making the biggest mistake of your life."

"Maybe so, but it's my mistake to make. I'm flying back to Rome tonight."

Ben took his bag and stormed out of the room. Rose grabbed her bags and hurried out the door. As serendipity would have it, the elevator was still on their floor. But when it opened back up, Rose stood face-to-face with Angelique, who grinned smugly.

"Leaving so soon, Rosie?" she mocked as Rose brushed by her.

***

Rose hailed a cab, and once inside its confines she started sobbing. She couldn't help herself. Oddly, Rose felt relieved but also sad, especially for the precious little girl, Emily. Rose hoped the child would become a better person than her parents. She also thought of Doris, who would explode with anger and tears at the news. A traffic jam, blaring horns, and several tissues later, Rose arrived at the airport.

Rose marched into the airport and looked down at the gawdy engagement ring. She suddenly felt embarrassed, wondering if she had, in fact, overreacted. She quickly stepped back outside and hailed a cab to take her back to Ben's apartment.

Her heart pounded for the next half hour as the cab bucked city traffic. She started to send Ben a text but thought twice. She hoped he had cooled off and they could talk things through. A sense of optimism returned.

Repeatedly tapping the elevator button as if it would hurry things up, Rose took a couple of deep breaths. When the door opened to her floor, she ran to the mirror to wipe the mascara out from under her puffy eyes. Clearly, she looked upset, but she didn't want their meeting to be melodramatic.

Bolstered by her belief she was doing the right thing, she used her key to open the door. Sounds of loud music jolted her. Rose took a few more steps inside and looked around. Two empty wine glasses caught her eye. Laughter emanated from the other room. She edged closer in a state of disbelief; there was a silk blouse thrown over the living room chair. Angelique and Ben were in his bedroom, together.

Rose pulled the ring off, ready to hurl it at Ben. In that instant, it occurred to her that it was worth a lot of money, as Ben had said. *Nope,* she decided, plunking it down on the countertop.

She sneaked over to Ben's briefcase in the living room and grabbed his laptop, which contained all of his contacts, research and client lists. Ben would have to meet her terms to get it back.

Chapter 18

ROSE WASTED NO TIME meeting with Beatrice. Beatrice picked Rose up at the airport, and they immediately went to her laboratory in the Vatican. Beatrice showed Rose the first drawing.

"That top corner section is getting thin, but, Rose, we've tested and retested the paper and it does date back to Michelangelo's time, so we are working with a historical find."

Rose leaned over the parchment and gasped, "Oh my God, I can't believe it!"

Beatrice took off her googles. "We've got an O-R-E-N-Z-O! All we need is the L."

"It would make sense; Lorenzo Medici was Michelangelo's mentor and friend. Michelangelo lived with him in the palace when he was a young man, and that's where his relationship with Lorenzo's daughter began. And it would make sense that he would name a potential son after his patron."

"I agree with your hypothesis," Beatrice said. "But it is just a theory. I'm hopeful we'll peel away more layers of the other writing to get to the truth."

For the next several days, Rose observed Beatrice painstakingly clean the heavily soiled sketches, seemingly one particle at a time. It was like an archeological dig. Beatrice moved like a surgeon, carefully applying a gel solution to the parchment with a long, thin Q-tip-like brush.

"I hope that we uncover the rest soon. This suspense is too much. It's like watching paint dry."

"Restorations can take years, Rose. If you rush them or do sloppy work, you can ruin the piece of art."

"I love watching you uncover a sliver of the past. It's absolutely thrilling, but I'm clear that this is not what I am cut out to do for a living!" Rose shook her head, mocking herself.

"That's the first real smile I've seen on your face since you got off the plane in Rome."

"I'm sorry for that, Beatrice. Thank you for letting me camp out in your apartment. You saved me."

"Glad I could help you out."

"I don't know what I would have done if you hadn't picked me up at the airport that night. I was a complete wreck."

"I understand," said Beatrice. "Your American friend sounds selfish and shallow; I do think these things work out for the best. Better you discovered his true character before you married him, or even worse, had children."

"I agree, and I'm sick of dodging him. He's been texting and calling all week. I need to get back to my life in Florence and make a fresh start."

"That's the spirit! He doesn't deserve someone like you."

"Thank you, Beatrice. I'm so lucky I met you. This whole process has been an incredible life experience. Even just sitting here in the inner sanctum of the Vatican is a privilege."

"Cardinal Baglioni wants to talk with you before you leave for Florence."

"Oh really. Do you have any idea why?"

"He didn't say."

"I'll let him know I'm available all afternoon."

***

Rose headed down a long corridor to get herself a cappuccino, and her phone buzzed again. Of course, it was Ben. She decided that she was ready to talk.

"Rose, please." His voice sounded hoarse and jagged. "Don't hang up. I'm so sorry."

Silence ensued.

"Thank you," she replied thoughtfully. "I appreciate the apology."

"It's not what you think!"

"Now that's a good one."

"Listen to me, I swear I'm telling you the truth. I was really upset when you left, and Angie came over. It wasn't planned. One thing led to another and—"

"Ben, stop lying. I was gone for one hour, Ben, maybe ninety minutes tops. I can't believe that you hopped in bed with your ex moments after I walked out the door. You wouldn't do that if you really loved me, so stop kidding yourself."

"Rose, please. Give me another chance. I promise that we can make this work."

"No."

"But—"

"It's over, Ben!"

"She was my wife. We have a child together. I don't love her."

"I don't trust you or the kind of person that you've become."

"That's such a mean comment."

"Well, that was quick switch from contrite to rude. You've changed, Ben, or maybe I never really knew you at all."

"Rose, my computer. Did you take it? I have a deadline, and I need my computer immediately! You stole it from me."

"I guess we're even, then. You tried to steal the drawings from me and failed. The difference is you can have your computer back, Ben, if and only if you meet my terms."

"What are they?" he snapped. "You know, I can have lawyers come after you."

"Oh, I hope not!" said Rose coyly. "That would be so stressful for me, which may affect my balance and, well, I'd hate to stumble and drop it in the Arno."

"What do you want?"

"I want you to sell my engagement ring and donate every penny of that money to charity."

"Are you kidding me? That's ridiculous!"

"Do it or no computer. You're going to give the money to Feedmore in Charlottesville, and as soon as I see a tax receipt, I'll send your computer. If I were you, I'd hurry up and make the sale."

Ben cursed under his breath, calling Rose a barrage of sexist names.

"Be careful, Ben, or your computer may just slip out of my fingers."

"I'll send you an email receipt in the next twenty-four hours."

"At least some good will come out of our relationship!"

***

The cardinal's receptionist called to say that he would like to see her. Rose gulped because she found him to be a rather kind yet imposing figure in his crimson robes. "I'll be right there," said Rose, who made her way to his office, marveling at the breathtaking masterpieces that lined the wall.

The cardinal seemed pleased to see her and motioned for her to take a seat across from his own.

"Rose," he said warmly. "I've been following the restoration process very closely and it may, in fact, prove our theory. We have long thought Michelangelo fathered a son who collaborated with him on the creation of the Sistine Chapel."

"That's so amazing! It looks like the name on the child picture is Lorenzo."

"Correct. I also think there's a strong possibility that the third drawing of the intertwined hands was executed by this supposed son and they would have discussed the image at length. They may have even disagreed, perhaps on how one of the most iconic images of the Renaissance should be portrayed." He rubbed his chin. "A discovery of this kind has the power to generate a lot of publicity and interest."

"I think art historians would be thrilled to know that there is more to the story. Has a decision been made on whether the Vatican will reveal the discovery?"

"No." He looked at her quizzically. "Why do you think you found them?"

"Oh my! I have no idea. That's a really intimidating and hard question to think about."

"I believe that you are meant for a higher purpose, Rose."

"Such as?"

"I'll explain momentarily." He paused. "Beatrice shared that you've been suffering from a broken heart from your American fiancé, I believe."

"Yes, Cardinal. He did not treat me well."

"Might I ask what happened to the young man who was with you on your last visit?"

"Oh," she said. "I'm afraid I chose the wrong person and Lyon is gone forever."

The cardinal's sympathetic look made Rose's eyes well up with tears.

"Might I be able to interest you in some humanitarian work in the coming weeks?"

"Um," she said, "I don't understand."

"We— I mean a Vatican task force is working on a project in Nairobi, Kenya, to find ways to employ the local people. One of the most important elements is education. Would you be interested in working in the school? They're desperately short staffed and I think you would be an ideal candidate to support our work there."

"That sounds interesting, but I've just moved abroad a short time ago and I've been dealing with a broken engagement. It's all been overwhelming. I haven't had time to adjust to life in Italy yet, so moving again to Africa just doesn't seem wise. I'm so sorry!"

"I understand and I respect your decision," he said. "What is it you would like to do in Florence?"

"I really want to learn and grow as an artist. I'm not sure how much talent I have, but I do want to explore it."

"Aha!" he said. "I know just the person to help you. His name is Antonio Romano and he's an excellent teacher, and a personal friend."

"Antonio Romano! I met him and his wife at a workshop two years ago when I was last in Florence. I tried to find them when I first arrived back here, but they moved, so I hit a dead end, so to speak."

"I can definitely be of assistance." The cardinal smiled. "Antonio is a dear friend."

For the first time in weeks, Rose felt a sense of lightness in her being. "Oh! Seeing Antonio and his wife would be fantastic." Rose beamed. "Yes, I would really appreciate any help you could give me."

"It would be my pleasure. I will write my letter of introduction and have you deliver it to Antonio yourself. The old-fashioned way is best in this situation, eh?"

"Thank you, Cardinal. Your introduction would be a dream come true for me!"

"Very good then," he said kindly. "As I said when we first met, God has a plan for all of us."

He clasped both of her hands in his, and Rose felt renewed. She walked back to the laboratory, eager to share the news with Beatrice, who wholeheartedly approved of the idea.

"I can't think of anything more perfect for you right now. What an enriching life experience!"

"I'm kind of nervous. It would be such a privilege to work with them, and I hope I can do it."

"You must try!"

"Well, I certainly have plenty of free time."

"What about Lyon? You should get in touch with him when you get back to Florence. He was such a great guy."

"Oh, Beatrice, I can't!"

"Why not?"

"I don't think he ever wants to see me again!"

Rose explained how Lyon had come over to her apartment minutes after Ben proposed and her mom and stepfather arrived. He had been really angry and surprised by the news.

"Tell him the truth. That you picked the wrong guy. You have nothing to lose!"

"How am I supposed to communicate with him? He told me never to contact him again."

"You'll find a way. I've got a hunch that your paths will cross."

"Okay, enough about my personal life. Let's talk about Michelangelo! What do you think the cardinal will do if you confirm the theory that he did father a son named Lorenzo who may have contributed in some way to the Sistine Chapel?"

"Rose, have you not considered that maybe it was the supposed Lorenzo's idea to have Adam and God's hands touching, and not Michelangelo's?"

Rose gulped. "That couldn't be!"

"Why not?" Beatrice raised one eyebrow. "It's certainly a consideration that the Vatican will have to take into account."

"It would cause a firestorm of media!"

"Precisely."

"Oh, and I couldn't bear to have anything distract from that image. Michelangelo can do no wrong!"

"Right again."

It was hard to say goodbye to Beatrice and get on the train

back to Florence. Rose felt scared and alone. She also dreaded the moment that her mother found out that she and Ben were not getting married. It was sure to be an ugly confrontation. But her father always taught her to "take the hard right over the easy wrong." It was a belief that was embedded in her character.

With a deep breath, Rose touched the cardinal's letter in her tote bag, feeling really excited to connect with Antonio and, hopefully, have an opportunity to study under him.

***

The tax receipt for the ring sale appeared in her inbox, and Rose felt a sense of finality with Ben. And then the dreaded call came from Doris.

"You're a fool," Doris hissed into the phone. Gone was any attempt at being maternal. "Don't you realize that this affects my life too?"

Rose swallowed hard. "Doris, I can see why you're upset, but Ben and I aren't meant for each other. I'm sorry for any awkwardness this may cause you."

"It must have been something you did," Doris barked.

"You're right. It was all me."

"He was a catch. I just knew you couldn't keep him."

Rose looked at the phone in disgust. Was this woman really her mother? Maybe she was switched at birth into this life with this mean-spirited woman who taught her how not to behave. *I made the right decision to move abroad.* "*Ciao*, Mother," she said, readily hanging up the phone.

It was liberating to package up Ben's computer and get it out of her apartment. As soon as she left it at the FedEx office around the corner, Rose used her Google maps to find the Romanos' studio at the address the cardinal provided. It was nestled on a side street hidden from any tourist traffic. There wasn't an actual sign on the window, just several Renaissance-looking canvases propped up on dark wooden tripods.

The vaguely familiar scent of lavender layered with linseed oil ignited her excitement at being back in the presence of this couple. A dark-haired young man with glasses greeted her, and Rose explained that she was interested in seeing the Romanos, and asked if a schedule of classes was available. The young man graciously agreed to show her around while she waited for Antonio.

The dark wood ceiling beams, white walls and the colorful front hall rug gave the space a cheerful vibe. Antonio appeared moments later, a short man with a shock of thick gray hair. They talked for a few minutes with Rose trying to explain that she had met him two years ago. The young man named Francesco who had greeted her helped interpret Rose's introduction and explain what she wanted. Antonio seemed disinterested, pointing to a schedule of classes and mumbling something to Francesco in Italian.

"He says there is a substantial waiting list; some people wait years to get a spot," explained Francesco apologetically.

Rose pulled out the cardinal's letter of introduction, and upon seeing the seal, Antonio looked at her thoughtfully. He read the note, nodded and said in English, "Be here tomorrow morning at nine. You can fill out the necessary paperwork and give us the payment then."

"Thank you," Rose exclaimed. "I'll be here on time and ready to work."

Rose was so excited about the news that she found herself walking toward Lyon's office, rehearsing what she would say to him. *I agreed to marry Ben because we grew up together and he's from my world. But you, on the other hand, were always so kind, free spirited and fun that our connection scared me. I adore your parents, and, well, will you please give me a second chance? Please. I know I blew it.*

She marched inside and decided she had nothing to lose by facing him and asking for forgiveness and another chance. Her heart pounded in her chest at the thought of seeing him again.

But, as it turned out, Lyon was away on business and would be back in a couple of weeks. Rose sighed heavily, wondering if she should send him a text, but that didn't feel right. She would wait for him to return, and hopefully they could talk then.

***

Sleep proved elusive that night as Rose questioned her sanity in signing up to take classes with one of the leading artists in Florence. Who did she think she was? The Doris in her head echoed a litany of negative thoughts. *I'm not good enough. I'm a complete fraud. I've made the biggest mistake of my life not forgiving Ben and getting married.* And the one that ate away at her soul: *I just knew you couldn't keep him.* Another "Doris Special" comment that stung.

Rose was so nervous the following morning that her hands shook as she put her things into a backpack; she added her trusty sketchpad, water, a power bar and a few of her brushes, reflecting on how the tables had turned and she was the student and no longer in charge. She pushed her fears aside as she checked her reflection in the mirror, added a little makeup for confidence, and made her way to the studio.

There were five other students; two of them looked young, probably college age, and then there was an older gentleman and two other women closer to her age. Much to her surprise, in the center of the room was a striking, dark-haired model dressed in a flowing, voluminous red gown that looked like red paint cascading in a line from her body. It would be thrilling to capture the sensation of movement in the gown's design. Francesco, the assistant, pointed Rose to a chair with a canvas and easel.

Rose hadn't taken formal classes since college, so she felt very awkward. The moment Antonio walked in the room, everyone began speaking torrents of Italian. Rose could understand very little of the conversation, the jokes, or pretty much everything for that matter.

Her cheeks burned and a slow roll of anxiety crept up her spine until a tingling sensation filled her hands and feet. This was supposed to be her moment, the instant that her dream became a reality, and she hadn't even thought of the language barrier.

Antonio began explaining the project, pointing and gesturing, and she hadn't a clue what he was telling them to do. Rose was frozen in her chair. Her eyes welled up with tears and she brushed them away.

"Are you alright? Could I get you a glass of water?" whispered Francesco as he leaned over to help.

"I don't know what to do. He's speaking too quickly."

"Ah, I see," he said with compassion. "I can help you. Try to draw the model using the charcoal first, paying particular attention to the layers of the gown."

Picking up her charcoal, she began studying the lines of the woman's dress, paying attention to the folds and patterns under the arms. As she observed the subject, instinct took over and she sketched the arm and the right hand.

As she sketched, Rose remembered a spring banquet at Bellfield. She and Zoey had led the girls in a celebrity-themed project, making over fifteen life-size figures. They had instructed each girl to pick someone she admired, and they began the process of tracing or drawing a six-foot figure for the stage. Rose's selection of Lady Diana surprised everyone, but she had always admired her. Her hands moved easily over the paper, and she completed the likeness quickly, then adding a jeweled crown on her head.

"I can't believe you just drew that, Miss Maning," exclaimed one student. "That's amazing! That looks professional."

The memory helped her relax, giving Rose the boost of confidence she needed to continue working on the drawing. As she studied the model, she lost herself in how to place the image on her canvas.

Just as she was sketching a fold in the gown, Antonio came over and began fussing at her in Italian. Francesco translated. "Slow down and pay attention to the details. The lines in her hands, the contour of her ear." Antonio spoke in a rush. "He says that you need to change the way you are looking at the subject and focus less on filling the blank canvas. Quality over quantity, to coin an American phrase."

Rose nodded, thinking that it was going to be a long day. Several hours later, she looked up to see some fellow students standing and some seated. The room was very quiet as Antonio walked around and evaluated their work. He came to stand beside her and studied the drawing.

Maybe it wasn't so bad that she didn't understand all of Antonio's critiques. She could make out the words "promise" and "good beginning," which lodged in her mind. It occurred to her that she might need to hire a translator and study conversational Italian.

And that is precisely what she did for the next few weeks. Rose signed up for Italian lessons at night and hired a translator to help her in the studio. Her days were long and hard, but she was challenged in a way that she had never been before, which was oddly satisfying. Rose's sole purpose was to create and become fluent in Italian. Her main contact in the States remained Zoey, who emailed her regularly with updates about the school and local gossip.

***

Fall arrived in a cacophony of color, and the days gradually became crisper. Rose's life took on a familiar routine as she devoted every minute of her time to her craft. She started her days with a cup of coffee and muffin on the balcony as she watched the sun rise over the city. As she walked to the studio on a beautiful October morning, she ran into Francesco, who greeted her warmly.

"Ciao," he said, kissing her on both cheeks. "Antonio has a surprise for everyone today!"

"Oh, don't tell me. He's going to say something positive about my work?" she joked. "I'm not sure I can take much more constructive criticism."

"You're very talented and a good student," said Francesco. "No one in that studio puts in the hours that you do. Don't be so hard on yourself."

"I used to tell my students something like that. Now I realize how ridiculous it sounds."

"Hopefully you don't plan to spend another weekend in the studio. I've got a group going out tonight. Why don't you join us?" He looked at her. "Come on, you need to get out."

"I don't know."

"I'll take that as a yes."

She smiled. "So, what does Antonio have in store for us? Maybe he'll let us use some colored paint."

Rose walked in the studio, dropped her backpack and looked up to see Lyon's mother, Faith, leaning over a canvas. She was surprised, delighted and scared all at once.

"Darling Rose," said Faith, who appeared equally taken aback by the meeting. She walked over to embrace her, kissing her on both cheeks.

"Faith, how are you? What are you doing here?"

"I'm the guest artist today. Antonio wanted his students to take a break from all the detailed drawing and have a contemporary lesson for fun. How do you say—shake things up a little."

"That's wonderful!"

Faith looked at Rose's ring finger, apologized, then offered, "I'm sorry, I don't mean to pry, but Lyon said that you were getting married to someone in the States."

"Um, not anymore," said Rose. "It was the shortest engagement on record." They laughed awkwardly. "The only things I'm committed to right now are my artwork and my Italian."

"I see. Wise choice. You have a lot of talent."

Rose was dying to ask about Lyon, but Antonio walked in the room along with three other students who were eager to get started. Stepping to the front of the room, Faith introduced herself to the class, giving a lovely introduction on where she gained her inspiration and how and when she loved to paint contemporary landscapes. For Rose, she spoke a bit slower, and Rose considered it a moment of personal growth that she was able to understand most of what Faith said.

The day, like her brushstrokes, flowed easily, and Rose found Faith's instruction a breeze compared to what she had been doing in class these last few months. Painting bright colors really appealed to her artistic sensibility. It was definitely something to consider. She suddenly recalled the series of drawings that she began at Faith's guest house that Lyon had really enjoyed. They were rolled up somewhere in her apartment, and Rose was determined to find them.

At the end of class, Rose took a moment to thank Faith for a wonderful experience. She was a bit surprised when Faith asked, "How about we have a drink together? I'm staying tonight in the city."

"Oh, that would be lovely. When and where?"

Francesco looked askance at her, and Rose felt horribly guilty that she had all but ignored his overtures of friendship these past few months.

"There's a little place around the corner called Le Vespe where we can grab a bite to eat. It's very casual. I'm going to freshen up and you can meet me there in say an hour."

"I'm looking forward to it."

"Very good then. I'll see you in a bit. *Ciao*."

***

With a spring in her step, Rose raced home to get ready. She felt as if she were stepping out of a bubble of her own making. While she had always admired Michelangelo's undeniable work ethic, sacrificing everything including his own personal hygiene for his craft, Rose wasn't convinced that she was meant to be any kind of renowned artist. The hot shower felt heavenly, as did discarding her paint-stained, smelly art student uniform that she had adopted.

From the inner dregs of her closet, she dug out a simple black dress and paired it with some black booties. Her hair was another matter entirely. It had grown long and unkempt, so Rose plowed a brush through her tangled mane, determined not to wear it in her usual braid. Looking in the mirror, Rose was pleased with her efforts to look presentable. Not to mention her secret hope that Faith could tell her how Lyon was doing. She willed herself not to get her hopes up because Faith might not be so forthcoming on his whereabouts.

The restaurant was bustling with the Friday crowd at the bar, and Rose spied Faith cheerfully waving to her from a corner booth.

"What a great class today!" Rose said, taking a seat across from her. "I'm glad Antonio gave us a break today to do something different. It was fun to paint with color and not focus on the drawing all day long."

"I'm glad you enjoyed the class. We have so much to talk about!" exclaimed Faith.

Moments later, the waiter served a carafe of Chianti along with some assorted cheeses and bread. Each tried the cheeses, sampling the goat with herbs and brie. Rose asked about the figs in the dish. Faith looked her in the eye and said, "Shall we get the elephant out of the room, so to speak?"

"Yes, please," said Rose, who admired her honesty. "I made a mistake. It all happened so fast. My first love came to Florence unexpectedly with my parents, and the next thing I knew, I was engaged to be married and my mother was crying with joy; it all seemed so perfect. And then it wasn't. Our relationship was not grounded in trust, and our differences were too great to build a life together. Believe me, I've spent the last few months living in a sea of regret."

"Darling, you're too young and vibrant to be so hard on yourself. I'm rather superstitious and believe things happen for a reason. Like us today. I'm so glad that we connected. You're a wonderful student and artist."

"Thank you. You have no idea how much that means to me." Rose took a sip of red wine to quell her anxiety. Finally, she got up the nerve. "Dare I ask about Lyon? I went to his office a few months ago and they said he was out of the country. I've called and left messages several times, but his assistant was not very helpful."

"He has other business interests, and . . . "

Silence.

"Don't tell me, there's someone else." Rose was overcome with emotion.

At the look of sympathy on Faith's face, she thought she might start to cry. Reining in her emotions, she said, "I see." A tear escaped, but Rose brushed it away, quickly changing the subject. "So, tell me, how do you know Antonio?"

"He was my teacher too when I first came to Italy. He can be a little gruff sometimes and the compliments are not forthcoming, but he's a genius. We both know that."

"I've learned so much already from him, but feel like I have so far to go. He's a very demanding teacher!"

"Of course he is. That's what makes him the best at what he does."

"I know I'm fortunate to be his student, but I wonder what's next?"

"Tell me, Rose, why does your generation always have to have all the answers and wrap them up in a neat package? Patience, my dear. Sometimes, it takes years for things to unfold."

"I'm someone who likes a plan," said Rose.

They enjoyed the cheese and continued chatting for a bit until Faith excused herself to take a call. Rose was casually checking her phone when she looked up to see Lyon.

"What are you doing here?" he said in a clipped tone.

"I could ask you the same question," she shot back.

"My mother asked me to meet her for a drink."

"Well, she invited me too. We've been here for over an hour. She just stepped away and I've got no idea where she went."

Lyon turned to leave but Rose reacted swiftly. "Please don't leave. I'd really like to talk to you for just a minute. I've called you many times to explain over the last few months. Did you know that?"

"I've been busy."

"Lyon, I really messed up and I wish you'd let me explain."

"Why?"

"Because you're a very special person to me."

"I suggest you do better than that or I'm leaving."

"Okay, I've been miserable without you and—"

"Nope, not good enough, Rose." He sat across from her, and Rose thought quickly.

"Hmmm. How was heaven when you left it?"

She got the beginnings of some lip movement out of him.

"You look like something carved by Michelangelo."

"You're going backwards on that one."

"Last try. I think you're the most handsome man I've ever met."

"Better," he said, glancing at his phone. He looked up at her. "So, my mother is suddenly tired and has decided to head to bed early. She must not like Marianne."

"Who's— Ouch!" said Rose, remembering that there might be someone else. "I suppose I deserved that comment on your girlfriend?"

"Uh-huh."

"I said I was wrong. I'm sorry. So, who's Marianne?"

"My best friend, and yes, I was hurt by how quickly you reunited with your American boyfriend."

"I can explain," she said, searching for the right words. "It was like being caught in a whirlwind. Everything happened all at once. I don't know how to tell you what it felt like to have my mother's approval for once . . . but really, who's Marianne?"

"Rose darling, I was kidding! Marianne is my new love; she's fifteen pounds of labradoodle puppy. We just got her. I was the, how do you say, babysitter for my mother today."

Relief flooded through Rose as she waited for him to show her a picture. "She's gorgeous!"

"Amazing how much you can love a puppy without a care," he said sincerely.

"I can tell," replied Rose. "So, it looks like I have some major competition to win you over."

"That you do," he said sincerely. "But it seems you've already cast your spell on my mother."

"She's an amazing person and an incredible artist. I really admire her." Rose went on to explain how she had gotten a letter of introduction from Cardinal Baglioni to take instruction from Antonio Romano and how she had been working hard on her drawing for the past few months and then, chance would have it, that his mother came to teach the class this morning.

"Aha! So that's how it all happened."

"Can you ever forgive me?"

"Maybe," he said with a wink as he reached for her hand across the table. "But you'll have to get Marianne's approval first. She's at my place if you want to meet her."

As they left the restaurant, Lyon easily guided her down the streets.

"I didn't realize that you were only a few short blocks away."

"I knew that when I sold you your apartment."

"What?" She gave him a look. "I could have easily picked Machiavelli's Mansion. You know how I love history. That would have been the most logical given my parameters."

"Too expensive," said Lyon, raising one eyebrow at her. "You're not someone who is going to go over budget, and the space was enormous for one person."

"How about the one with the chef's kitchen? That modern loft that you showed me first?"

"That place was going to appeal to an individual or couple who are foodies. As a matter of fact, this fantastic German couple, both of whom are chefs, ended up buying it. They promised to make me dinner on a regular basis."

The moment Lyon unlocked the door to his apartment, Rose was enthusiastically greeted by a gorgeous, tail-wagging puppy bouncing up and down. She scooped Marianne up into her arms and had her face showered with kisses. "She's so precious," exclaimed Rose. "I love her!"

Moments later, Marianne leapt into Lyon's arms. Then she proceeded to flop down and pee all over his shoes. Rose couldn't help herself; she started laughing hysterically.

"I'll get a paper towel."

Lyon threw off his shoes and turned on a few more lights. His place was filled with dark leather furniture, mahogany floor-to-ceiling bookcases, white walls and a modern kitchen. Faith's beautiful paintings decorated the walls with a symphony of color.

Their eyes met and they held each other's gaze for a long time. Marianne started whining, and Rose scooped the puppy up in her arms to quiet her down.

"You seem to be winning over the women in my life today."

"What about you?"

"I haven't decided yet."

"Whether we can start over?"

"I was thinking something more along the lines of finishing what we started."

Rose caught the twinkle in his eye, and she reached for him, longing to hold him close. Their lips met in a long, slow, hot passionate kiss that nearly took her breath away. His lips grazed her throat and her neck as he pulled her closer. He ran his hands through her hair and whispered her name. The intensity of their connection brought tears to Rose's eyes at how close she had come to losing him forever.

"I missed you so much."

Seeing her emotional response, he slowly and deliberately kissed her.

The promise of things to come abruptly ended when the puppy jumped between them. In a swift motion, Lyon scratched the puppy's ears, got her a treat and put her in the crate in the kitchen.

"Well done," said Rose.

Lyon devoured her with his eyes. "So beautiful," he said, taking her into his arms.

Suddenly, her phone buzzed several times, and she reached for it.

There were three text messages from Beatrice telling her to get to Rome immediately. She turned to Lyon. "It's Beatrice. She's found something. She wants me to come to Rome as soon as possible. Would you come with me? I don't know what she's found, but I want you to be there."

"Of course."

"I haven't heard from her in weeks, and now this urgency is strange."

"Maybe nothing. You have to be prepared for all outcomes."

"You're right. It could just be a courtesy. But three texts?" Rose thought for a minute. "She could have discovered something really important but, then again"—she smiled—"I think what we've recaptured is far greater."

Chapter 19

A LINE OF TOURISTS circled the block of the Vatican, waiting to view interior rooms filled with breathtaking artworks by such masters as Raphael, Michelangelo, Caravaggio and Leonardo da Vinci. Beatrice met Rose and Lyon at the side entrance and ushered them to a private conference room in the laboratory; Cardinal Baglioni arrived shortly thereafter. He greeted Lyon with a warm handshake. "Hello again, young man. I'm glad that you're here."

Beatrice asked them all to take a seat and turned on a large screen, which illuminated the first of the three drawings. The drawing was beautiful, and Rose felt a wave of excitement at seeing it restored.

"I'll get right to the point. As we all know, Michelangelo is known for his study of the male nude figure and he spent his lifetime achieving greatness in his art. He was a genius and a master draftsman who was celebrated for his excellence in drawing. His contemporaries called him *Il Divinio* or 'the divine one.' In the first drawing note the roundness of the stomach and child's legs and compare it to this unfinished cartoon of the *Virgin and Child*. This looks like the hand of Michelangelo, and yet it is not the baby Jesus if you note the detail in the eyes, brows and prominent nose. The comparative drawing is currently owned by the Casa Buonarroti in Florence.

"The inscription we found on the right corner reads *My Lorenzo*, which can be interpreted several ways. As you may know, Lorenzo the Magnificent was the supreme ruler of Florence with his brother Giuliano from 1469 to 1478 and sole ruler from 1478 until his death in 1492. Most importantly, he was Michelangelo's patron. Perhaps this was a commission from him. But the title *My Lorenzo* does suggest an intimate relationship between the artist and his subject. That being said, our research leads us to believe that this is not the Christ Child, which was an often-favored subject of Michelangelo. There's a possibility that this could have been the artist's child, but we have no way to substantiate the initial theory through this drawing."

The cardinal nodded his approval for her to continue with her analysis. Rose's eyes were glued to the screen, and she barely noticed that Lyon had taken her hand for moral support. Beatrice then displayed the second drawing alongside a well-known picture of Andrea Quaratesi that was currently owned by the British Museum.

"The second drawing, in which the young man is fully clothed with an almost ethereal expression on his face, is even more puzzling than the first, for many reasons. It was a rare occasion that Michelangelo painted his subjects clothed."

Everyone laughed.

"In the second drawing you found, this young man looks like perhaps an early version of Michelangelo's famous portrait of Andrea Quaratesi that, as you can see, is exquisitely beautiful in its simplicity. The boy in the drawing Rose found does share the same prominent nose and dark penetrating eyes as the child. However, this portrait of a young boy of, say, age twelve or so is definitely *not* Quaratesi, the son of a Florentine banker, or anyone we know." Beatrice used a laser pointer with a red light to go back to the drawing Rose found and highlight the nose. "So, there is a strong possibility that these first two drawings are related but, again, we can't confirm with complete certainty that Michelangelo drew portraits of his own son."

"But is there a chance he did?" asked Rose.

"Absolutely. Someone saved these pictures and passed them down from generation to generation for a reason. They do tell a story, but not one I can verify at this point. Note the worn edges on all of them. It looks like they were once in frames. But let's get back to the analysis. These drawings hint at the hypothesis that Michelangelo fathered a son, but they do not have the power to substantiate a claim of this magnitude."

"What about the third drawing that shows God and Adam's hands together rather than their fingers touching?" asked Rose.

"Actually, that's where I get excited!" Beatrice took a deep breath. "I think we can conclude that this was a primary idea considered by Michelangelo as he painted the Sistine Chapel. It's a beautiful message and one that would work as seamlessly as the current one."

"It's clear we have no way of proving that Michelangelo had a son involved in some of his artistic accomplishments. Is it safe to say that art historians could better understand his creative process by seeing the third drawing?" exclaimed Rose.

"Indeed," said the cardinal. "So, this is where a new story begins." He stood. "It's a message of love and peace and it must be shared!"

"You mean, the Vatican is going to release the discovery of this drawing?!"

"The vote was unanimous! We think that our world needs more positive messages right now. This story and these hands would be thrilling for tourists and pilgrims alike to view."

The news brought tears to Rose's eyes.

"But what about the other two drawings?" asked Lyon quizzically.

"I believe there will be a time and a place for them as well. Beatrice has agreed to stay on this project and continue her research." He looked at Beatrice and said, "Well done."

"When do you think you'll announce the discovery?"

"First, we want to involve several noted scholars and conduct some additional research before we go public. It's all very exciting."

"Maybe that's the time I should head to Africa," joked Rose.

"So, you have given my offer more thought," said Cardinal Baglioni.

"What offer?" asked Lyon.

"I thought that Rose would be an ideal person to get involved in some of our mission work in Nairobi, Kenya. The school needs more qualified teachers; they also could benefit from a larger facility." The cardinal eyed both Rose and Lyon. "How is your study with Antonio Romano going?"

"Very well," said Rose. "I must admit it's been really challenging for me to work with him. He can be gruff at times."

"That doesn't surprise me."

"Fortunately, my Italian is coming along. I wonder, now that you're going to make the discovery public, I'd like to show you a concept that I've been working on. I had an idea to paint the intertwined hands with people from all ages and all races coming together as one."

"Go on."

"I had a vision of bright colors and intertwined hands on wall-sized canvases."

"Have you shared this idea with Antonio?"

"Not yet."

"Perhaps he could help you achieve this vision."

"So, you like the idea?"

"Yes, very much." He looked at Lyon and Rose. "I have a feeling I'm going to be seeing the two of you again soon."

"I hope so," said Rose.

***

After the meeting, Lyon and Rose climbed the Spanish Steps and walked along a beautiful path, admiring the stone busts; the

Borghese Garden was breathtaking.

"I'm actually surprised the cardinal plans to go public with the third drawing," said Lyon.

"Me too. I still say there's more to the story on the first two, but I'm going to leave that to the experts."

"They may want you to recount how you found the drawings."

"I'm not sure I want to talk to anyone about it. I'm a very private person; it would be hard for me." She paused. "I'll certainly never tell anyone about the dream."

"Why not?"

"Again, it's all so intimate, like seeing into my soul. I believe I was meant to safeguard those drawings, and they'll be available for the next generation of scholars to debate and analyze."

"I respect your integrity."

"Thank you. That means a lot to me."

"We have some time before the museums close. How about we have a look at the *Pietà* today and grab some dinner?"

"You read my mind."

A visit to St. Peter's to view Michelangelo's stunning *Pietà* was the perfect way to end the day. Rose was mesmerized as she stared at the figures behind the glass case. "Sheer genius," she said, recalling the class she taught on the sculpture at Bellfield. A picture didn't do it justice.

"Did you know that when Michelangelo conceived this sculpture, it was all a rather awkward position?" Rose asked Lyon. "You have the body of a full-grown man in the arms of his mother. You see, look at his peaceful expression, which does not give away any of the horror that just happened. Michelangelo was a master at combining the spiritual with the natural world. All that shines through is a mother's love for her child."

Lyon took her hand. "Your friend Zoey was right. The way to your heart is through your passion for the life and works of Michelangelo."

"Actually, the way to my heart right now is a large margherita pizza. I'm starving!"

"Let's go then!"

"I want to make this project happen. The cardinal liked my idea of bright-colored intertwined hands of people of all ages and races coming together for peace and unity. Do you think your mother would be willing to help me?"

"Are you kidding me? She'd love it. And clearly you've won her over since she's the one who engineered last night."

"Have you forgiven me?" Rose asked nervously.

"Nope. I'm still thinking of how you can make it up to me."

He took her in his arms and kissed her passionately—so much so that someone in the gallery whistled. They reluctantly broke apart. After a short walk, they came upon the Trevi Fountain, a Baroque extravaganza of Greek statues with water cascading skyward in the center, gleaming in the evening light.

"Come on, let's make a wish. Doesn't legend have it that if you throw the coin over your left shoulder, you get to return to Rome?"

Lyon handed her a euro. Rose delighted in throwing it behind her.

"What did you wish for?" he asked, taking her hand again.

"I can't tell you or it won't come true."

***

Rose had no trouble garnering support from Faith and Antonio for her wall-sized canvas idea of people of all races, young and old and all walks of life holding hands. She knew her role would ultimately take a back seat to Antonio's and Faith's talent, but she didn't care. Her message would be clear and positive. The image lodged in her mind, and she threw herself into creating the canvas, with Antonio's precise instruction. He set up a room inside his studio for the project, and Rose practically camped out there as she worked around the clock to bring her vision to life.

"You are doing a beautiful job," said Faith, standing in the doorway of the studio.

Rose savored the compliment. "Thanks!" She put down her paintbrush. "I want to get the images in my head on the paper before they disappear."

"Spoken like a true artist."

"I don't see myself that way."

"I believe in you."

Tears misted Rose's eyes, and she looked across the room at Faith. "You have no idea how much your support means to me. I know I have a lot to learn."

"We are all always learning. Even your hero Michelangelo had his moments of insecurity with his rival Leonardo da Vinci."

Rose laughed. "I still find that somewhat ridiculous."

"You have to trust yourself and your vision."

Rose nodded, knowing how much more confident she had become over the past few months.

"And on that note, I'll let you get back to painting. It is all going to be wonderful."

Rose forgot about everything as the hours passed easily. As she drew the intertwined hands of an old man and a young Asian boy, it became clear that she would have to draw their entire figures for it to look right—a far bigger idea than she had first envisioned, and one that would be extremely challenging to execute. Rose looked up to find Lyon in the doorway staring at her. Their eyes met and he stepped in to peek.

"It looks *fantastico!*"

"Nice turn of phrase," joked Rose, getting up to greet him. He swooped her up in his arms and kissed her passionately.

They were interrupted by Faith, who said, "Darlings, I have some news!"

"What is it?" said Rose, trying to wriggle out of Lyon's arms.

"My gallery thinks this is a brilliant idea and they're willing to put on an exhibition next spring! But there's a catch . . . They want to devote the whole gallery to it! That means at least two more canvases."

"Whoa, Mother! You can't be serious. How are you guys going to pull that off?"

"It'll take a lot of work, but I'm confident that we'll get it done," said Rose.

"That's the spirit," exclaimed Faith.

For the next few months, Rose worked almost constantly day and night with total focus, trying to complete the project which she had aptly named *Humanity*. Antonio, the perfectionist, slowed the process, constantly correcting Rose with Italian accented by rapid hand gestures. His constant criticism was difficult to take, but she could see he was right.

Rose worked nearly every day, exhausting herself to the point of becoming ill. Faith could see her enthusiasm waning, and so could Lyon.

"Rose, this has been going on long enough. You're taking the weekend off!"

"Lyon, I'd love to, but I can't. Not now!"

"My parents have invited us to spend the weekend in Tuscany and even my mother agrees that you need a break. You must rest or you'll burn out."

"You're right. These past few months have been crazy, haven't they?"

"Hopefully, you mean that as a compliment," said Lyon, taking her into his arms. "I've loved watching your passion come to life. The exhibition is going to be brilliant."

"If Antonio doesn't fire me first," she joked. "No matter how hard I try, he finds fault with everything I do."

"You're working alongside Italy's top artist, and its most demanding. That is in and of itself an accomplishment. But it's a demanding one."

"You're right. Maybe I'm just exhausted, but your enthusiasm and support have helped keep me motivated."

"Well, there's something else we need to talk about that has to do with my feelings for you, Rose." He pulled out a pretty blue box.

"What's that?"

"A promise to love you forever. Will you marry me?"

Rose gasped. "Yes!" she cried as their lips met in a tender kiss.

Lyon opened the box to reveal a gorgeous emerald flanked by two diamonds.

"I've never seen anything so beautiful," she cried.

"I could say the same about you. Beautiful inside and out."

"Oh, Lyon, you've stolen my heart. I love you so much."

He placed the ring on her finger and explained, "This ring has been in my mother's family for generations."

"It fits perfectly."

"I thought so." He kissed her again. "My parents would like us to join them this weekend in the country. My father has a special bottle of bubbly he's been working on to celebrate." He paused. "My brother, Peter, and my sister, Katherine, are coming in as well."

"I'd love to."

***

Lyon's father, Joseph, and Faith were eagerly waiting for them, and their warm welcome was something that Rose would never forget. The dining room table was elegantly set for a celebratory lunch. The table was awash in all white with winter white lilies and white roses in a silver vase in the center. Faith approached Rose and embraced her. "I'm so excited! Now, I have another daughter. You're so special to me."

"That means so much to me. I love you," said Rose. At last, she had a real mother who genuinely cared for her. It was a true blessing.

Lyon's sister, Kathryn, and her husband, Giovanni, arrived

about the same time as Peter and his wife, Natalie, with their two little girls. Rose took in the scene, feeling so grateful to be part of such a vibrant and loving family. They talked and talked until Rose fell into bed that night, staring at the beautiful ring on her finger.

Despite the time difference, Rose called Jack and Zoey; her best friend was not in the slightest bit surprised.

"I knew it!" Zoey exclaimed. "I saw the way he looked at you when you were house hunting."

Jack was thrilled for his sister and looking forward to flying over to meet Lyon, but he did ask whether she had told their mother.

"Not yet," said Rose. "She was so incredibly rude to me when Ben and I broke up. She blamed me for it."

"Ah, Rose." Jack sighed. "You know Ben and his ex reconciled, right?"

"I do. I saw it on the cover of some tabloid on my way to the studio a few weeks ago. Poor Doris. Her dreams are dashed," she added sarcastically.

"She does love you, Rose."

"Really? It's always been all about her."

"Rose, I think you should reconsider reaching out to our mother. You're engaged now and starting a whole new life."

"Don't be so mature, Jack," joked Rose as she finished up her conversation with him, asking for more pictures of her nieces. "It's always been different for you, Jack, but I'll think about it."

Rose wasn't sure how to go about mending her relationship with her mother. But as she looked at the ring on her finger, she guessed she owed it to herself to try and work things out. Doris would never apologize, so Rose decided a long letter sharing her news was the smartest way to deal with her. It seemed rather antiquated and strange to put pen to paper, but she was able to say that Lyon was the best thing that had ever happened to her, that she was happily settled in Florence, and then she suggested that perhaps they could find a time for her and Eric to meet Lyon.

***

Progress on the exhibition was slow and steady, and Rose's days were filled with the joy of painting and seeing her vision appear on canvas. She dreamed about a beautiful wedding in the Tuscan countryside and felt truly blessed. Faith took over the studio when she was in class, and Rose always joined her during lunchtime and late day. It was Rose's favorite time as the two women collaborated on the overall look and feel of each canvas. But it was Lyon who suggested that they add some technical advancements to the project that included a light shining intermittently on various parts of the canvas to give the illusion of movement.

"The millennials are much more computer oriented, so you'll want it to be more exciting."

"I love this idea," said Rose.

Antonio, of course, hated the concept of modern lighting and had one of his usual tirades. Back and forth the three artists went as dozens of figures emerged on the canvas in various shapes, sizes, colors and genders, all coming together to form a whole.

A call from the cardinal brought unexpected news; he planned to attend their exhibition and throw his support behind the project.

"You are sharing a master's beautiful idea with the world and the cardinal knows it," Lyon said.

"I love your optimism. If for a minute I even thought about our opening that way, I'd get a terrible case of stage fright. I'm far from a genius, and a respectable artist at best."

"I think what you're doing is fantastic," he replied, kissing her.

"You always know what to say to make me feel special. Thank you."

"I'll never get tired of being with you."

Rose felt renewed every time she finished a section of the canvas, despite Antonio's gripes. It all was coming together so well, and she started to think they would make the June opening. Jack called and planned to be there along with Doris and Eric. Rose couldn't help but feel anxious. Lyon did not fit Doris's image of the perfect son-in-law; only Ben could fit that bill. And yet, she hoped she would behave.

"How do you feel about being a September bride?"

"I can't wait that long," joked Rose, who scrubbed her hands, trying to get all of the paint off. "I want to marry you right away, but, seriously, it all sounds lovely. Getting married at your parents' home in Tuscany is so generous of them, and I love the idea of having our celebration be small and intimate." She added, "About my mother."

"What about her?"

"I'm warning you; she's difficult."

"I can handle it," he laughed. "There are far worse things in life."

***

The details of the exhibition consumed Rose, and they all worked feverishly to finish on time. She was walking to the studio on a sunny June morning when she spied a billboard on a bus with the intertwined hands announcing the event. She got chills up her spine when she saw how beautiful it looked and practically raced to class, thrilled to be part of this amazing accomplishment.

When the final painting was installed in the gallery, Rose was both excited and nervous about the opening reception. Several media outlets had asked to take pictures of the enormous installation, which was generating a lot of excitement. The paintings were a mix of traditional figures with contemporary bright colors that radiated beauty and joy. Whatever the critics' views of the work, Rose concluded, she was extremely proud of the project and its positive message of unity.

Crowds were waiting at the door as Lyon escorted her inside the gallery lit with high-tech equipment that flashed intermittent soft LED lights on various parts of the four wall-sized canvases.

"It's absolutely brilliant!" gushed Faith, coming over to embrace her. "Look how many people are flooding in through the front door."

"I can't believe it," said Rose with a sigh of relief. "It all came together so flawlessly."

Even Antonio and Valentina seemed pleased as they were strolling around the pictures hand in hand.

"Look, what a novelty," Rose said. "He's not speaking in torrents of Italian telling me to fix something."

Faith gave her a hug. "He wouldn't have participated in the project if he didn't believe in it. Antonio has high standards and he knew he could push you to a higher level of expertise. You did an amazing job. I'm so proud of everything you've accomplished. Rose, you are an artist and I hope you are proud of yourself."

Her words were so good for Rose's soul.

"Now," she said, taking Rose and Lyon by the hands. "You two are going to enjoy this summer and start planning a wedding!"

Rose and Lyon kissed tenderly until they were interrupted by Jack, who came over to give her a big hug and offer his congratulations. "This is incredible, little sis."

"It wasn't just me, Jack. I'd like you to meet Lyon, my fiancé, and Faith, my future mother-in-law."

Rose felt as if she were in a dream. Suddenly, Doris arrived in a shocking hot-pink dress that screamed "pay attention to me." Her stilettos were sky high. She strutted over to where Rose and Lyon stood with a circle of friends and announced herself by cooing loudly, "Daaahling, this is fantastic!"

Before long, Doris was the center of attention, basking in praise as the artist's Southern mother. Lyon whispered, "She does know how to make an entrance."

"Mother, this is Lyon, my fiancé."

"It's nice to meet you." Doris eyed him and then gave him a big hug. "Welcome to the family."

"Thank you," said Lyon.

A triumph of color, vision and a positive message of love, even for her mother.

Later, Jack came to stand beside her. "Lyon seems like a great guy! He asked me about the construction business and the girls. He seemed genuinely interested in getting to know me. We're off to a good start."

"I'm not surprised. We're really happy. Let me introduce you to his parents."

Rose scanned the room and bristled when she saw Lyon leaning against a wall talking to Dominique. She excused herself from her brother and walked over as if to take a victory lap.

"Rose, you remember my old friend Dominique," Lyon said nervously.

"How could I forget?" Rose smiled. "What brings you here, old friend? Did you come with your husband?"

Dominique swallowed hard. "I came because . . . well, to congratulate you on your work and Lyon on your engagement. I guess you got what you wanted after all."

"*We* both did," said Lyon.

Just then the cardinal approached, shaking Lyon's hand and hugging Rose. Dominique quietly slipped away.

"Ah, my dear, you've really impressed me with this vision," the cardinal said. "I think this is something that will garner attention all over Italy, and who knows, maybe all over the world! Congratulations!"

"Thank you so much, Cardinal. I appreciate that."

"I wanted to mention that I'm heading to Kenya next week to check on the project there. If you're interested, you could come and see the school there and perhaps meet the locals."

"Well, I might just consider that idea, but only if Lyon consents to join me."

"I hope so," the cardinal said, gazing at Lyon, who had moved away to chat with someone. "You could really make a difference in the lives of those children."

"You have no idea how much your moral support means to me. I hope you don't mind me saying that you remind me a bit of my father."

"I don't mind at all," said the cardinal, who smiled warmly at her.

***

Rose headed to the restroom to freshen up. She was still a bit unnerved from seeing Dominique, her mother, and from all of the attention from admirers.

Beatrice walked in and said, "Rose, I've been looking everywhere for you. The show is absolutely first class!" She paused, looking at her pale face. "Are you alright?"

"Yes. Yes. Just feeling a bit overwhelmed." She paused. "I saw Lyon talking to Dominique and I got annoyed."

"All that says to me is that you are crazy about him. A good problem to have. If anything was going on, she certainly wouldn't have shown up here. You need to have more confidence in him, and yourself. Please enjoy your success. You and Lyon are an absolutely fantastic couple. I've never seen two people more in love."

"I definitely got a little jealous. That woman bugs me."

"So what? Today is about you, and you have Lyon. I'm sure you're exhausted from all of the work and late nights leading up to tonight."

"Oh, Beatrice, you're so right! My mother always sets me on edge."

"I want you to pull it together and go enjoy yourself. It's a gorgeous summer night and you need to go have fun."

"Absolutely." She hugged Beatrice and told her how much she appreciated her friendship.

Rose searched for Lyon, but he was nowhere to be found. She waded through the crowds of people and cut upstairs, but there was no sign of him. The whole thing felt very strange, and she grew increasingly nervous that he had left. Rose looked over the balcony to see him deep in conversation with the cardinal. Rose practically raced back down the steps to join them. Lyon put his arm around her and kissed the top of her head and held her tight. He mouthed the words, *I'm sorry.*

"I was telling Lyon that I've invited both of you to go to Africa with me to see the marvelous mission work that's being done there by our team."

"I'd like to go this summer," Rose blurted out. "I'm ready."

"So would I," said Lyon. "I've talked with the cardinal, and I can help design and build the new school."

"Is there a space for the children to do art?" she asked. "I think I have some money from a certain sale that needs to be put to good use."

Cardinal Baglioni put his hand on her shoulder. "You've made me very happy and proud tonight, Rose. But I'm not surprised. Currently, we have a one-room schoolhouse, but perhaps we could create a place for children to grow and learn in a good environment."

"It would be a privilege for us to change that!" said Lyon.

The cardinal clapped his hands in joy. "Very good then. I think we'll make a very good team." He smiled warmly.

When the cardinal left to chat with another guest, Lyon said, "I'm really proud of you and this exhibition."

"Thanks," she replied.

"I can't wait to work with the cardinal. Then, I'm going to take you on safari. Seeing the raw beauty of Africa and its people is going to change your life."

"Really? I thought moving to Florence was the game changer."
She smiled. "Oh, I meant to say, moving to Florence and finding
you."

Lyon squeezed her hand. "True. But look at these beautiful
canvases. Darling, I think it's safe to say that you found yourself
when you moved here!"

At that moment, Antonio came over and kissed her on both
cheeks. He was thrilled with the exhibition and had been basking
in the praise of his fellow artists and the media attention. Then,
he turned to her and in heavily accented English said, "Well
done, Rose! Together, we sent out a message of love and unity
to our world."

Rose savored his praise, taking in all that she had accomplished
under his direction. She looked over at Cardinal Baglioni, who
turned to her and said, "Rose, you and I were destined to meet.
We can spread the message that *love is love*. We do not have to
earn it. Everyone is entitled to it and it's always there for us. Oh
yes, I think this is just the beginning of our story."

"Really?"

"Together, we can help others heal in our broken world."

"I'd like that, Cardinal."

Rose looked around her at the crowded exhibition, seeing
the intertwined hands, and felt a sense of purpose. As if on cue,
Lyon clasped her hand.

Acknowledgements

"The greatest danger for most of us lies not in setting our aim too high and falling short, but in setting our aim too low and achieving our mark."
~ Michelangelo

These words from the Master inspired me these last few years while I researched and wrote.

A heartfelt thank-you to my wonderful husband, Bagley, who has always supported my writing and my dreams. He was the one who encouraged me to write what I wanted to write, and this story came from my heart. My daughters, Ellie and Susanna, gave me great suggestions!

A special shout-out to my Sisters in the Word who helped me find that creative spark again. Thank you, Becky Page, for being my first reader and offering numerous suggestions. For dear sweet Dorothy, your courage and grace inspire me to write about God's glory.

And cheers to my new friends at Koehler Books!